"You do this all the [...] shook her head. "I'[...]

And wasn't that the understatement of the year? Logan couldn't stop his gaze from roaming over her, starting at her wide brown eyes and wandering down to her graceful hands, stopping to linger on everything in between. Olivia was a woman built for civilized pursuits, not the machinations of a ruthless drug cartel.

"No, you aren't," he agreed. Seeing her here in his office, looking lost, tugged at something deep inside his chest.

"Would you feel better if I went with you?"

She grabbed his hand, squeezing hard. "I *would* feel better if you were with me." Her words made him want to puff out his chest, but he controlled the urge.

"So you'll do it?" he asked, trying not to sound too eager.

"Yes, I'll do it."

"Excellent." Logan couldn't stop a grin. Finally, they had a solid chance to bring these guys down! It was the operation of a lifetime, and he would make sure they succeeded.

Or die trying.

* * *

We hope you enjoyed a first look at a brand-new, electrifying miniseries, Doctors in Danger!

* * *

If you're on Twitter, tell us what you think of Harlequin Romantic Suspense! #harlequinromsuspense

Dear Reader,

I love to travel! I'm lucky enough to have visited the rain forest twice—once in Central America, and once in South America. Both times, I was awed by the magnitude of the forest, and by the sheer number and variety of plants, animals and insects, all of them fascinating and not nearly as interested in me as I was in them.

I really enjoyed revisiting the forest while writing this book. Olivia and Logan get up close and personal with the jungle, which only makes their lives even more complicated. I hope you enjoy reading about their adventures! I know I'd love to hear from you—feel free to email me and tell me your favorite vacation spot!

All the best!

Lara Lacombe

ENTICED BY THE OPERATIVE

Lara Lacombe

HARLEQUIN® ROMANTIC SUSPENSE

Recycling programs
for this product may
not exist in your area.

ISBN-13: 978-0-373-27995-1

Enticed by the Operative

Copyright © 2016 by Lara Kingeter

All rights reserved. Except for use in any review, the reproduction or utilization of this work in whole or in part in any form by any electronic, mechanical or other means, now known or hereinafter invented, including xerography, photocopying and recording, or in any information storage or retrieval system, is forbidden without the written permission of the publisher, Harlequin Enterprises Limited, 225 Duncan Mill Road, Don Mills, Ontario M3B 3K9, Canada.

This is a work of fiction. Names, characters, places and incidents are either the product of the author's imagination or are used fictitiously, and any resemblance to actual persons, living or dead, business establishments, events or locales is entirely coincidental.

This edition published by arrangement with Harlequin Books S.A.

For questions and comments about the quality of this book, please contact us at CustomerService@Harlequin.com.

® and TM are trademarks of Harlequin Enterprises Limited or its corporate affiliates. Trademarks indicated with ® are registered in the United States Patent and Trademark Office, the Canadian Intellectual Property Office and in other countries.

Printed in U.S.A.

www.Harlequin.com

Lara Lacombe earned a PhD in microbiology and immunology and worked in several labs across the country before moving into the classroom. Her day job as a college science professor gives her time to pursue her other love—writing fast-paced romantic suspense with smart, nerdy heroines and dangerously attractive heroes. She loves to hear from readers! Find her on the web or contact her at laralacombewriter@gmail.com.

Books by Lara Lacombe

Harlequin Romantic Suspense

Doctors in Danger

Enticed by the Operative

The Coltons of Texas

Colton Baby Homecoming

Deadly Contact
Fatal Fallout
Lethal Lies
Killer Exposure
Killer Season

Visit the Author Profile page at Harlequin.com for more titles.

For Mister, my favorite traveling companion.

Chapter 1

"Is it time for our next girls' weekend yet?"

Olivia Sandoval couldn't help but laugh at the plaintive note in her friend Avery's voice. "That bad, huh?"

"I'm just ready for a break."

Olivia moved the phone to her other ear and used her free hand to massage a kink in her neck. Avery and Mallory had been her best friends since they'd met in medical school ten years ago, and they'd all shared an apartment. They had managed to live together during their residencies, and then one by one, they had each moved away to take jobs—Avery Thatcher to Atlanta for her job at the Centers for Disease Control and Prevention, Mallory Watkins to Los Angeles to work with a cruise ship company, and Olivia to Washington, DC, where she practiced plastic surgery. They had wildly different careers, but they were still close and made it a point to get together twice a year to catch up. Olivia looked forward to their biannual trips all year, and she knew Avery and Mallory felt the same way.

"I hear you. I bet Mallory is, too."

"Are you kidding me? She's a doctor on a cruise ship, for crying out loud! Her whole life is a vacation."

"Jealous, much?"

"Yes." Avery didn't bother to deny it, which made Olivia smile.

"You get to travel for your job," she pointed out.

"Yeah, but not to any fun locations. I'm leaving tomorrow for a small town in Kansas. Apparently there's some kind of respiratory thing going on there."

"Kansas is nice," Olivia pointed out. "Lots of friendly people."

"But no ocean view," Avery grumbled.

"Well, no. But there's more to life than salt water."

"Says the woman going to Colombia in a few weeks."

"Hey, I'd love for you to join me. We could always use another pair of hands down there."

"I wish I could go," Avery said wistfully. "But I'm not a surgeon like you. I've spent too many years holed up in my office at the CDC—my clinical skills aren't what they used to be. I wouldn't be much help for you."

"You'd be surprised," Olivia replied. "If you remember how to do a physical, you're halfway there. The need for basic medical care is so great, anything is better than nothing. Just think about it," she added. "Colombia is beautiful, and it would be a great experience for you."

Avery was silent for a moment. "I'll sleep on it," she said, a note of interest in her voice. "Maybe I could finagle the time off."

A spark of excitement flared to life in Olivia's stomach. Having one of her best friends come on her annual charity trip would be wonderful. It would be great to spend the time with Avery, and more important, having another clinician on site would really increase the number of patients they could treat during their stay. She opened her mouth to tell Avery as much when the intercom on her desk buzzed to life.

"Dr. Sandoval? Your next patient is here."

"And that's my cue," Avery spoke into her ear. "I'll call you later, okay?"

"Sounds good. Have a safe trip."

Olivia hung up and pressed the button on her desk. "Thanks, Carrie. Please send him in."

"Sure thing."

She stood, running her hand down the front of her blouse to smooth out the wrinkles. As a plastic surgeon, appearances mattered. She had to project confidence and competence, especially for a first meeting. Patients needed to see her as a calm, composed figure who could help transform their physical imperfections into assets. One of the first things they did was judge her own appearance, so she was always careful to make sure her hair and makeup looked good before every meeting.

A soft knock announced her patient's arrival. She opened the door with a smile, ushering the man in and taking his file from Carrie, the office assistant. "Thank you," she said softly to the other woman.

Olivia glanced at the chart before turning her attention to the man who had entered her office. Carlos Martinez. Her gaze tracked over his face as she gestured for him to take a seat. He was a few inches shorter than her, but he carried himself well. His eyes were clear and dark, and silver strands threaded through his black hair, lending him an air of sophistication. His skin had lost some elasticity due to age, and there were fine wrinkles fanning from the corners of his eyes and mouth. *Face-lift*, she thought automatically. A little pulling, a little stretching, and he'd look ten years younger in no time. *And maybe a nose job*, she added, focusing on the slight angle to his nose that hinted of a long-ago break that hadn't healed properly.

She glanced at his body, wondering if he wanted some kind of liposuction, as well. He looked trim, but she knew from experience that a well-tailored suit like the one he was sporting could hide a multitude of sins.

"Mr. Martinez, I'm Dr. Sandoval." She smiled as she extended her hand. His grip was firm but not painful.

"Nice to meet you." His words carried a soft, lilting accent that told her English was not his first language. It reminded her of her father's speech, the rolled *r*'s that sounded almost like a purr, the way his words strung together in a smooth rhythm. She was half-tempted to respond in Spanish, but decided against it. Spanish was the language of her family, the language of home. English helped her remember this was a business meeting and she had to keep things professional.

Olivia rounded her desk and sat, opening his file to a blank page so she could take notes. She liked to spend the first meeting talking to her patients, getting to know them and listening to what they wanted to change about their bodies. It was important that she keep their expectations realistic, especially from the beginning. A lot of people walked into her office looking like an average Joe and wanted to walk out looking like a supermodel. And although Olivia was very good at her job, some things were just not possible.

Although she didn't love performing cosmetic procedures, it paid her bills and allowed her the freedom to pursue her true passion—helping those who truly needed plastic surgery to live a normal life. The burn patients, the children with cleft palates, the women who had suffered severe facial damage at the hands of abusive partners. She was lucky to have found a practice that allowed her to take on a lot of pro-bono work, and even better, they didn't bat an eye when she took a month off every year to do charity work in Colombia.

She was really looking forward to her upcoming trip, but right now she needed to focus on the patient in front of her.

"What brings you to my office, Mr. Martinez?"

"I have business proposition for you."

She lifted a brow at his unexpected reply. "I'm sorry, I thought you were here as a patient." Had Carrie gotten her appointments mixed up? The office manager usually ran a tight ship, but everyone made mistakes.

Mr. Martinez waved a hand, as if the misunderstanding were of no consequence. "I didn't specify when I made the appointment. I simply needed to see you."

"Oh?" This was highly unorthodox. Olivia usually didn't meet with potential business partners on her own—that was something all the members of the practice did together, to ensure everyone had equal input on decisions that might affect them all. "Can we reschedule this meeting so the other doctors can hear your proposal? That's generally how we do things here."

"There is no need," Mr. Martinez replied smoothly. "This proposal is for your ears only."

That was unusual. Olivia had joined the office five

years ago, but she was far from being the senior doctor on staff. What could this man possibly want with her?

"All right," she said, deciding to hear him out. His eyes held a glint that told her he was determined to say his piece. Better to listen and usher him out the door as quickly as possible so she could get on with her day.

"I understand you travel to Colombia every year, and spend a month doing pro bono work there."

"Yes." She leaned forward, excitement making her fingertips tingle. Did he want to donate? The medical charity she partnered with was always in need of funds for supplies, and the more money they raised, the more patients they could treat in Colombia and elsewhere in the world. The need for their services seemed to grow every year, a fact that broke her heart. "Are you interested in making a contribution?" It was a bold question, but subtlety had never been Olivia's strong suit, especially when children in need were concerned.

"In a manner of speaking." He spread his hands out, palms up, as if to say *I'm a reasonable man.*

"I have a proposal that I think will benefit both of us," he continued.

"And what does it involve?" *Would he just get to the point?*

"What I am suggesting is merely that you act as a courier for my employer."

"A courier?" Olivia felt the fine hairs on the back of her neck rise, and she suppressed a shudder. The man in front of her looked polished, but his continued use of euphemisms was suspicious.

"My employer has a business arrangement with partners in Colombia, but what they lack is a reliable transporter. If you accept this offer, you will simply carry funds and once there, exchange them for product. Upon your return, you will deliver the product to me."

Olivia leaned back, wanting to get as far away from this man as possible. He hadn't said anything overtly incriminating, but she wasn't stupid. *Product* was just a nice word for drugs. "No," she said flatly, faking a confidence she didn't feel. She couldn't afford to show weakness—it was clear the man in her office had unsavory connections, and she didn't want to be seen as a target. "I'm not interested."

"I think you will find our offer is very generous," Mr. Martinez replied, ignoring her words. "I know you have extensive debt, both from your medical training and your parents' hospital bills. We can make that go away."

Olivia felt a spike of pain at the mention of her parents. Two years ago, they had been driving home in the middle of a storm when her father had lost control of the car and slid off the road into a tree. Both her parents had been seriously hurt and had lingered in intensive care for weeks before finally succumbing to their injuries. Losing them had almost broken Olivia, but over time, her blinding grief had morphed into a determination to live a life that would make them proud. Her pro bono work in Colombia was one way she found comfort, going back to her father's home country to help those who needed it most.

The fact that this man was asking her to corrupt the work of her heart triggered a black wave of anger in her chest. How dare he try to use the loss of her parents against her? Did he really think she was so desperate for money that she would resort to carrying drugs to pay her debts? She wanted to lash out, to scream at him to leave and then call the police to report him.

But she didn't. Despite her swirling emotions and racing thoughts, she was very aware of the man in front of her. His gaze was locked on her, and though he appeared calm, there was a predatory gleam in his dark eyes. He looked like a snake, waiting and watching for the right time to strike. A trickle of fear skittered down her back, and she realized that she needed to tread very carefully. Something about his demeanor told her that this was not a man who accepted the word *no*.

"I appreciate your offer," she said slowly, almost choking on the lie. *Just get him out of here!* her mind screamed. "But I don't think I'm the right person for this job. My medical supplies are inspected both going to and coming from Colombia. I don't see how I'd be able to bring your product back into the country without attracting the wrong kind of attention." It was the truth, and hopefully he'd accept it.

Her heart sank when he waved away her excuse. "We have provisions in place to make sure that doesn't happen. I assure you, this job is entirely safe. We chose you because you are the last person anyone would suspect. You have a history of travel to the region, and your reputation as a selfless healer puts you above reproach. We will ensure you receive appropriate compensation for your efforts." Then he named a figure that sucked the breath out of her lungs. "We'll pay you half up front, and half upon delivery of the product."

She looked away and ran her hands down her thighs, stopping to grip her knees tightly. Did her fear show on her face? Could he tell how scared she was? She tried to keep her expression neutral, hoping she wasn't giving anything away.

Her mind raced, scrambling for a response. Carlos

was an unknown quantity, and she didn't want to make him angry. *But really*, said a small, subversive voice in her head. *What can he do to me?* She'd already lost her parents, she had no siblings and her two best friends lived in different states. He could always hurt her, but somehow she doubted he would try that tactic. If he wanted her cooperation, she had to be healthy enough to travel. And it would take more than a few bruises to convince her to work for this man.

A strange calm settled over Olivia as she realized that she held all the power here, not the man in front of her. Yes, he worked for drug traffickers, and she watched enough news to know those were dangerous people. But he had come to her, which meant he needed her. And he had no leverage to force her to accept his offer.

She met his gaze. "No."

He smiled, as if he'd expected this reaction. "Dr. Sandoval, I think you should reconsider."

"No," she repeated. "I will not be a part of your business."

Carlos leaned back, his brows lifted in surprise. "That sounds very final."

"It is."

He shook his head. "In my experience, such answers never are."

Olivia opened her mouth to reply, but he waved it off and stood. She rose as well, unwilling to let him tower over her. "It was a pleasure meeting you today. I will give you a little time to think about your answer." He reached into his suit jacket, and Olivia froze, adrenaline making her heart kick hard against her breastbone. Oh, God, was he going to shoot her?

Carlos caught her expression and smirked. He withdrew his hand slowly and set a card on her desk. "My number," he said. "I expect to hear from you soon."

"You won't." The words sounded strangled, and she cleared her throat. "As I said, my answer is final."

He smiled, but his eyes remained cold. "As you say." He walked to the door and stopped, turning back. "I admire your spirit. It will serve you well."

She held her breath until the door closed behind him, then she rocked forward until her palms landed flat against the solid weight of her desk. *It's okay*, she told herself, repeating the words over and over again until she no longer felt like her heart was trying to beat out of her chest. *He's gone.*

But for how long?

The rest of her day passed in a blur. Olivia tried to focus on her job, but the memory of Carlos Martinez was front and center in her mind, an unwelcome and disturbing distraction. Fortunately, she had no scheduled surgeries so her impaired attention was no danger to her patients.

She had to report him to the authorities. It was her only option. The thought of him targeting someone else, someone who might not be able to refuse his offer, weighed on her. Could she really live with herself, knowing he was free to continue hurting people?

But who should she call? Would the police help her? Or did she need to try the FBI? And how could she convince them she was telling the truth? After all, she hadn't recorded their conversation. It was her word against his.

"It doesn't matter," she muttered to herself as she

navigated the evening traffic. "I have to tell someone. What they do with the information is on them." At least she'd be able to sleep at night, knowing she'd done all she could.

She'd tucked his business card and his medical file in her bag before leaving the office. When she got home, she pulled them both out and started up her computer, determined to find the number to the local police. She'd start there, and if the police didn't take her seriously, she'd move on to the FBI or some other organization.

The doorbell rang just as she pulled up the web page for the Alexandria, Virginia, police department. Good—her dinner was here. She'd ordered takeout before leaving the office so she wouldn't have to cobble together a sad meal of crackers and stale cheese. Grabbing her wallet, she headed for the door and glanced through the peephole. A young man stood on her stoop, holding a bag that contained her food.

Olivia opened her door with a smile and extended a hand to take the bag, holding out a few bills in payment. "Thanks," she said, the word dying in her throat as a shadowy figure moved up the walk and into the glow cast by her porch light. She took a reflexive step back, but the delivery boy pulled on the bag, halting her progress.

Carlos Martinez stopped just behind the young man, a wry smile on his lips. "Dr. Sandoval, so good to see you again. We took the liberty of paying for your food so it wouldn't grow cold. May we come in?"

She glanced around wildly, hoping to see lights on in the house next door. Her neighbor, Logan Murray, was a large, fit man, and if she could somehow scream loudly enough to get his attention, perhaps he could help her... But his windows were dark. She was on her own.

"No." Her heart in her throat, Olivia dropped the bag and stepped inside. She grabbed the edge of the door and tried to slam it shut, but the young man stuck his foot in the jamb and forced his way into her house, Carlos close on his heels.

Olivia stumbled backward, trying to keep her gaze on the intruders while she got as far away as possible. A weapon, she needed a weapon—something, *anything*, she could use to defend herself. Her hands ran across the back of her sofa, the end table, the wall. Her fingers swept along the candles standing on the hall table, and she grabbed her mother's silver candlestick, brandishing it like a bat. Why, oh why, had she left her cell phone next to the computer?

"Dr. Sandoval," Carlos said, his tone disapproving. "Please. We are not here for violence. Can we not sit and have a civilized chat?"

Her throat too tight for words, Olivia shook her head.

He let out a deep sigh. "Well, then." He made a sharp gesture with his hand, and the younger man reached behind his back and retrieved a gun that he pointed at Olivia with a confidence that made her stomach drop. *Oh, God.*

Carlos settled into her recliner and gestured for her to take a seat on the couch, facing him. Olivia half walked, half stumbled over, her legs gone numb with fear and her attention focused on the lethal-looking gun pointed at her head. She sank onto the sofa, gripping the candlestick so hard she thought it might snap in her hands.

"I thought we might revisit our conversation from this afternoon."

Olivia cut her gaze to Carlos, then back to the man with the gun. "I have nothing to say to you while I'm being held at gunpoint." Her voice wavered a bit, but she was proud of herself for getting the words out. Her fear of getting shot weighed heavy on her chest, making it so hard to breathe she felt like she was drowning. If he would just put the gun away, she might be able to actually think!

Carlos tilted his head, a slight smile playing at the corners of his mouth. He was enjoying her fear, damn him! Olivia straightened her spine and clamped her mouth shut, determined not to give him any more satisfaction. After a moment, he nodded at the younger man. She refused to turn her head to look at him, but she caught movement from the corner of her eye and breathed a silent sigh of relief as he returned his gun to its hiding place.

"Now, then," Carlos said. "As I was saying. Have you had time to reconsider my earlier offer?"

"My answer hasn't changed," Olivia replied. The other man moved, and she fought the urge to flinch. But he simply walked around the couch and took the rocking chair in the corner of the room, his gaze watchful. At least he wasn't threatening her again.

Carlos merely nodded. "I thought you might say that. So I brought along some additional material for you to examine." He reached into his jacket pocket and withdrew an envelope, holding it out for her. She refused to take it from him, so he dropped it on the table between them and leaned back. "I think you will want to see what's inside," he said, with a nod at the envelope.

Keeping her eyes on the men in front of her, Olivia leaned forward and brushed the table with her fingertips, catching the edge of the paper. She reluctantly set the candlestick on the seat next to her, but really, what good was it against a gun?

The envelope wasn't sealed, and she lifted the flap to find a stack of photographs. The bottom dropped out of her stomach when she saw Avery's face, and she quickly flipped through several of the pictures. Avery at work. Avery at the gym. At the grocery store. At home. The last one had been taken through her bedroom window as her friend packed a suitcase on the bed.

I'm leaving tomorrow for a small town in Kansas...

Olivia moved to the next picture, her fingers so stiff she almost dropped the stack. Tears sprang to her eyes as she saw her other best friend, Mallory. She'd thought Mallory of all people would be safe, since she worked on a cruise ship and was always gone. But apparently Carlos had eyes and ears everywhere.

When she reached the end of the stack, she glanced up to find him watching her. "So you see," he said, as if they'd been talking all along, "you may feel that because your parents are dead, you are safe. But I hope you realize that is not the case."

Olivia swallowed hard. "You can't be serious." Would they really go after her best friends? That was the kind of thing that happened in movies, but not real life. Right?

"Dr. Sandoval, I assure you I am deadly serious. If you do not agree to cooperate, we will target your friends. If that doesn't work, we will move on to their families, as well. Would you really risk the safety of innocents for the sake of your precious pride?"

Her heart sank as she realized the full gravity of his threat. She couldn't bear to think of a world without

Avery and Mallory in it. They'd been best friends since medical school, and Olivia thought of them as family. The only family she had left, in fact.

Helplessness crashed over her, bringing with it a wave of weakness that made her head feel too heavy for her neck. She stared down at her lap, lacking the strength to even meet Carlos's eyes. What choice did she have now? If she refused, she had no doubt Carlos would follow through with his threats. He was never going to go away. He was never going to leave her alone. She'd been so arrogant earlier, assuming he'd just accept her refusal and slink away. But now she realized she was nothing more than a pawn to him, and he was going to play this game with or without her consent.

Anger flared to life deep inside her chest, sending tendrils of heat through her limbs. Sweat gathered at the back of her neck, and she reached up to lift her hair, exposing her skin to the cool air of the room. She eyed the candlestick next to her—could she club Carlos with it? The idea was distasteful and went against the vows she'd taken to do no harm, but in this case, she might be willing to make an exception.

Her eyes shifted to the young man in the chair. He was watching her with dark eyes, his gaze alert. No. If she made any kind of move toward Carlos, he'd shoot her before she could harm his boss. She was well and truly stuck.

"Fine." She spat the word at him, her acceptance leaving a bitter taste in her mouth. "I'll do it. But I want your guarantee that you won't harm them."

Carlos lifted one shoulder in an elegant shrug. "If you fulfill your responsibilities, I will forget all about them."

It was as close to a promise as she was likely to get, and while she didn't trust him, she had to believe he was telling the truth. Why target her friends unless absolutely necessary? It would draw too much attention, and Carlos seemed like the type who didn't make a move unless it was going to benefit him.

He stood and smoothed a hand over his jacket. The young man rose as well and moved to stand beside his boss. Carlos smiled down at her. "I am so glad we were able to come to an agreement," he said solicitously. "You are an intelligent woman, and I knew you would see reason."

Olivia stood but didn't reply. She had nothing to say to him and didn't trust herself to speak. The last thing she needed was to antagonize him just as he was leaving. He might lash out at one of the innocent people in her life just to teach her a lesson in manners.

Her silence didn't seem to bother him. He gestured to the young man, and together they moved to her door. Olivia stayed where she was, turning to watch them go.

He glanced back at her before walking out the door, his eyes going cold when he saw her expression. He looked at his partner and nodded once. Before Olivia realized what was happening, the younger man closed the distance between them and slapped her hard across the face.

Her head snapped back and tears flooded her eyes. She staggered, grabbing onto the back of the couch for support to keep from falling down.

"What was that for?" she said, pressing her hand against her throbbing cheek.

"Consider it a warning," he replied. "You work for us now. We won't tolerate insubordination."

"I didn't say anything," she protested.

He smiled, but it didn't reach his eyes. "You have a very expressive face, Dr. Sandoval. You must learn to control it. The next time, I will not be so kind."

Chapter 2

Logan Murray pulled into his driveway with a sigh, glad to finally be home. It had been a beast of a day, and he was looking forward to a cold beer and a little mindless TV to help him unwind. Most days, he enjoyed his job as a DEA officer. Taking out drug dealers and breaking up smuggling rings was incredibly satisfying, but not every day was an adventure. And after spending the last week buried in paperwork he was ready for something—*anything*—to break the monotonous routine.

He climbed out of the car and headed for his mailbox, glancing at the house next door as he walked. The windows gave off a warm glow, indicating Olivia Sandoval was home. *One of these days*, he thought wryly. She was an attractive woman, and he'd been meaning to connect with her for a while. But the timing was never right. He was off on assignment, or she was out of town. Or they were both too busy to run into each other. Still, part of him held on to the fantasy that they'd magically connect and just click, the way his friend and his soon-to-be-fiancée had while in line at the grocery store. If it could happen to Greg, it could happen to him. Right?

He peeked into his mailbox and tugged out the pile of papers shoved inside. Bill. Junk mail. Card from Mom. He really should call her—it had been too long since they'd talked. And what was this? More stuff for Olivia.

A groan escaped his throat. He needed to call the post office to complain—he'd lost count of the number of times the mail carrier had delivered Olivia's mail to his box. He had a pile of her stuff on his kitchen counter, just waiting to be delivered. Casting another glance at her house, he decided it was time to hand over her correspondence.

Ducking into his house, he dropped his bag on the kitchen table and scooped up Olivia's mail. Maybe he could talk her into having dinner with him while he was over there—it was a long shot on such short notice, but worth a try.

He rang her doorbell, then wiped damp palms on his pants. Why was he nervous? He faced down drug dealers and violent criminals every day in his job, so why did the thought of talking to a beautiful woman make his heart pound in his ears?

Probably because it's been a while, he thought wryly. Five years, to be exact. Ever since he'd arrived home to find his fiancée, Emma, in bed with his best friend, Chris.

Make that his *former* best friend.

The old, familiar anger began to well up in his chest

and he pushed it down, dismissing the pair of them from his thoughts. He'd dated a few women casually since Emma's betrayal, but his heart hadn't been in it. Still, maybe it was time to try again, to let down his guard and give love another chance. He knew Olivia was a doctor. Maybe he'd tell her his story and ask if she wanted to help heal his broken heart.

Real smooth, he thought, mentally rolling his eyes. Shaking his head at his foolishness, he waited for a moment. Had she heard the bell? Maybe she was busy—in the back of the house, or in the garage. *Or the bathtub*, he thought, the image popping into his head before he could stop himself. He strangled the fantasy before it could take flight, unwilling to think about her tawny skin, wet and glowing in candlelight, her heart-shaped face framed by damp ringlets of dark curls...

Looking for a distraction, he pressed the bell again. He'd give her a few more minutes, then come back another time. They were bound to run into each other eventually.

He had just about given up when he heard a soft sound coming from inside her house. Music? No, that wasn't right. He stepped closer to the door, angling his head to hear better. It was the sound of a woman, that much was clear. But something seemed off. Even though the noise was faint and muffled, he could tell from the tone that it wasn't laughter or arousal he heard. It was distress. Something was wrong.

"Olivia?" He raised his voice, hoping she could hear through the thick wood of the front door. "Olivia, it's Logan. Are you okay?"

The noise stopped, so he spoke again. "I just came by to drop off some of your mail. I can leave it on the porch if you like." He hated to go, knowing she was upset, but Olivia struck him as a private person and she probably wouldn't want anyone to see her crying. Besides, what could he really do to help?

After a few seconds of silence, he knelt to place the mail on her welcome mat. Just as he set it down, the lock scraped and she opened the door.

If she was surprised to see him kneeling on her porch, she didn't show it. She stared down at him, her eyes dull and red-rimmed, the tip of her nose pink. Logan gathered up the mail again and slowly rose to his feet, sensing that any sudden movements would spook her into retreat. "Hey, there," he said softly. "Are you all right?"

Olivia merely shrugged one shoulder in an elegant gesture that managed to both answer his question and convey a sense of hopeless surrender.

"I have some of your mail." He extended the bundle, but she merely stared at it for a few seconds, as if trying to recognize what he held and why he was trying to give it to her. Then she reached out to take it, her movements jerky and painful-looking.

"Thanks," she said, her voice as subdued and lifeless as her eyes.

"No problem." He cast about for something to say, but before he could come up with something comforting or helpful, Olivia shrank back into the house, her expression one of horror.

Logan whirled around to see a car driving past, its headlights sweeping up the yard as it turned. The illumination showed nothing amiss—no lurking stalkers hiding in the bushes, no threatening dogs slavering up her driveway, hungry for a bite of her flesh. Just a normal lawn on a normal street. Why then did she look like she'd seen a ghost?

He turned back to see her leaning against the wall, hanging on to the doorknob for support. Her knuckles showed white under the skin, betraying the strength of her grip. It was clear she was on the verge of falling, so Logan reached out to steady her. As soon as his hand made contact with her shoulder, Olivia jerked away, her dark brown eyes going wide and unfocused.

"No!" She took a step back, stumbled over a rug and went down hard on the tiled floor of her entryway.

Wincing, Logan moved forward and crouched down next to her. His arms ached to pull her up and support her, but given her violent reaction to his touch, he didn't want to risk hurting her. "Olivia," he said softly. "Please let me help you."

She was curled in a ball, her arms wrapped tight about her middle. Had she hurt herself? Or was she simply trying to protect herself from him? His heart twisted at the thought that she was afraid of him— never in a million years would he want to give her that impression. Her actions reminded him of children who were left behind in the aftermath of some drug busts, those innocents who were so traumatized they turned inward to block out the world. "I'm going to put my hand on your shoulder and help you sit up," he continued, keeping his tone even. "I'm not going to hurt you. I just want to get you off the floor."

She didn't speak, but he caught her quick nod. Good. She wasn't going to panic. Moving slowly and deliberately, he did as he'd said, moving her into a sitting position. He let her adjust for a moment, watching her face for any signs of newly realized pain.

"Did you hurt yourself?"

She shook her head. "Just my pride," she muttered, pushing her dark brown curls away from her face.

He offered her his hand, and she pulled against him as she rose to her feet. They stood together, their bodies only inches apart. He knew he should move back, give her some personal space. But she still seemed fragile, like a young sapling at the mercy of the wind. She looked like she could go down again at a moment's notice, and given the fact she had yet to release his hand, she probably felt that way, too.

"I'm sorry," she said, keeping her eyes on the floor. "I don't know what came over me."

"It's okay," he assured her. "I'm just glad you didn't get hurt." That much was true, but her reaction troubled him. Her response to his touch had been over-the-top, a fight-or-flight instinct most people only displayed in response to a mortal threat. The fact that her first impulse had been to run made him think she had been hurt in the past, maybe even abused. Was that the problem? Had she had a run-in with a bad former boyfriend tonight?

The thought made his muscles tense, and he glanced around, his training kicking in as he looked for any evidence of a physical encounter. Men who hurt women were lower than scum, and Logan would have no trouble stepping between Olivia and that kind of danger.

His eyes trailed across the entryway table that sat flush against the wall. There were some small tokens arranged on the table's surface, but they looked out of place, as if they'd been knocked askew. Three narrow parallel lines made tracks in the thin layer of dust on the table, and he realized with a shock they were the impressions made by a hand skimming across the surface. Had Olivia run her hand along the table, searching for a weapon?

At the end of the table, a small square impression was left in the dust. Something had sat here, but what? A dark shape on the floor caught his eye, and he focused on it to discover it was a long, thin candle. It had rolled under the table, but he saw a waxy spot on the tile where it had first made impact. So the square impression must have been a candlestick. But where was it now?

Olivia cleared her throat, interrupting his musings. "Ah, thanks for bringing the mail over." She picked up the scattered papers and stacked them on the hall table, then turned to face him. She had regained her composure and was quickly rebuilding her defenses. That was good, but it meant he was losing his chance to find out what kind of trouble she was in.

"Is that Chinese food I smell?" He took a step farther into her house, following his nose. "Man, I haven't eaten all day. Do you mind if I crash your dinner?" It was a lame excuse, but it was the best he could do on short notice.

Olivia stiffened, but when she met his gaze he put on his best "who, me?" expression, hoping it would earn him a spot at her table. His stomach chose that moment to growl audibly, further advancing his case. He smiled sheepishly and was rewarded by a small smile from Olivia.

"Sure," she said. "It'll be nice to have some company."

She led him through the living room and into the kitchen. He caught a glimpse of the candlestick lying on the sofa cushions. Interesting. Had Olivia sat there earlier, facing off against a threat? He inhaled deeply as he walked through the room and caught the faint hint of men's cologne lingering in the air. So someone had been here, someone Olivia had felt the need to defend herself against, using only a candlestick for protection.

Logan waited until Olivia had retrieved plates and silverware and placed them on her kitchen table.

"Olivia, are you in trouble?"

She went pale and dropped the silverware in a noisy clatter against the plates. "No."

"That's not what it looks like to me."

Her dark eyes flicked up to his face before she returned her attention to dishing up the food. "And I suppose you're some kind of detective." She pushed a plate in his direction and sat, and he did the same, taking the chair across from her.

"Something like that," he replied easily.

"What do you do again? You're in security, right?"

"I'm an agent with the Drug Enforcement Administration."

Her hands clenched and she pushed back from the table, the chair legs screeching on the tile floor. "I have to go," she said abruptly.

Logan stood, as well. "Olivia, I don't think that's a good idea."

She shook her head. "No, I really need to get out of here."

He took a step to the side, effectively blocking her exit. She reared back to keep from running into him, and he held out his hands, trying to appear nonthreatening. "Here's the deal," he said, striving for a comforting tone. "It's clear to me that something has happened tonight, something that has you upset. And while I'm not trying to dig into your private life, I would like to know why you're so distressed by the fact that I work for the DEA."

She stared up at him for a moment, worrying her bottom lip with her teeth. It was an incredibly sensuous gesture, but Logan knew she didn't mean anything by it. "I really can't talk about it."

He merely watched her, knowing there wasn't anything he could say to make her trust him. She had to decide that on her own—no amount of pretty words would convince her.

Finally she dropped into her chair, her shoulders slumping in defeat. "You can't help me. No one can."

"That sounds pretty final to me. In my experience, few things are."

She shuddered at his words, as if they'd brought up a bad memory. "If I tell you, will you leave me alone?" She sounded utterly destroyed and he could tell her resolve to stay silent was crumbling.

Not a chance, he thought. But he needed her to talk, so he tilted his head to the side, hoping she would interpret the gesture as agreement. "You can talk to me," he said softly.

She shook her head, pressing her lips together in a pale line. Then she laughed, a harsh, grating sound that was totally void of humor. "What the hell?" she said, the edge in her voice sharper than a sliver of glass. "Just promise me this—keep my friends safe. Will you do that for me?"

Logan frowned, the finality in her tone troubling. "I'll do my best. Why do you sound like you'll be missing them?"

Olivia met his gaze then, and the hopelessness in her brown eyes nearly broke his heart.

"Because in a few weeks, I'll be dead."

* * *

Logan's green eyes widened at her outburst, but he recovered quickly. "I'm sure it's not as bad as you think," he started, his tone making it clear he thought she was being a drama queen. His obvious doubt annoyed her, but she tried not to hold it against him. She did sound like one of those characters on the telenovelas her Nana had loved to watch. Under different circumstances, she might have found the whole thing amusing.

"Do you want me to talk to you or not?"

He hesitated a moment, clearly trying to decide what to say. Then he simply nodded.

Olivia took a deep breath, pushing aside her doubts. Logan worked for the DEA, so he was probably the best person to talk to about Carlos and his offer. Besides, she didn't really have any other options at this point.

To his credit, he didn't interrupt her. He sat there quietly, his large hands folded on the table and his broad shoulders looking like they could hold the weight of the world. She felt a small spurt of satisfaction when he sat up straight at the mention of Carlos—*See? I'm not crazy*, she wanted to say—but he remained silent until she finished telling him the whole story.

"Have you contacted your friends?"

Olivia stared at him, feeling drained of all emotion. "No. Avery would know something is wrong just by the sound of my voice. And Mallory is in the Caribbean somewhere on her cruise ship. But even if I could get ahold of her, I don't want to put either of them at further risk."

He acknowledged her point with a nod. "Fair enough. I just thought you might feel better if you talked to them, reassured yourself that they're still okay."

She looked down at her plate, the food blurring as tears filled her eyes. "I would," she admitted. "But I'm too scared to try right now."

After a moment, she raised her head and met Logan's gaze. Sympathy was bright in his eyes, but he didn't try to offer her empty reassurances or hollow promises. He simply let her process things without trying to brush away her emotions, a fact that she appreciated. She ran her gaze over his strong chin and long, straight nose, then up to his eyebrows, twin brown arches over his deep green eyes. He was a very attractive man, a fact she was finding harder to ignore...

"Okay. Let's talk about Carlos. Can you tell me what he looked like?"

Olivia took a deep breath, appreciating the distraction. "Here's the paperwork he filled out at my office." She slid the folder across the table, then took a second to recall his face and rattled off a description of the other man. "If that's even his real name," she finished.

"Probably not," Logan agreed, glancing through the forms she'd given him. "But he sounds like a guy we've been interested in for a while."

"You know him? Does that mean you know where he is?" This could all be over soon! If the DEA knew where to find Carlos, they could arrest him and her friends would be safe.

Her hope must have shown on her face, because Logan shook his head. "We don't have that kind of information yet," he said gently. "We know he's involved with an organization called Fantasmas del Mal, but we don't yet have specifics about where he lives or who he associates with."

"Fantasmas del Mal," she repeated. The name triggered a dim spark of recognition in the recesses of her brain. She tried not to get involved in that aspect of Colombian life, but no one who spent time in the country could long ignore the collection of organizations that operated in the shadows. "The Evil Ghosts? Is that some kind of drug cartel?"

Logan lifted one shoulder. "In a manner of speaking. The Colombian cartel system isn't what it once was, but the power vacuum left behind by the deaths of Pablo Escobar and his rivals didn't last long. Fantasmas del Mal is one of several militant organizations that stepped in to fight over control of the drug trade."

So it was as bad as she had feared. "That's a rather poetic name."

A small smile flitted across his face. "It is, indeed. Rumor has it the locals coined it because the members of the cartel sweep in to mete out punishments, then disappear like fading ghosts."

She swallowed hard. "I see."

"Olivia, I need to ask you something." He pressed his lips together and looked away, as if he were searching for the right words. "Why didn't you go to the authorities after Carlos came to your office? We could have moved on this, started the process earlier if you'd said something."

"Would it really have mattered?" She walked over to the coffee table, picked up the photos of her friends and held them out for Logan. "Those pictures aren't all from today or even yesterday. Someone has been following my friends for weeks, if not longer. They've been in danger this whole time. What good would a few hours have done?"

He reached up and gently touched her cheek. The

pain from the slap had faded, but the memory of it made her shudder. "That's a fair point," he said softly. "Now that we know they're being threatened, I can make sure they have protection."

Some of the tension left her body at his assurance, but then a horrible thought entered her mind. "What if Carlos's men see their guards? Won't that tip him off that I spoke to you?" She started to pace, wrapping her arms around her waist as she walked. If the police suddenly showed up at Avery's home or office, it would definitely be noticed. And she had no doubts that Carlos was ruthless enough to take out a couple of patrol officers if it meant killing her friends, too. That was just the kind of message he'd love to send, and something told her he wouldn't hesitate to act.

Had she just signed a death warrant for her best friends?

A terrible squeezing band of pressure wrapped around her chest, and she struggled to breathe. *I shouldn't have said anything.* Damn her emotions! They had made her weak, made her seek out the comfort of an understanding listener. She'd thought Logan could help her, but now she realized getting him involved had been a huge mistake, one that would cost her friends the ultimate price.

Black spots danced in her vision, and the roar of blood filled her ears. Something grabbed her shoulders, and then she was pushed down, her fall broken suddenly by a solid structure underneath her. A warm weight pressed against her back, guiding her head forward until she was nearly bent over.

After a moment she registered a low voice, close to her ear. "Take it easy. You're okay. Just keep breathing for me." It was Logan, his breath warm as it fanned across her cheek.

He sounded so calm, so soothing. She felt the pressure in her chest ease, and the whooshing sound in her ears receded as she focused on his voice.

"There you are," he said, after a moment. "Glad to have you back."

"You have to leave Avery and Mallory alone." She gripped his arm and squeezed hard, trying to make him understand how important this was. As much as it pained her to think of her friends being under surveillance by the cartel, at least they were still alive. If the police suddenly showed up, it would do more harm than good.

"Whoa," he said, placing his hand over hers. "Slow down. You're jumping to conclusions here."

"I can't risk their safety. I'd never forgive myself if something happened to them."

"It won't," he said, his tone brooking no argument. "This isn't my first rodeo. I'm not going to have uniformed officers suddenly start following your friends around like lost puppies. The type of protection I'm talking about is more subtle than that. These guys hang back and watch. They focus more on the cartel's men than your friends, making sure the bad guys don't try anything."

"So Carlos won't know they're around?"

Logan shook his head. "Think of them as guardian angels. They're around, but invisible to most people."

That sounded better. Olivia took a deep breath and felt her heartbeat slow as she considered his words. It would be nice to know someone was watching over them, someone who was trained to keep them safe.

And if they could do it without tipping off Carlos and his men? All the better.

"Okay," she said. "I'm sorry I doubted you."

He smiled, his gaze warming as he looked at her. She felt drawn in by his eyes, their mossy green color reminding her of the jungles of Colombia. Was that why she had started talking to him? Because her subconscious had made a connection to her familial home?

For the first time, Olivia became aware of Logan as more than her nice neighbor. He was a handsome, strong man, and he seemed to be very interested in helping her deal with her problems. Her stomach did a funny little flip as the implications of that sank in. It had been a long time—*too long*, her libido chimed in— since she had noticed a man and been noticed in return. She'd been in a serious relationship once. But Scott had dumped her after the deaths of her parents, saying she'd changed too much. Maybe he'd had a point. At first, her grief over their loss had been so raw it kept her from doing much more than surviving. Scott had accused her of shutting down and had pushed her to move on. When she resisted, he'd left, saying he didn't want to be tied down to someone who could give up so easily.

His departure had been another painful blow to her heart, and Olivia hadn't dated since. She couldn't bring herself to trust another man, but she was also a little afraid: if she didn't open her heart to new people, she wouldn't be hurt by their inevitable losses. Avery and Mallory had made it clear they thought she was making a mistake, but in truth, Olivia hadn't met anyone who made her want to take that risk.

Logan spoke again, interrupting her thoughts and reminding her this was no time to get distracted. "There's another possibility you should consider."

"What's that?"

"Your friends may not be under constant cartel surveillance at this time. Carlos may have had his men follow them to get the pictures he showed you, but that doesn't mean they're still being trailed."

His words lit a candle of hope in the darkness of her thoughts. "Do you think so?"

Logan lifted one shoulder in a shrug. "Following people takes time and ties up resources. I'm not saying your friends are in the clear, but Carlos probably feels pretty confident that he can find them. Why waste time having men shadow their every move when he can just pick up the phone and get them back on the radar at a moment's notice?"

A growing sense of excitement made Olivia's skin tingle. Were Avery and Mallory safer than she thought right now? If that was the case, maybe she could somehow warn them, get them to run far away until the danger had passed.

Her thoughts must have shown on her face, because Logan held up a hand as if to slow her down. "I can't be sure they aren't being followed," he began, but Olivia cut him off.

"What if I somehow got a message to them, let them know what was going on? They could hide until we figure out what to do about Carlos."

Logan shook his head, his mouth flattening in sympathy. "Too risky. Carlos is going to be hyperaware of your actions until you're in Colombia. I know you're worried about your friends, but trust me, staying away is the best thing you can do for them right now."

Olivia sank back into her chair, her enthusiasm waning. "How can I be sure he hasn't killed them already?"

"Believe me, you'd know." He sounded quite certain, but Olivia didn't share his conviction.

"How do you figure that?"

Logan grimaced. "These are the kind of people who send graphic videos accompanied by body parts. If your friends were already dead, Carlos would make sure you were aware of that fact."

Olivia felt the blood drain from her face. "Oh, God."

"Try not to think about it."

Oh, sure. Like her imagination was something she could just switch off on command. Maybe that was how Logan dealt with such matters, but Olivia's mind didn't work that way.

She glanced around the room, looking for something to distract her from thoughts of Avery and Mallory being tortured at the hands of vicious strangers. Logan seemed to sense her trouble, and he reached out to grab her hand with his own.

"I know it seems hopeless now, but we will find a way to make sure everyone comes through this safely. Especially you." He punctuated his words with a gentle squeeze, and warmth traveled from her hand up her arm and into her chest. Although she didn't know him very well, Logan's presence was a comfort. It might have been the fact that he was so calm when her emotions were all over the place. Or it might have been the confidence he projected, as if he could take on the problems of the world and put them to rights. Or perhaps it was just the peace that came from being touched by another person seeking to offer reassurance, something she hadn't felt since Scott's departure. Either way, Olivia closed her eyes and allowed herself a moment to savor the contact.

When she opened her eyes, she saw that Logan was watching her. His expression was one of concern, and she had the fleeting sensation that he really and truly cared about her and her problems. But that was probably just wishful thinking on her part. After all, they barely knew each other, so why would he care about her on a personal level? He was likely interested in her story as it pertained to his job, but nothing more.

Disappointment felt like a stone in her stomach, but she ignored it. It was her own fault she had to turn to a neighbor she barely knew for help.

Pushing aside those thoughts, she refocused on Logan. "What happens now?" The words were unfamiliar in her mouth. As a doctor, she was used to having complete control over a situation. In her office, in the operating room—even in Colombia—she was in charge. People looked to her for guidance and direction, and she had no problem stepping up and taking the reins. But this was a situation she didn't understand and didn't know how to navigate. She felt like she'd been dropped in a foreign country, with no idea of the customs or how to speak the language.

He frowned slightly. "Two things. First, I need to call this in and inform the team what we're dealing with here."

"Wait a minute," Olivia replied, disentangling her hand from his and holding it up. "I'm not willing to risk the safety of my friends like that." Had she made a mistake after all?

Logan's expression was a mix of pity and kindness. "We'll do everything in our power to keep them safe," he said. "But I have a responsibility to report this, and the only way we can find out what's really going on is if we launch an official investigation."

"Won't that alert the bad guys that I talked to you?" Panic clawed up from her chest, threatening to strangle her. Things were moving too fast, spinning out of control. If Logan got more people involved, it increased the chances of Carlos finding out and killing her friends.

"We won't do anything to tip our hand."

"What's the second thing?" At his puzzled look, she continued. "You said there were two things that need to happen next. What's the second?"

He nodded. "We're going to find a way to keep you alive while you carry this out."

Olivia wanted to believe him, but she didn't dare get her hopes up.

"Do you really think that's possible?"

Logan apparently heard the resignation in her voice. He reached out and placed his hand under her chin, tipping her head up until she met his eyes.

"You're going to get through this, Olivia. I will make sure of it."

Chapter 3

She was quiet on the drive in. Logan couldn't tell if she was shutting down, or merely being considerate since he spent most of the time on the phone. He made a few calls to some key players, people who needed to know what was going on and would help decide what to do about it. He didn't want to bring everyone in just yet—not until he knew exactly what they were dealing with. He didn't want to have to tell Olivia this, but the threats from Carlos could be a false alarm, or it might be too late for her friends. Either way, he wasn't going to pull the trigger on a massive operation without a little more confirmation.

He glanced over, hoping to get a read on her mood. But she was turned away from him, staring out the window at the passing buildings. It was just as well. He didn't exactly have a script of comforting words to draw from, and he certainly didn't want to make things worse for her by saying the wrong thing.

Part of him was glad she wasn't looking at him. He'd had a hard enough time containing his reaction at the kitchen table. As soon as she'd told him her story, complete with mention of the mysterious Carlos Martinez, his skin had started to tingle as if he'd been dropped into a pool of champagne. Her description of the man had fit perfectly with the profile they had on one of the US operatives for Fantasmas del Mal. The administration had been working for ages trying to gather more intel on this guy and his associates. If they could stop the US cell of this organization, it would be a major blow to the Colombian crime lords. Furthermore, crippling the US arm of Fantasmas del Mal might just weaken them enough that their competition would finish off the cartel.

But first things first. They had to figure out a way to keep her alive while she did the group's dirty work.

Once again, his protective instincts fired up at the thought of Olivia in danger. He wasn't quite sure why she elicited such a strong reaction from him, but he wasn't going to dismiss the feeling. It had been so long since he'd felt much of anything that he welcomed the emotion, even though he knew it would only make matters more complicated.

Some things were worth the trouble.

The way he saw it, the only way her friends stood a chance of getting out alive was if Olivia carried the cartel's money and exchanged it for drugs. A simple plan, except for one obvious flaw: Olivia wasn't trained to handle this kind of situation.

And the bad guys knew it.

Logan tightened his grip on the steering wheel as he thought about her, alone and helpless, sent to deliver a pile of money in exchange for a suitcase full of drugs. She would be like a lamb to slaughter. The suppliers would likely give her the drugs—fear of Fantasmas del Mal ran deep in Colombia. But that didn't mean they wouldn't hurt Olivia in the process. Everyone knew these exchanges were dangerous. And as long as Olivia didn't die... No harm, no foul, at least as far as the cartel was concerned.

Besides, unless he missed his guess, Carlos Martinez or another mystery man would probably kill her once she got back and delivered their product. She was clearly reluctant to participate, and they didn't need anyone with a conscience knowing too much about their business. Once Olivia had completed the job, she'd be considered a loose end, someone to dispose of quickly before she could do any damage.

He shook his head. No matter what she did, she was damned. He clenched his jaw, hating the thought of her being treated like a loose end. She was so much more than that...

Did she realize the magnitude of the danger she was in? He glanced at her out of the corner of his eye, but her posture hadn't changed. From what he could tell, she was a smart woman. They didn't exactly hand out medical school diplomas, and he imagined plastic surgery was a demanding specialty. But book smarts didn't always translate into street smarts, and it was possible Olivia hadn't thought that far ahead.

"There's no happy ending here, is there?"

Or maybe she had.

He winced, but really, it was better this way. He'd

much prefer her to be informed than to be ignorant of the risks and realities of her situation. And a big part of him was relieved that he didn't have to be the one to crush her hopes. Call him old-fashioned, but he really hated to be the guy who made a woman cry.

"We don't know all the facts yet," he cautioned. "There's a lot of information we still need before we act."

Olivia turned to face him then, her wide mouth pressed into a thin line. "You and I both know that the only way I'll ever see my friends again is if I do what they want. That's assuming the cartel doesn't kill them just to make a point."

Logan didn't reply. He couldn't deny the truth of her words, but he didn't want to confirm them, either.

"So the only way to get out of this is for me to work with the devil. Which will probably get me killed."

"Not necessarily," he interjected. For some reason, it was important to him that she not give up hope. The odds were not in their favor, but there was always a chance.

And he was going to do his best to make that chance a reality.

She smiled, but it didn't reach her eyes. "I'm not stupid," she said softly. "And while I don't know much about this organization, I doubt they're the type to let me walk away. I refused them once, and they made it clear that to do so again would be a bad idea." She ran her fingertips along her cheek as she spoke, and for the first time he noticed a faint darkening there, like the beginnings of a bruise. Had they hit her? He nearly snorted in disgust. He wouldn't put it past Carlos or his men. From what he knew of them, they weren't above bullying a woman to get what they wanted.

Logan was quiet as he pulled into the parking lot. He found a spot close to the door and cut the engine, then turned to face Olivia. "Can I ask you a question?"

She shrugged. "Sure."

"What's the worst case you've ever had?"

Her brows drew together. "Worst in what way? Most difficult, or most frustrating?"

"I mean worst, as in you thought there was nothing you could do."

Olivia's eyes dropped to her lap, and he knew she was thinking. "There was a child in Colombia," she said. "He was about six and had a cleft palate. The surgery itself wasn't terribly complicated, as these things go, but once we got him onto the table everything went wrong. We lost power, his pulse dropped dangerously low, and the anesthesiologist had no way to truly measure his state of consciousness. I thought for sure we were going to lose him."

"Did you?"

"No." She shook her head, then lifted her eyes to meet his. "We didn't. We pulled out all the stops, and by some miracle we were able to save him and complete the operation."

"It wasn't a miracle," he replied. "It was your talent and the skills of those on your team."

Olivia tilted her head. "I suppose that's one way of looking at it."

"I know this is a lot to ask. I know you don't know me, and you don't know the members of my team. But please try to trust me. Things look bleak now, but I will find a way to get you and your friends through this."

"How can you be sure?" The words were barely more than a whisper, but he heard them loud and clear in the quiet car. "I want to believe you—I do. But I'm so afraid."

"I know," he said, just as softly. "But it's my job to make sure the bad guys don't win." *Especially where you're concerned.* For some reason, Olivia's dilemma was more than just another case to him—protecting her was something he felt compelled to do. "Is this the part where you tell me you're the best there is?" She gave him a shaky smile, trying to pass the question off as a joke. But he saw the curiosity in her eyes, the burning need to know if he really could deliver on his promises.

"Would you feel better if I did?" He could rattle off a list of his accomplishments in his sleep, but that's not what she needed to hear. Besides, he knew better than anyone that words were meaningless. He had to show her by his actions that he was capable of keeping her safe.

"I honestly can't say."

Without thinking, Logan reached over and brushed a thick tendril of glossy brown hair behind her ear. "Tell you what. Let's go inside and have a conversation with some of my friends. You can listen to what we come up with, and I'll let you decide if I'm good at my job."

She nodded, and they climbed out of the car. He walked around the hood and put his hand on the small of her back to guide her into the building. It fit perfectly, as if that spot on her body had been made for his touch.

Don't even go there, he told himself. Olivia was a woman in trouble, and while his inner hero was thrilled to be the one to ride to her rescue, he had no business entertaining those kinds of thoughts. His personal feelings had no place in this situation, a fact he couldn't afford to forget. Things were bad enough—one slipup on his part could cost several lives.

It was a sobering realization, and one that got his brain back on track.

Time to go to work.

Olivia was beginning to regret her decision to stay in Logan's office.

It was a nice enough place, but being alone with her thoughts only gave her the opportunity to obsess about Avery and Mallory—where they were, if the cartel had kidnapped them yet. If they were all going to make it out alive.

Logan hadn't been gone long. "You're welcome to sit with us as we hash this out," he'd said.

"No, thanks." She didn't need to be in the room while he and his friends talked candidly about her situation. She wanted them to feel free to come up with a plan, and if they were trying to be sensitive to her feelings, they might not discuss all their options.

"Want some coffee?"

She'd declined his offer. She was jittery enough already—if she added caffeine to the mix, she just might vibrate right out of her skin.

He'd given her a sympathetic look. "I'll come back for you soon."

She'd merely nodded, and he'd turned and left the room.

To pass the time, Olivia stood and walked over to the wall behind his desk. It was filled with pictures and plaques, physical evidence of his commendations and awards. She stepped closer, peering at a photo that showed a group of men sitting on a large pile of plastic-covered bundles. *Drugs*, she realized. It took a second to find him, but Logan was sitting on the right-hand side, grinning widely underneath his sunglasses. There were several other similar photos on the wall, making her wonder just how many successful operations he'd conducted. Her heart lightened a bit at the proof that Logan really was as good as she'd hoped. Maybe she and her friends would get through this after all.

Her gaze flickered over to a formal picture, one of Logan in a suit, standing next to a dignitary who looked vaguely familiar. He was quite handsome when he dressed the part, but her eyes kept going back to the more casual shots of Logan with his team. There was something about those images that drew her to him. Maybe it was his tanned skin, his tangled hair or even his knockout grin. Perhaps it was the combination of all three. But the longer she studied the pictures, the more she realized she liked looking at him like this because he appeared to be happy. The photos had captured a man who truly enjoyed his work, one who was totally comfortable in his own skin. It was a rare quality these days, especially in her field. She was so used to being around people who hated some aspect of their appearance that some of their negativity had rubbed off on her, making her forget that not everyone was unhappy. No wonder she had found Logan attractive from the beginning—he was the natural antidote to the melancholy of her daily job.

Not that it was all bad. Her trips to Colombia made the daily grind worth it. There was nothing like using her skills to change someone's life for the better. These were not people who felt a little too fat or a little too wrinkled to be pretty. These were patients who couldn't eat properly because of cleft palates, people who had massive scars, people who truly needed help. Fixing them gave her the only peace she'd felt since her parents had died, and she lived off the sense of contentment for the rest of the year.

Olivia rubbed her hands up and down her arms, suddenly feeling cold. Logan had a light jacket hanging off the back of his chair, and she reached for it, vowing to return it to its rightful place before he caught her wearing his clothes. She shrugged it on, rolling up the sleeves so her hands were free. It hung off her shoulders and halfway down her thighs, but she felt immediately warmer. Breathing in, she caught a hint of laundry detergent, male body wash and a faint, clean note that could only be his skin. It was a pleasant scent and she closed her eyes, taking a deeper breath. Being wrapped up in his jacket made her feel secure, and as she stood there snuggling into the fabric, her heart rate slowed and her muscles began to relax. For the first time since Carlos's appearance in her office, she felt normal.

A soft knock at the door interrupted her sanctuary. She turned to find Logan standing in the doorway, his eyes dark and unreadable.

"We're ready for you now."

She swallowed, her heart in her throat. "Okay." She took a step toward him, then realized she still wore his jacket. With a small sound of embarrassment, she moved to take it off.

Logan held out his hand, stalling her. "Leave it," he said. He eyed her up and down, the corner of his mouth lifting in a half smile that was too sexy for her liking. "It looks good on you."

Goose bumps broke out along her arms, making her glad the long sleeves covered her completely. Logan was here as a favor to her, and the last thing she wanted was to make things awkward between them.

"Did you come up with something?"

Logan's eyes sparkled as he looked down at her. "We did, indeed. Come on—I'll introduce you to the team."

She would make a terrible poker player, Logan thought to himself. Olivia sat and listened patiently while the other men spoke, but her furrowed brows and turned-down lips made it very clear what she thought of their plan.

He was fairly proud of his team and the strategy they'd come up with, especially given the short time in which they'd had to work. It was a decent approach, but Olivia's terrified expression made him start to second-guess their work.

Did we miss something? Should we try another angle? Possibly, but he and the rest of the team had hashed out several options before settling on this one. It was by no means perfect, but it was a damn good strategy to build upon.

Keith finished talking, and the men fell silent. All eyes were on Olivia as she considered their explanations. He could practically feel the tension ratchet up in the room as the guys waited for her to speak. Her face betrayed her thoughts, but they all wanted to hear if she would agree, despite her obvious reservations. Since she was an integral part of the operation, it was crucial she felt comfortable participating in the plan. If not, they would need to go back to the drawing board.

After a pregnant pause, Olivia exhaled in a gust of

breath. Logan found himself holding his own breath in response, not wanting to miss her reply. He forced himself to breathe with a little mental kick. Why was he so nervous? This certainly wasn't his first operation, and he usually didn't get so wound up when proposing a plan of action. Why should this be any different?

Because it's personal, he realized. He didn't know Olivia well, that was true, but she was his neighbor. She belonged in the "home" category in his mind, and it bothered him that something from his career had bled over to stain that compartment of his world.

"I want to make sure I understand what you're proposing," Olivia said, jerking him out of his thoughts and back into the room. "You want me to do exactly what the bad guys have asked. The first step has me carrying a large amount of cash into Colombia. How exactly am I going to get that into the country without raising suspicions?"

"That's our problem," Keith assured her. "Don't worry about it—we'll make sure you don't have any trouble on that end."

"Okay." She sounded anything but convinced, but she didn't protest. "What about the exchange? Won't they kill me and just take the money?"

Alan shook his head. "That's highly unlikely. They know if they cross Fantasmas del Mal the cartel will pull no punches when it comes to retribution."

"Oh, of course," she replied, sarcasm leaking into her voice. "So I'll just exchange the money for drugs, and then waltz back into the US, clearing Customs without a second glance?"

"Well…" Keith, Alan and Joseph shared a glance. "Basically, yeah," Joseph finished. "I know it's hard to believe, but we'll smooth the way for you. We need you to come back here and give the goods to Carlos, so we can apprehend him."

"Why can't you grab him when he gives me the money? Why do I have to go through all of it if you're just going to arrest him in the end?"

"Because," Logan interjected, sensing she was at the end of her patience. "If we arrest him before you complete the job, they'll kill your friends. Plus, waiting gives us even more time to gather information on him, and our partners in Colombia will continue to investigate his associates. By working together, we'll be able to build a much stronger case, so when we do arrest him, we'll have even more charges to bring against him and his collaborators."

Olivia shot him a look that told him as clear as any words that she couldn't care less about the legal ramifications of waiting to arrest Carlos. He expected her to fire back a retort, but she simply bit her bottom lip and remained silent.

The men glanced at each other again, their uncertainty plain. Olivia didn't sound too happy at this point—did they need to come up with something else?

"Gentlemen, can you give us a moment please?" Olivia clearly wanted to say something, but Logan had the sense she didn't want to talk in front of his team. Maybe if it was just the two of them, she'd open up a little more.

The guys rose as one from the table and filed out of the room, each one looking slightly relieved at being out of the line of fire. Logan had the distinct urge to laugh as these experienced men rushed to get away from one upset woman, leaving him behind to handle the situation. So much for loyalty!

After the door shut behind them, Logan studied Olivia, trying to gain insight into her frame of mind. "Want to tell me what's bothering you?" he asked softly.

She huffed out a laugh. "Where should I begin?"

He ducked his head in acknowledgment. "Fair enough. What do you think of the plan?"

One slim shoulder jerked up, then disappeared into the folds of his jacket. Seeing her wear his clothing did something funny to his stomach, like he'd just chugged a two-liter bottle of soda before spinning in circles. *Focus*, he chided himself. *Find out what's bothering her.*

"It seems fairly straightforward," she replied, sounding a little hesitant.

"That's usually the best way to do things. Less chance of mistakes."

"For you, maybe. You do this all the time. But me?" She shook her head. "I'm not built for this."

And wasn't that the understatement of the year? Logan couldn't stop his gaze from roaming over her, starting at her wide brown eyes and wandering down to her graceful hands, stopping to linger on everything in between. Olivia was a woman built for civilized pursuits, not the machinations of a ruthless drug cartel.

"No, you aren't," he agreed. Seeing her here in his office, drowning in his jacket and looking lost, tugged at something deep inside his chest. Could he really ask her to do this on her own? Sure, the DEA would be watching from afar—they couldn't get too close because they didn't want to betray their involvement and spook the bad guys. But was that enough?

No, he decided. It wasn't. Olivia deserved more.

"Would you feel better if I went with you?"

Her head jerked up at that, her eyes brightening with hope. "Can you do that?"

He nodded, mentally preparing himself for the battle that was sure to come when he announced this change of plan to the rest of the guys. "If it would make you feel better."

She grabbed his hand, squeezing hard. "You'd do that for me?"

"We take care of our own," he replied, squeezing back. "And if you do this, you're definitely on the team."

She smiled at that, her eyes bright with unshed tears. "I never thought I'd be part of a posse before."

"Please," he scoffed. "We're a little more organized than that."

"That's true," she said. She studied him a moment, her expression growing serious. "Are you sure you can do this? It won't mess up the surveillance the other guys were talking about?"

"It'll be fine," he assured her. "If anything, it will be good to have eyes and ears on you, so I can make sure nothing bad happens." Besides, the surveillance team wouldn't be able to respond quickly if necessary, whereas he'd be right there, ready to act if things got too hairy.

"I would feel better if you were with me," she murmured, almost to herself. Her words made him want to throw his shoulders back and grin, but he controlled the urge.

"So you'll do it?" he asked, trying not to sound too eager.

She nodded, meeting his gaze. "If you can really come with me, then yes, I'll do it."

"Excellent." Logan couldn't stop the smile spreading across his face. Finally, they had a solid chance to bring these guys down! It was the operation of a lifetime, and he would make sure they succeeded.

Or die trying.

Chapter 4

Olivia ran her hands down the front of her pants, wiping away the sweat that was making her skin feel clammy. *This will be over in just a few minutes*, she told herself. It didn't help. She had been dreading this moment since Logan had asked her to call Carlos and set up another meeting at her office, and even the knowledge that Keith and Alan, two of Logan's fellow DEA agents, were sitting in the waiting room did nothing to help calm her anxiety.

"Why can't you be there, too?" she'd asked him. She'd heard the fear in her own voice, but if Logan had noticed, he hadn't commented.

"I don't want Carlos or any of his men to see me before I accompany you on the trip. We can't risk raising their suspicions," he'd explained patiently. "Besides, Keith and Alan are two of the finest men on my team.

I trust them, and I know they'll keep you safe. But it won't come to that."

He'd been so confident that Carlos wouldn't try to hurt her at this meeting, a fact she'd appreciated at the time. But now that she was moments away from seeing the man again, her nerves were starting to get the better of her.

Would he be able to tell she'd gone to the authorities? He had said her thoughts showed on her face. What if Carlos took one look at her and knew the DEA was involved? Would he simply kill her now, or go after Avery and Mallory first? Olivia's stomach dropped to the floor and her knees began to wobble. She sank onto her desk chair and sucked in a breath, trying to push back against a sudden surge of nausea.

"I can't do this," she whispered, her heart beating wildly against her breastbone. Her head felt curiously light, as if it was a balloon that could float away at any moment. It was an unsettling sensation, and Olivia gripped her desk hard, afraid that if she let go she would rise off the ground and be lost.

A shrill ring pierced the fog of her panic and made her jump. It took her a moment to place the sound, then she realized it was coming from the phone Logan had given her last night. A burner, he'd called it. Almost impossible to trace, and since the cartel didn't know she had it, it was safe to use.

"Hello?" She could barely get the word out.

"Olivia." Logan's warm, deep voice flowed across the line. "How are you?"

She wanted to laugh at the ordinary question, but couldn't manage it. That was probably for the best, the small, rational part of her brain realized. She was on the cusp of hysteria and if she started to laugh now, she might never stop.

Fortunately, Logan seemed to understand. "Listen to me," he said, his tone soothing. "You're going to be all right. I know you're scared, but you can do this."

"What if he figures it out?" she whispered loudly. It was silly, she knew, but she was afraid that if she gave voice to her suspicions, Carlos would indeed realize she had talked to someone. "What if he reads it on my face?"

Logan didn't respond right away, and Olivia felt the blood drain from her head. *He agrees*, she thought numbly. *He knows I'm going to give it away without saying a word.*

"You do tend to let your thoughts show on your face," he said finally. "But that's not necessarily a bad thing here."

"What?" she squeaked. "How do you figure that? He'll kill my friends!"

"Let me finish," Logan said patiently. "You're scared, right? That's normal. Let the fear show. It would be strange if you weren't afraid. Besides, Carlos thinks he's beaten you, that he controls you. If you act too confident, it will clue him in that something is off."

"There is no chance of me acting too confident," she assured him.

"What happened to your anger?" Logan challenged. "The woman I saw last night was afraid, yes, but underneath the fear she was spitting mad that she'd been manipulated. Where did that fighting spirit go?"

"I can't risk my friends," she said, but Logan cut her off.

"If you don't find your anger, they're as good as dead," he said bluntly.

Olivia bit back a cry, but he didn't stop to offer an apology. "If you let your fear control your actions, you will lose. If you spend this time worried, Carlos will know about our plan, and your face and demeanor will communicate that to him louder than any words. It's a self-fulfilling prophecy."

"What am I supposed to do?"

"Dig deep and find the strength I know you possess," he replied. "You can do this, Olivia. You are a smart, savvy woman. And you are not alone. Don't let this gangster get the better of you. You're smarter than he is."

Tears sprang to her eyes and she blinked hard to keep them from falling. Did Logan really see her that way? Or was he just giving her a pep talk so she didn't blow the operation before they'd even gotten started? Either way, his confidence was seeping into her, shoring up the cracks in her defenses and making her feel like maybe she could get through this after all.

"I wish you were here with me," she said, realizing too late how that sounded. She winced, hoping Logan wouldn't think she was hitting on him.

"I do, too," he said. "But this is the last time you'll have to face Carlos. I'll be by your side every moment we're in Colombia. You'll be sick of me by the time we're done," he said, laughing softly.

Not likely, she thought reflexively. Then she shook her head. That was just her insecurities talking, she decided. Logan was a strong and confident presence, and he made her feel safe. It was only natural she wanted him around while she dealt with the unknown quantity that was the cartel.

"We'll see about that," she replied, trying to sound natural.

Logan was quiet, as if digesting her words. "I'm going to hang up now," he said, sounding a little rueful. "Remember, you can do this. And your backup is just down the hall. It's going to be okay."

Olivia closed her eyes and let his voice wash over her, diluting the worst of her fears. "Thank you," she said simply.

"Don't mention it. I'll see you after." It was a statement, but she grabbed on to it like a promise.

"I'm going to hold you to that."

"I hope you do."

Then he was gone, and she felt a wave of loneliness at the loss of his presence. Even though he hadn't physically been near, just hearing his voice had been enough to quell her rioting emotions. She'd never been affected like that by anyone before, and the fact that Logan, a relative stranger, held such sway over her should have bothered her.

Instead, it was a comfort. And given all the uncertainty in her life right now, Olivia wasn't inclined to question this gift.

She slipped the cell phone into her desk drawer just as her office line rang. She took one last deep breath to steady herself and answered.

"Dr. Sandoval? Your next patient is here."

Logan's face flashed in her mind, along with his encouraging words. *You can do this.* She was going to have to, because in addition to keeping her friends safe, Olivia didn't want to let him down. This was his chance to take out a major player in the drug trade, and she wouldn't let herself be the one to mess things up.

Feeling a little like her old self again, Olivia straightened her spine. "Send him in, please."

"Look alive, guys. I've got eyes on him."

Joseph's voice buzzed in Logan's ear, triggering a jolt of adrenaline that made Logan's heart pick up speed.

"Pictures?" Logan asked. Even though Olivia's description of Carlos was spot-on, it would be good to have photographic confirmation of his involvement.

"Got 'em," Joseph replied. He was parked down the street with the best telephoto lens money could buy, snapping shots of anyone entering and leaving the building that housed Olivia's office. "It's our guy.

"He's in the building," Joseph continued. "Headed your way, Keith."

There was a rumble of acknowledgment as Keith cleared his throat. He and Alan were sitting in the waiting room, posing as patients. Technically, their presence wasn't required, but Logan felt better knowing two of his team members were only a few feet away from Olivia. Carlos was an unpredictable man, and Logan didn't want Olivia to have to deal with him alone if there was any trouble.

Logan leaned forward and adjusted the blinds, carefully checking to make sure the sun didn't reflect off his own set of lenses. He had a direct line of sight into Olivia's office from his perch across the street. Normally he'd be the one inside, right in the thick of things while Keith took care of this end of the operation. But since Logan was going to pose as a potential investor on the trip, he didn't want to show his face beforehand

and risk Carlos recognizing him later. So today it was his job to collect more photographs and to record the conversation, using the department's powerful audio surveillance equipment.

It would have been easier to fit Olivia with a wire. More enjoyable, too, his libido pointed out, as it was the perfect excuse to get his hands on her body. But it just wasn't worth the risk. If Carlos discovered it, he'd kill her without a second thought.

And so Logan sat in his nest of wires and cables, trying to keep his frustration under control. This kind of watching and waiting was a crucial part of the job, but it had never been his favorite. He much preferred the fieldwork—the thrill of the chase and the adrenaline rush that flooded his system every time he confronted danger.

His team teased him about his need to constantly keep moving, but Logan had learned that if he didn't stop, he didn't have time or energy to think about *her*.

His ex-fiancée's betrayal with his best friend had cut deep, and even though five years had passed, the pain was still with him. After kicking Emma out, Logan had thrown himself into the job, using the never-ending demands of his career as an excuse to neglect his personal life. Olivia was the first woman who'd caught his eye in what seemed like forever, and even now, he couldn't put his finger on what exactly drew him to her.

A movement across the street caught his eye, interrupting his musings. He focused the camera on Olivia as she stood and smoothed the front of her blouse. He hadn't told her he was watching from across the way—he didn't want to make her feel self-conscious. She was nervous enough already.

"You can do this," he muttered, knowing she couldn't hear him but wanting to say the words nonetheless. She was holding up remarkably well under the circumstances, but he held his breath as her office door opened and Carlos stepped inside. If she could just get through these next few minutes...

"Dr. Sandoval, so good to see you again."

Logan adjusted the volume of the microphone, tuning it slightly to improve the signal as he did so. Then he double-checked that it was recording. So far, so good.

He could tell by Olivia's body language that she wasn't happy. Still, she nodded in reply, the gesture only a little stiff. "Good afternoon."

She sat behind her desk and Carlos unbuttoned his suit jacket before taking one of the chairs across from her. "I am so glad we could meet to discuss the details of our business together," he said smoothly. "But first, if you will permit me?"

He reached into his jacket, and Logan's gut twisted in warning. Was Carlos going for a weapon? Had he somehow guessed the DEA was watching?

Apparently, Olivia had the same fear. She leaned back in her chair and lifted her hands as if to defend herself. But she was a sitting duck behind her desk, totally at the mercy of the man in her office.

Logan's heart shot into his throat and he opened his mouth to give Keith the signal to go. But just as the words formed on his tongue, Carlos withdrew his hand to reveal not a gun, but a small black object that he placed on the desk.

Olivia swallowed hard, regaining her composure quickly. "What is that?"

"A simple jamming device to ensure our conversa-

tion remains private. One can never be too careful,"
Carlos said. Then he pressed a button on the device,
and Logan's audio feed went dead.

Damn!

Chapter 5

Olivia couldn't take her eyes off the small black device on her desk. *Breathe*, she told herself, trying to keep the alarm off her face.

"Why did you bring that?" Her voice shook a little, but hopefully not enough to arouse Carlos's suspicions.

He tilted his head to the side, his gaze sharpening as he studied her. "This bothers you?" He leaned back, a small smile playing at the corners of his mouth. "Why? Do you have something to hide?"

The question hit a little too close to home, but Olivia held back an instinctive flinch. *What does he know?* she wondered. He must suspect someone was listening, which meant he had to think she'd gone to the authorities. But if he had any proof she had talked to the DEA, surely he wouldn't bother with the facade of this meeting. From everything Logan and his men had told her, the cartel wasted no time meting out retribution. And Carlos didn't seem like the type to get his hands dirty, so it was unlikely he was planning on killing her in her own office. He was probably just fishing for information, wanting to see how she responded.

His question hung in the air between them, and Olivia realized the danger of this moment. If her denial was too strident, he would suspect she was hiding something. Too casual, and it would seem like she had lost her fear of him. Given the way he'd reacted the last time she'd shown any kind of attitude, he likely wouldn't hesitate to punish her again. She had to walk a very fine line to make sure she didn't trip his radar or trigger his temper.

It was enough to make her palms sweat and her mouth go dry. But then Logan's voice echoed in her head. *Find your anger.*

Olivia met Carlos's gaze. "I have nothing to hide. But I'm curious—why did you bring this now? You had no problem speaking freely in my office before. Are you afraid of something?"

The subtle taunt hit its mark. Carlos narrowed his eyes and straightened in the chair. "Be careful, Dr. Sandoval. Do not forget who you are dealing with here."

She nodded at the device. "I don't appreciate the implications of that. I told you I wouldn't contact the police, and I haven't." It was the truth, and it showed on her face. Logan had come to her, and he was DEA, not a cop. "You didn't use that in my office the other day or in my home later that night. What changed?"

"Today, we discuss the details of our business. There can be no chance of eavesdropping."

So he *didn't* know anything—he was just being paranoid. Olivia let out a silent sigh, the tension leaving her body along with her breath.

"Let's get this over with," she said, reaching for a notepad and pen.

Carlos held up a hand and she jerked back, her heart leaping into her throat.

He smirked at her reaction, but merely placed his hand on the notepad, sliding it away from her. "No records," he said. "Nothing gets written down."

"How am I supposed to remember the details?" she protested. "It's not like I have experience doing this."

He lifted one brow. "You're an intelligent woman, Doctor," he said softly. "I'm sure you can handle it. And if not…" He waved his hand in a dismissive gesture that suggested the alternative was just as acceptable. The message was clear: either she memorized his instructions, or she died.

Anxiety was a tight band around her chest, making it hard to breathe. The blood rushed through her ears, and she struggled to focus on what Carlos was saying. She had to get this right so she could tell Logan and his men exactly what was going to happen and when. If she left out even the smallest detail, it could compromise the entire mission.

The men she was to meet worked in a processing station deep in the jungle, turning raw *coca* extract into cocaine. She would be told when and where to meet them once she was in Colombia, but he gave her basic information regarding the approximate location of the meet.

Carlos was surprisingly patient with her, repeating his instructions several times and asking her to say them back to him. Only after she had parroted his words verbatim several times did he seem satisfied.

"Do they know you are sending me?"

He nodded. "Of course. This is not a surprise to them."

Olivia shook her head. "No, I mean do they know you are sending a woman?" Her mother had told her stories of how hard she'd fought to be taken seriously by the men in Colombia. While things had improved, there was still a distinct possibility the male members of the cartel would either refuse to deal with her, or perhaps even shortchange her because they thought she didn't know better.

Which was the truth.

"You needn't concern yourself," Carlos said, sounding confident. "The suppliers know better than to question our processes."

One less thing to worry about, assuming he was right. Still, it was one thing for him to promise compliance from a cushy urban setting thousands of miles away. The jungle was a wilder place, not subject to the laws of men.

She added the issue to her growing list of concerns, but there was nothing to be done about it now.

Carlos stood, signaling an end to their conversation. "Safe travels, Dr. Sandoval. We will meet again upon your return."

Olivia rose and gathered her courage. She had to tell him now, before he walked out. There wouldn't be another chance. "There's just one more thing."

He paused in the act of buttoning his suit jacket. "Yes?"

"I have a guest coming on this trip."

"A guest?" he repeated.

She nodded. "A potential investor has asked to accompany me so he can see firsthand what our needs are and the people we are helping." It was the cover story they'd concocted to explain Logan's presence on the trip. It was a pretty good one, as far as lies went. Now she just had to sell it.

"Unacceptable." Carlos shook his head. "You must tell him he cannot come."

"I can't do that," Olivia said. "We made the arrangements months ago. If I tell him he can't come, it will be highly suspicious."

"I do not care if this man wonders why you have canceled. He cannot go."

"You don't understand." Olivia spread her hands in a placating gesture. "He has ties to a major pharmaceutical company. His company is donating most of the supplies, and one of the conditions of this donation was that he come with me. If I tell him he can't join us, he will pull the supplies and I will have to cancel my trip." She leaned forward slightly, resting her hands on the desk. "I'm sure you don't want that to happen."

Carlos clenched his jaw and was silent for a moment. "What is this man's name?"

"Logan Marshall." They had decided to keep his first name the same, so Olivia wouldn't accidentally trip up and blow his cover in Colombia. According to Logan, it had taken the men in the tech department a matter of hours to create a plausible identity for "Logan Marshall," complete with credit history, employment records and even a few parking tickets to boot. If Carlos decided to check him out, he would find exactly what they wanted him to see: an upper management pharmaceutical employee tasked with improving the PR image of his company by participating in charitable works.

"Very well." Carlos sounded like he was speaking around a mouthful of broken glass. "Make sure he sees nothing, is that clear? Because if he does, his death will be your fault."

Even though she knew Logan was already involved, a chill raced through her at the threat. "I will be careful."

Carlos gave her a cruel smile. "I know you will. Because I will be watching you the whole time."

"What?" How was that possible? Was he going to plant cameras in the money? On the heels of that thought came another more horrifying question: Had he already bugged her home and office? Did she have any privacy, or was she constantly being monitored now? And if so, how was she going to speak to Logan and his men without giving everything away?

He shook his head. "Do you honestly think we would trust you with two million dollars? Surely even you are not that naive."

"I don't understand." The thought that her every move was under observation triggered a cloying sense of claustrophobia, and her heart began to pound against her breastbone.

"We have eyes everywhere," Carlos said, his voice soft. "I will know when you sleep, when you wake. What you have for breakfast. Even the number of sweat drops on your forehead. Nothing will be hidden from me."

Olivia felt her eyes widen as the implications of his words sank in. How many spies did the cartel employ? Was there any way to know who was a true friend and who had the cartel on speed dial, ready to betray her at the first opportunity?

"Remember what we discussed," Carlos said, gathering up his jamming device. "We will meet again upon your return."

Olivia waited until the door clicked shut behind him before lowering herself into the chair. She opened her desk drawer and fished out the antacids, then choked down a couple of the chalky tablets in the hopes of calming her roiling stomach. Things were worse than she'd originally thought.

Logan had made it sound like he and his men had the situation under control and that he would keep her safe. But now that Olivia knew how extensive the cartel's influence was, did they even stand a chance?

"If you could just sign here, Dr. Sandoval." Logan made a show of pointing to a spot on the clipboard, then winked at her. "This authorizes us to spray your property. You said you were seeing a lot of ants in your home?"

"Uh, yes," Olivia replied, shooting him a puzzled look. He held up a finger to stall her questions, and after a moment Alan spoke from the other room.

"All clear."

Logan tossed the clipboard on the sofa and gestured for Olivia to follow him into the dining room. She eyed his hat as they sat down.

"Capital City Pest Control?" she asked dubiously.

He shrugged. "Gets the job done. And if anyone is watching they won't question why we're here."

"Are you sure it's safe for us to talk?" Her eyes darted around the room, as if she expected cartel enforcers to pop out from behind the curtains at any moment.

"We're fine," he assured her. "We swept for bugs,

and the house came up clean. No one is listening in on our conversation."

She leaned back in her chair, her shoulders relaxing a bit. "That's good. It feels like I've been living under a microscope ever since Carlos came to my office." She reached for a stray pen on the table and spun it this way and that, her fingers betraying her nervousness.

Logan reached out and placed his hand over hers, stalling her movements. She glanced up at him with wide eyes and he offered her a smile. After a few heartbeats, her hand relaxed under his and she smiled back at him. "Sorry."

"It's okay," he said. "This can't be easy on you."

"I've had better days, that's for sure." She rotated her hand until their fingers were entwined, then squeezed. His heart did a funny little flip at the contact, and for a moment he felt like they were the only two people in the world.

Alan pulled out a chair and sat, and Logan tugged his hand free. Something flashed in Olivia's eyes—was it disappointment?—but it was gone in an instant and she nodded a greeting at his teammate.

Logan wiped his hand against the leg of his pants, feeling the ghost of her touch on his skin. It would have been nice to keep holding her hand, but he couldn't afford the distraction. Especially not in front of his guys.

Keith pulled a small recorder from his pocket and placed it on the table. Olivia glanced from it to him, and Logan nodded. "We need to record your story so we can enter it into the official case files. Plus, it allows us to go back and relisten to key points."

"Do you just want me to talk, or do you have specific questions for me?"

"Why don't you just tell us what happened first? We can ask our questions once you've gone over everything first."

Olivia nodded. "Okay." She took a deep breath and started speaking.

Logan kept his mouth shut while she told them about Carlos's visit to her office. She recited her instructions, and Logan could tell from the language she used that she had memorized exactly what the other man had said. That was good, as it meant she wasn't inadvertently leaving out any details.

The exchange itself would be simple. She was to take the money to a campsite in the Amazon jungle. These were fairly common setups, where cocaine was isolated, purified and sometimes packaged for export. Once she arrived, she was to exchange the money for a few kilos of the drug, which she was to hand over to Carlos once she'd made it back to the States.

"Did he tell you the location of the site?" Keith asked.

Olivia shook her head. "He said I would be told that once I was in Colombia."

Logan bit his lip to keep from frowning. Olivia didn't seem to realize it, but the instructions Carlos had given her basically guaranteed she would be terminated upon her return to the US. After all, she would know the exact location of the prep site, a piece of information that was a closely guarded secret. The cartel couldn't risk that she might tell someone where to find the camp after this was all over. Logan didn't want to be the one to let her know, but if Carlos and his men had meant for Olivia to survive, they would have set up an exchange at a neutral location. By sending her to the production site, they were essentially signing her death warrant.

"What is it?" He looked up to find Olivia's eyes on him, her expression worried.

He shook his head. "Nothing," he replied automatically. "Everything's fine."

She merely stared at him, her expression making it clear she wasn't buying it. "You're lying."

Logan cast a quick, pleading glance at Alan and Keith, but the other men shrugged slightly as if to say "It's all on you."

Traitors.

"I'm just curious as to why they're sending you to the production site, rather than setting up a meet elsewhere."

"Is that a problem?"

"No," he assured her. "It's actually better for us. If we know the exact location, we can go in later and shut it down." Or rather, the Colombians could, if there was a police unit left standing that hadn't been bought by the cartels. Corruption of government officials was better compared to the bad old days, when Pablo Escobar and his cronies had reigned supreme, but it was still an issue of concern.

"They can't be too worried about you finding it if they're telling me exactly where it is," she remarked. "So either they've paid off everyone, or they're just going to kill me." Her tone was matter-of-fact, reminding him of their earlier car ride when she'd seen through his vague platitudes. His respect for her went up another notch, and he realized that from now on it would be best for him to be totally honest. Olivia was a smart woman, and if they were going to work together on this operation, he had to trust her with the truth.

"I told you, I'm not going to let you die." He wanted

to grab her hand again to reassure her with his touch as well as his words, but he settled for holding her gaze instead.

Olivia's big brown eyes searched his and after a moment she nodded slightly. "There's more," she said, worry creeping back into her voice.

"What is it?" Alan sat forward, his pen poised to take notes.

"Carlos said they have eyes everywhere. That my every move will be watched and reported to him." She started fiddling with the pen again, glancing at him and then Alan. "Is he exaggerating, or do they really have spies everywhere?"

"It might be a little of both," Logan replied. "The cartel certainly has people on the payroll, but I don't think everyone you'll meet is in their pocket. Still, it's best to be careful."

"How are we going to do that?" She worried her bottom lip with her teeth. "You and I are supposed to stay close to each other—won't it seem strange for me to spend all my time with you?"

"Not necessarily," Alan said, a speculative gleam in his eyes. "What if Logan poses as more than just a corporate sponsor?"

"What do you mean?" Olivia frowned slightly, and Logan's stomach dropped. Was Alan actually suggesting he pretend to have a more personal relationship with Olivia?

"The two of you could pretend to be a couple," Alan suggested, confirming Logan's fears.

Oh, no. No way. Bad idea. Personal emotions never mixed well with professional obligations. He was having a hard enough time keeping his burgeoning attraction for Olivia under control. If he had to pretend to be her boyfriend, it would be almost impossible to stay totally focused on the job at hand.

Besides, Olivia probably wanted no part of such a deception. They barely knew each other. Surely she had no desire to act the part of the doting girlfriend for a relative stranger.

Logan opened his mouth to shoot down Alan's crazy suggestion, but before he could speak, Olivia nodded enthusiastically.

"I'll do it."

Alan and Keith both grinned, and Logan's palm itched with the urge to smack those knowing smiles right off their faces. They didn't know about Emma—he hadn't told anyone at work about it. But his lack of a dating life had been noticed on more than one occasion, and the team had taken to calling him "Monk," a nickname he tolerated if only to keep them from coming up with something worse. They'd been trying to set him up for ages with cousins, friends of wives or girlfriends, even neighbors. But Logan had always refused without explanation.

Leave it to these guys to force his hand now, even though the whole thing would be fake.

"So it's settled then," Keith said.

"Sounds like it to me," Alan replied.

"What do you think?" Olivia asked. She was watching him again, taking in everything as she studied his reaction to this proposal.

Logan scrambled to come up with an objection to the plan that wouldn't make him sound like a complete ass. He didn't want Olivia to think he was rejecting the idea because he didn't find her attractive—far from it. But he also didn't want her to know that he was worried about staying focused on the job. If he made it sound like he couldn't keep things professional she might worry she was going to Colombia with a Grade A creeper.

He glared at Alan and Keith, wishing they'd kept their mouths shut. The guys generally had some good ideas, but this one was a real dud.

"I don't want you to do anything that would make you feel uncomfortable," he said, hoping that sounded good.

Olivia huffed out a laugh. "I'm being blackmailed into acting as a drug mule for a notorious Colombian cartel. We're way past uncomfortable here."

"Fair enough," he conceded. "But you don't have to add to your troubles by pretending to like me."

She tilted her head to the side, a faint smile playing at the corners of her mouth. "Maybe not, but it's the only way to plausibly explain why we're joined at the hip."

Logan didn't respond. As much as he hated to admit it, she and the guys were right.

"Don't worry," Olivia added, a spark of humor lighting her eyes. "Your virtue is safe with me."

"Ha-ha," he said, ignoring the snorts of suppressed laughter coming from Alan and Keith. "Are you sure you really want to do this?"

Olivia nodded, determination settling over her face. "Absolutely."

Chapter 6

"Are there any other developments?"

The question was not unexpected, but it still made Carlos's stomach turn. He took a deep breath as he debated his next words. Would it be better for him to reveal this latest wrinkle, or should he pretend as if everything was proceeding as planned? He hated to show any kind of flaw—if his employers thought he was mishandling the situation, there would be hell to pay. But if they thought he was being less than truthful, his punishment would be extreme. In the end, he decided honesty was worth the risk.

"Olivia Sandoval has agreed to act as a courier, just as you thought she would. But there is another person accompanying her on the trip."

The man on the other end of the line was silent for a moment, giving Carlos plenty of time to imagine his reaction. He would be displeased, but he wouldn't let his temper show. There was always a chance that someone was listening, and El Jefe was not stupid. He had led Fantasmas for the past ten years with a calculating ruthlessness that left no room for emotion. His ice-cold control was one of the most terrifying things about him, and Carlos had always considered him the personification of that American colloquialism "Don't get mad, get even."

"Who?"

"She claims the man is an investor who insists on going with her so he can see how his company's money is spent."

"His name?"

"Logan Marshall. I am currently investigating his background." Carlos typed as he spoke, entering the name into the search engine. After a few endless seconds, the results popped up.

"Is there anything unusual I should know about?"

Carlos scanned the information quickly, cursing himself for not having done this sooner. But he hadn't had the time, and he hadn't had the guts to let the phone ring. When El Jefe called, you answered.

"Nothing that I see so far."

"Good. Keep me updated."

"Of course."

There was a click as the man disconnected, and Carlos let out a sigh, his shoulders slumping as some of the tension left his body. He hadn't wanted to discuss this latest development until he'd done due diligence on Logan Marshall and determined what kind of threat the man was. Now El Jefe would think him unprepared at best, incapable at worst.

He shook his head, trying to dispel the growing fear that he was on the verge of disaster. He had served Fantasmas for the better part of five years, and had done his job well. It was why he was still alive. El Jefe knew he was a good soldier, and he wasn't likely to have him eliminated on the basis of one small mistake.

Besides, it wasn't really his mistake to begin with. He'd had no way of knowing an investor was involved in Olivia Sandoval's upcoming trip. She'd never taken one with her before. *No*, he thought, feeling some of his confidence return. *This is not my fault.*

He turned his attention back to the computer screen. The addition of this new player was unexpected, but perhaps it would prove a useful development. After all, it was one more innocent life he could threaten to ensure Dr. Sandoval's cooperation. She had responded well to the threats against her friends; adding one more potential victim to the mix would increase the pressure on her and give him additional leverage, which was always a good thing.

Carlos scanned the search results with a more critical eye, giving the information his full attention. Logan Marshall was employed in the public relations department of one of the bigger pharmaceutical companies, and based on his résumé, he was an expert in corporate spin. A necessary skill, considering the PR nightmare his company was experiencing after its exorbitant price-gouging tactics had been exposed.

He clicked over to see the photos that had popped up from his search and frowned. The page was flooded with images, each one of a different person. It would take too long to sift through everything in the hopes of finding the right Logan Marshall. Rather than waste the time, he logged in to the state's Motor Vehicle Administration site, courtesy of a password provided to him by an employee on the cartel's payroll. He smiled to himself as he searched again—the government had no idea how many of its employees were bought and paid for by "illegal organizations."

After a few seconds, a picture of Logan Marshall's driver's license appeared on the screen. Carlos studied the image, narrowing his eyes. Something about this man looked familiar...

The hairs on the back of his neck rose and the feeling of déjà vu intensified. He had seen this man before. But where? How had their paths crossed?

He leaned back from the desk and closed his eyes, clearing his mind of all extraneous thought. Experience had taught him that trying to chase after information only buried it deeper in his brain. Better to calm himself and let the knowledge float to the top so he could examine it more closely.

His mind began to wander, looking over memories and discarding those that didn't apply. Had he bumped into Logan Marshall in an ordinary fashion, while at the grocery store or running errands? No...that would not have caused the man's face to stick in his mind. It had to be something else. Something professional then, which meant Logan Marshall was not who he seemed...

Most of Carlos's meetings with associates were quiet, low-key affairs. It wasn't smart to draw the attention of prying eyes, and so everyone conducted themselves calmly and rationally— an outside observer would look at their group and see a handful of businessmen out for a working lunch. They always spoke in coded Spanish, which further helped to obscure their dealings. Washington, DC, was a cosmopolitan enough city that a table of Spanish-speaking men didn't draw comment, but most of the Americans surrounding them were stubborn monoglots, and the few who did speak Spanish were far from fluent. It was the perfect cover.

The meetings usually took place at an upscale restaurant, thanks to an ill-timed raid that had taken place two years before. The cartels had grown worried about increasing violence on American soil. It was one thing to kill indiscriminately in Colombia, but the United States authorities were not so forgiving when their citizens were targeted. In a rare show of solidarity, the cartels had agreed to a temporary truce to work out the details of turf distribution on US soil. If they could agree to terms, much of the violence in the US could be curtailed, which would take the spotlight off the cartels. The American police forces tended to focus only on immediate problems. If the cartels dropped off their radar again, things would be much easier.

A hotel had been chosen as the site for negotiations, and on the appointed day two years ago, representatives from each of the major cartels had arrived. The meeting was disguised as a conference of Latin American pharmaceutical investors so as not to draw suspicion. But somehow, the DEA had gotten wind of the true nature of the meeting.

Carlos had stepped out to relieve himself when the raid happened. He was still in the bathroom when the shouting began, and he hid in the stall until the initial burst of activity passed. Thinking quickly, he stripped off his suit jacket and tie, leaving him in dark pants and a white dress shirt—a close approximation of the hotel staff uniform. He slipped out of the bathroom and managed to snag a catering jacket off an abandoned cart. The employees were gathered at the end of the hall, gawking at the activity, so no one noticed him glide by.

He walked right through a thicket of DEA agents and police, his head held high and his pace measured so as not to draw suspicion. He was almost out—he wouldn't let a careless mistake cost him his freedom now.

He glanced back as he rounded the corner, and his shoulder struck something hard. Turning, his stomach dropped as he found he had run into a DEA agent.

"Excuse me," he murmured, nodding politely.

The other man nodded back. "My fault," he said. He studied Carlos's face for a second and his eyes narrowed, as if he was trying to recall something. Carlos felt his pulse spike—he had to get out of here before he was recognized. He offered a small smile and began walking away, feeling the weight of the other man's eyes on his back. He knew with absolute certainty that if he turned around the agent would be watching him, but to do so would only confirm the other man's suspicions.

Footsteps sounded behind him, and he realized the agent had started to follow him. He took a deep breath and forced his feet to move at a normal pace, resisting the rising panic that demanded he run.

"Logan!"

The footsteps paused, and he heard the man's voice behind him. "What?"

"We need you in here."

There was a muttered curse, and Carlos imagined the man standing there, torn. He kept walking, putting more and more distance between them. Finally, he rounded another corner and risked a glance back.

The man was gone.

Sitting at his desk now, Carlos frowned. The DEA agent's name was Logan. Not a very common moniker. He dove back into the memory and focused on the man's face...

Realization struck like a bolt of lightning and an electric tingle traveled from the top of his head down to his toes. He opened his eyes to stare at the picture on the screen again.

It couldn't be...

But it was.

Logan Marshall was the same man he'd bumped into two years ago. A DEA agent. Which meant Olivia Sandoval had talked.

Anger flooded him in a hot rush, and he reached up to loosen his tie. That bitch.

His first instinct was to punish her. He reached for the phone to give the order to kill her friends, but a thought struck him before he dialed. What if he could use this to his advantage?

The DEA was off-limits in the United States. To put a hit out on an agent who was on American soil was suicide. But Logan wouldn't be here for much longer. He was going to Colombia, and everyone knew that was a dangerous place.

A slow smile spread across his lips as he considered the possibilities. A DEA agent, alone except for one woman and undercover in Colombia. It was a gift really, and one he couldn't pass up. El Jefe would be pleased at such an unexpected windfall. They would interrogate him, find out exactly what the Americans knew and what they planned to do about it. Anticipation was a sweet burn in his chest. There were so many ways to make a man talk...

And then, once they had wrung every last drop of information from him, they would kill him. There were hundreds of thousands of square miles of jungle in Colombia—the Americans would never find his body. He would be one more drop in the ocean of lives lost in the drug trade.

He fixed his tie, whistling softly to himself. He would have to move quickly, but the prize was worth the rush. Pleasure flooded his system as he imagined presenting a DEA agent to El Jefe. It would be the diamond in his crown of achievements. El Jefe would be very pleased indeed.

And Carlos would reap the rewards.

"You've really never flown first-class before?"

Olivia shook her head and took a sip of champagne, enjoying the effervescent tingling as the bubbles danced across her tongue. She wasn't normally a big drinker, but the flight attendant had come by with a tray of flutes just as she'd taken her seat, and the novelty of it was too fun to pass up. When in Rome...

"Why not?"

She glanced over to find Logan eyeing her with open curiosity. "These tickets are expensive," she said. "The money I would spend on a cushier seat buys a lot of bandages."

He tilted his head to the side, acknowledging her point. "I didn't think of it that way."

"How did you get them to spring for these seats?" From everything she'd heard, the government wasn't in the habit of paying for civil servants to travel in such style.

Logan lifted one brow and smiled. "A pharmaceuti-

cal executive such as myself has an image to maintain."
Then he leaned forward and lowered his voice. "Plus, I
called in a few favors." He winked at her, which made
her stomach do a little flip.

Olivia leaned back in her seat, putting a few inches
of distance between them. "That was nice of you," she
said, hoping she sounded normal. When she'd agreed to
pose as Logan's girlfriend, she hadn't stopped to consider all that would involve. Being near him. Sharing
conversations. Touching him. Kissing him?

Whoa, she thought, cutting off the thought before
it could take root in her imagination. In the immediate aftermath of Carlos and his threats, she had seen
Logan as a potential solution to the problem, a way to
keep Avery and Mallory alive and safe while she did
the cartel's dirty work. But now that things had calmed
down a bit, she saw him as more than a DEA agent. She
was becoming acutely aware of him as a man, and unfortunately for her brain, her body liked what she saw.

Just how much acting would they have to do to convince people they were together? And more important,
could she keep her emotions separate from her actions?
The last thing she needed was to believe the lies and
truly fall for Logan. He was here doing a job, and no
matter how attractive he was or how much his eyes
sparkled when he looked at her, she had to remember
it wasn't real. The last thing she needed was to get attached to another person who was going to leave her.

Her parents hadn't meant to die, of course. She realized that. But Scott had chosen to leave her. And even
though she knew deep down she was better off without him, his desertion still stung. She felt the pain anew
every time she thought of him, and she wasn't up for

making connections with new people. It wasn't worth the pain of disappointment later.

"Happy to do it," he said easily. "And I'm doubly glad to know it's such a treat for you."

Her stomach flipped again, and Olivia set down the glass of champagne. The bubbles had to be affecting her—that was the only explanation. "So how does this work?" she asked, hoping that shifting the focus to business would help settle her nerves.

Logan took a sip of his own champagne and frowned slightly. "How does what work?"

Olivia gestured between them. "You and me. How do we approach the whole 'fake couple' thing?" If she knew what to expect, she could better guard against a sneak attack from her emotions.

Logan's expression cleared. "Ah," he said. He set the glass down and looked at her, his expression thoughtful. "To be honest, I'm not quite sure. This is the first time I've done anything like this."

"You've never had to go undercover before?"

"Not like this. Usually, it's the female agents who are tasked with faking a relationship. As far as I know, I'm the first guy to be put in this position."

Olivia couldn't help but smile. "I take it your coworkers were sufficiently amused?"

He lifted one shoulder. "You saw how Alan and Keith acted. They think it's funny as hell."

There was a note in his voice that caught her attention and made her think there was a bigger issue at play here. "Because of the novelty of it?"

Logan shifted in his seat. Perhaps he was just trying to get comfortable, but Olivia thought it was something more. "That's part of it," he said.

Meaning, her instincts were correct—there was something else going on, and it probably explained why Logan had initially resisted the idea.

"Do you have a girlfriend?" Was that the problem? Maybe he was dating someone, and having to pretend to be in a relationship made him uncomfortable. It was a reasonable explanation.

"No." He shook his head firmly. "I'm single."

Olivia let out the breath she didn't realize she'd been holding. She hadn't thought to consider Logan might have someone waiting at home for him. Now she didn't have to feel guilty about taking him away and forcing him to pretend to be in love with her.

"What about you?" His gaze was probing as he searched her face. "Surely a beautiful, intelligent woman such as yourself has no shortage of dates."

He thinks I'm beautiful? The compliment was a boost to her ego, and her inner twelve-year-old let out a little squeal of pleasure. "Not really," she began, feeling her cheeks warm. "For starters, I don't have much time in my schedule. I've dated some, but I've never found someone who wanted to stick around for the long haul." She reached for the champagne and took a fortifying sip, hoping he wouldn't press for more details. She didn't feel up to sharing the whole sad story with him at the moment.

"And now it's your turn," she said, lifting a brow. "You're handsome, employed and you don't live in your parents' basement. Quite the catch, by anyone's standards. So why are you still alone?"

He was saved from having to answer right away by the arrival of the flight attendant, who collected their glasses. Logan stared after her, and Olivia got the distinct impression he was hoping she would come back to provide another distraction. *Did I go too far?* she wondered. Perhaps Logan didn't want to share something so personal with her. Still, he had asked her first, and turnabout was fair play...

His silence stretched on, making her uncomfortable. Just as she was about to apologize for asking the question, he took a deep breath.

"There was someone," he said quietly. "Her name was Emma. We were engaged."

Oh, God, had she died? Olivia reached out and put her hand on Logan's arm, feeling like the worst sort of idiot. He was probably still grieving, and she'd brought his pain to the surface. No wonder he'd hesitated to agree to this arrangement! "I'm so sorry for your loss."

He glanced up, startled by her words. Then understanding dawned in his green eyes. "She's still alive," he said. A hint of bitterness crept into his voice. "And as far as I know, she and my former best friend are quite happy together."

She had cheated on him? Olivia shook her head. The woman had to be some kind of crazy to give up a guy like Logan. Even though she didn't know him all that well yet, it didn't take a rocket scientist to see he was a good man. "Sounds like you're better off without them."

He nodded. "I know that. It's just hard to remember, some days."

She squeezed his arm, understanding perfectly. Even though his former fiancée was still alive, he had suffered a loss, and she knew all too well what that felt like.

There were still times, two years after their deaths, that Olivia found herself driving home, her mind cataloging the list of topics she wanted to discuss with her parents. A joke a patient had told her. Her plans to re-paint the kitchen. That new recipe she wanted to try over the weekend. And then she would remember they were gone and her grief would rise up in a fresh wave, no less powerful than the first time it had hit her. She kept waiting for the day when thinking of them didn't bring such pain, but perhaps it would never come.

"Let's move on," Logan suggested, running a hand through his hair. "I didn't mean to let things get so de-pressing."

"That's life," Olivia said with a shrug. "No need to apologize."

"I appreciate your understanding. But talking about Emma always puts me in a bad mood, and I'm not about to waste my one and probably only government-sponsored trip in first class being grumpy. Besides," he added with a small smile, "we have homework to tackle."

"I can't believe they actually gave us packets," Olivia said, accepting his change of topic. She leaned down and retrieved her backpack. The folder was a little crumpled from its time among her books, granola bars and other travel necessities, but it was still intact.

Logan produced his own folder and pulled out the stapled packet of pages within. He slid her a glance. "Did you get everything filled out?"

"Mostly," Olivia replied, trying not to sound defen-sive. In truth, she hadn't had time to answer every single question, and some of them were downright ridiculous. How exactly was knowing her mother's maiden name going to help Logan more convincingly play her boy-friend? But she had tried her best, not wanting to let him down. "What about you?"

The tips of his ears turned pink. "I answered them all." Olivia felt her eyebrows lift, and he shrugged. "I was always a good student." He passed her his packet with a smile. "I don't know if this will really help, but it's worth a shot."

Olivia slid her papers over to him in exchange. "If nothing else, you should be able to figure out all my internet passwords with this information."

He laughed at that, and nodded at the pages in her hand. "Likewise. Promise you won't hack into my bank account?"

She pretended to consider the question. "What's it worth to you?"

A teasing glint entered his eyes. "How about another free drink?"

Olivia batted her eyelashes at him. "You sure know how to treat a girl."

"That's nothing," he said, leaning forward to speak over the noise of the revving engines. "I brought some chocolate along, specifically for you."

"Really?"

Logan grabbed his bag and opened it, revealing the contents. Sure enough, a bar of chocolate sat on top of a stack of books. The sight of it triggered a warm rush in her chest. The fact that he'd thought to bring her a treat meant a lot, and she suddenly wished she had thought to bring a gift for him.

The sentiment must have shown on her face. "Don't worry," he told her, zipping the bag closed again. "You can share it with me."

She narrowed her eyes slightly. She wasn't feeling *that* guilty. "We'll see," she said with mock seriousness.

He laughed, a deep, melodic sound that thrummed

through her and sent pleasant tingles down her arms and legs. "I wouldn't dream of coming between a woman and her chocolate."

"I'm pretty sure wars have started over less serious offenses."

"I'll consider myself warned," he said. He leaned back and gestured to the papers they held. "What do you say we get to it? Might as well be productive on this flight."

Olivia nodded. "Okay. But be gentle." Answering the personal questions had been easy enough, but having to sit next to Logan while he read her responses made her feel uncomfortably exposed.

He flashed her another one of those heart-stopping grins. "I was just about to say the same thing to you."

"Good to know we're on the same page then," she said, unable to keep from smiling in return. She couldn't imagine what Logan had to be nervous about, but it made her feel better knowing she wasn't the only one who found this situation awkward.

She started reading the packet and soon lost herself in the back and forth of the questions and his responses. Most of it was just a catalog of facts: his favorite color, favorite food, favorite movie, that kind of thing. But rather than reply with one-word answers, Logan had taken the time to write paragraphs of information that gave her great insight into his personality. She smiled as she read about his fascination with fire trucks as a child, and how he had never lost his love of the color red. Or his memories of Sunday night dinner with his family, when his Italian grandmother had cooked mouthwatering meals from scratch. Her specialty had been spaghetti Bolognese, and Oliva's stomach growled as she read his description of the flavors and textures of the homemade pasta and sauce.

It went on like this for pages, and Olivia found herself lingering over his writing, not wanting to reach the end. Reading his answers made her feel closer to him, the same way she'd felt while wearing his jacket in his office. It was nice to see this unguarded version of Logan, to learn about things that probably never came up in casual conversation. It was as if they were taking the fast track to emotional intimacy, and she took a deep breath, reminding herself that it was all an act. Logan had shared these memories with her because it was his job, not because he truly wanted to build a bond with her. While she felt more drawn to him than ever before, she had to keep her distance for the sake of their safety.

If she couldn't keep her head about her, this whole operation was going to blow up in their faces.

Chapter 7

Logan watched Olivia doze, happy to see her finally relaxed. He could tell from the dark circles under her eyes she hadn't been sleeping well, and he hoped this nap helped. Based on what she'd told him about her work in Colombia, she wasn't going to get much rest after they arrived.

He scanned through the questionnaire again, pausing here and there to linger over some of her answers. He'd practically memorized her responses, but the repetition gave him something to do. Besides, it was important he remained vigilant. If he let himself relax on this assignment it could mean the death of a lot of innocent people. So he read and reread her words, burning them into his brain. It seemed like a lot of effort for a random collection of facts, but it was easy to dismiss the risk from the safety of the airplane. Once they were on site, knowing exactly how Olivia took her coffee could be the difference between success or failure.

She was very precise in her answers, he noted. Her favorite color wasn't just blue, it was the blue of a cloudless summer sky. Her favorite drink was mint tea sweetened with honey and poured over ice. She didn't take sugar in her coffee, but instead added cream until it was the color of a brown paper bag. He smiled to himself, enjoying the images her descriptions evoked. It was a good thing she'd been so forthcoming in her replies, as it made his job a lot easier.

And it was a job, he reminded himself. Even though he found her incredibly attractive, even though the more he learned about her personally, the more he wanted to know, even though she was in danger and he instinctively wanted to protect her, he couldn't afford to lose sight of the fact that once they returned to the US, they would go back to being neighbors who were too busy to really connect. It was a disappointing thought, but it was better to acknowledge the truth now than be surprised by it later. He wasn't going to let a woman hurt him again.

Except... Olivia seemed different. There was no artifice in her gaze, no hint of falseness. Emma, on the other hand, had been a master of manipulation. He'd once marveled at her ability to work a crowd. She worked for an animal rescue charity, and once upon a time he'd been proud to watch her schmooze money out of donors, thinking she was a true believer in the goodness of her cause. She could charm the birds from the trees, and his mistake had been thinking her machinations didn't extend to their relationship. He'd been so naive. Emma's work made her a socially acceptable con artist. Sure, she didn't rob people outright, but she played on their sympathies to separate them from their money, often lying to their faces if it meant getting a bigger check. He'd finally realized she enjoyed her job not because she was making a difference, but because she viewed it as a game. She got a rush from tricking people, and there had been no end to her capacity for deception. She'd seen everyone as a potential mark, and he'd been the biggest fool of all.

Looking back, he could see all the warning signs he'd missed before. But that was the point of hindsight, wasn't it? Recognizing what you'd done wrong so you didn't do it again. Except in his case, all his hard-learned lessons were fading from his mind as he spent more time with the woman next to him.

Olivia shifted in her seat, then settled into a new position with a sigh. It was a small, intimate noise, the kind a woman made in the middle of the night while lying in bed. It had been a long time since he'd been privy to such private sounds, and hearing one now triggered a wave of longing so intense it made him ache. What he wouldn't give for the touch of a hand on his body! But he knew from experience that meaningless sex was not the solution to his problem. Scratching a physical itch did nothing to ease the loneliness in his soul, and he always walked away from the encounter feeling emptier. It was why he'd given up dating in the wake of Emma's betrayal—until he was ready to really trust another woman, being with someone just made him feel worse.

He glanced out the window, but the cotton-candy clouds obscured most of his view. This was going to be a difficult assignment, but he'd never backed down from a challenge before. He wasn't about to start now, especially under these circumstances. His team had been tracking cartel activity for the past several years, doing its best to cut off the supply chain in the United States. They'd had some successes, but the satisfaction that came from intercepting a few thousand kilos of dope was tempered by the knowledge that there was a seemingly endless supply waiting in the wings. If they could cripple Fantasmas del Mal, it would go a long way to reducing the amount of cocaine entering the country. They'd never been able to get close to the cartel's operations before, but now...

He slid another glance at Olivia, tracing the delicate lines of her brow and cheekbones with his gaze. He hadn't really talked about just how important this operation was because he didn't want to put any added pressure on her. She was under enough stress already, worrying about the lives of her friends. But if the DEA could confirm the location of one of the cartel's jungle super-labs? It would be a huge coup for them. The Colombians could shut the operation down, which would cause the cartel some major pain. Furthermore, the lab itself was most likely an intelligence gold mine.

He let his mind wander, imagining how one bust would lead to another, and another... If they played their cards right, they might even be able to bring down the whole organization. The power vacuum wouldn't last long, but they could do a lot of good in the interim and it would send a message to the other cartels that the DEA never gave up.

Olivia shifted again and Logan tucked his daydreams away. He couldn't let himself get caught up in that imagined future, or else he'd miss what had to be done in the present. As much as he wanted to be the one to lead the charge, his job on this operation was to gather the necessary intelligence so they could mount a successful takedown. It was vital to find out as much as possible now so there were no surprises later. Normally, this part of the job went smoothly.

But then again, he normally didn't have to worry about protecting a civilian.

Fortunately, he didn't think Olivia would be much of a burden. Sure, she had no operational training to speak of and didn't know the first thing about gathering the type of information the DEA needed, but she was an intelligent woman who kept her cool under pressure. It was an important skill, one that not everyone possessed. In fact, in Logan's opinion, it was the only thing that mattered. Everything else was trainable.

Not that they would have much time for that kind of thing. He might be able to teach her some basic self-defense moves, but that was about it. Certainly not enough so she could hold her own in a fight, if it came to that. All the more reason to stay close to her. The thought filled him with a perverse satisfaction that he didn't want to examine too closely. *Keep it superficial*, he reminded himself.

It was a message he was going to have to keep repeating if he wanted it to sink in.

Olivia inhaled deeply, drawing the rich, loamy scent of the jungle into her lungs. The air was thick with humidity, but it still felt refreshing after spending so much time in the cold, stale air of the plane. She slid a glance at Logan to gauge his reaction and hid a smile as he mopped at his brow. Hopefully it wouldn't take him too long to adjust to the climate—she didn't want him to be uncomfortable the entire trip.

The Jeep hit a divot in the road so hard it made her teeth clack together painfully. She grabbed the door for support and tightened her grip on the backpack at her feet. The cartel's money lined the bottom of the bag, and while she had managed to put it out of her mind on the plane, now that they were in Colombia she was acutely aware of the risk she was taking. If the bag was lost or stolen, it would mean the death of her friends.

Fortunately, Logan was here to help her keep an eye on it.

He laid his hand on her arm and squeezed, the gesture a sweet reassurance that she wasn't alone. "You can relax," he said softly. "It's not going anywhere."

She nodded, acknowledging his point. Besides, if she didn't stop worrying, she was going to drive herself mad. She let go of the bag and put her hand back in her lap.

Logan reached over and threaded his fingers through hers. A thrill shot through her at the contact, but she tamped it down. It was part of the act, she reminded herself. They had to maintain a consistent image now that they were in Colombia—there was no way to know who was spying for the cartel.

She turned and smiled at him, scooting closer until their legs touched. He draped his arm around her shoulders, holding her in place as the Jeep bounced along the road.

"How much longer?"

She lifted one shoulder. "Maybe half an hour. It depends on the road quality."

He grimaced. "You call this a road? Looks more like an overgrown deer trail to me."

"You're in the jungle," she replied simply. "What did you expect?"

"Fair enough." He was quiet a moment. "It really is beautiful, though."

Her heart warmed at his words. She'd fallen in love with the lush growth of the rain forest on her first visit to Colombia as a child. Her grandmother's home had backed up to a section of the forest, and she'd taken many walks among the trees with her parents, marveling at the exotic plants and animals, so different from anything she'd seen in Virginia. The fact that Logan seemed to appreciate it as well made her happy and also a tiny bit proud. Even though she'd grown up in the United States, her parents had been raised in Colombia and the country had always held a special place in her heart.

The Jeep slowed to navigate a particularly tricky curve. Logan leaned over to peer out the window. "Are those monkeys in the trees?" He sounded incredulous and a little bit excited.

Olivia leaned over, as well. "Yep," she confirmed, seeing the familiar auburn shapes. "Howlers. You'll hear them in the morning—that's when they're really chatty."

A look of wonder crossed his face. "That's so cool."

She laughed. "You think that now. But trust me, they're like an alarm clock you can't turn off."

The driver, having evidently picked up on their conversation, chose that moment to let out a loud wail that was a halfway decent impersonation of the monkey's famous cry. Logan and Olivia both jumped, and the man grinned at them in the rearview mirror.

"Bulla, sí?" he asked with a wink.

Olivia nodded. *"Sí,"* she replied, then turned to Logan. "He said they're noisy."

"So I gathered," he replied drily. "My Spanish isn't that bad, you know."

"If I were you, I'd keep that to myself," she advised quietly. "People tend to be freer with their words if they think you can't understand them, and since you are a stereotypical *gringo*, you just might overhear something interesting."

"Good idea," he said, leaning over to press a quick kiss against her temple. "We might make an agent out of you yet," he whispered.

His breath was hot in her ear and the intimacy of it made her shudder slightly. Logan felt the tremor of her body, but apparently mistook its meaning. "Don't worry," he teased. "I'll still be your backup."

"That's good," she said, striving to keep her tone light. "I need all the help I can get."

They spent the rest of the drive making small talk and marveling at the plants and wildlife visible from the Jeep as they bumped along the road. As they got closer to the village, Olivia's anticipation grew, fizzing in her stomach and making her feel a little giddy. She looked forward to this trip all year long, and she was determined not to let Carlos and the specter of the cartel steal her joy. Even though they were making her do an evil thing, she was here to changes lives for the better. It was a humbling task, but one she was proud and grateful to take on.

The density of the jungle began to thin, and eventually they entered a clearing in the thick growth. Their driver slowed as they approached the village, and a group of children who had been playing nearby abandoned their game to run after them as they entered the village proper.

"It's bigger than I expected," Logan remarked, leaning over to get a better look out the window.

Olivia thought back to her first trip here and how her stomach had quivered with a combination of excitement and fear when she'd caught sight of the white adobe buildings that lined the streets. The town was postcard-picture worthy with its cobblestone streets, clay tile roofs and brightly painted doors. But the beautiful facade hid a bone-crushing poverty that prevented many people from having access to health care. And although she was only one woman, she was able to change dozens of lives in the time she spent here every year. It never felt like enough, but it was better than nothing.

"The medical charity chose this town as our home base because it has a fairly stable connection to the power grid."

"That makes sense. I imagine it's kind of hard to do surgery without electricity."

She shuddered, thinking back to the operation she'd told him about before. "It's definitely not my idea of a good time."

"Do all your patients live here?"

"No. Some of them are local, but some of them come from miles away. I've been making this trip for several years now, so word has gotten out that I'm here during this time of year. There are always a few patients who have traveled long distances to get here, hoping I can help."

"And do you?" There was no judgment in his tone, only curiosity.

"I try my best." But there were some people she couldn't help, and it always broke her heart. That was the downside of coming here—there were limits to her abilities, and she couldn't save everyone.

They pulled up to the hospital, a large two-story building on the corner of a block. A bright blue stripe was painted along the bottom half of the walls and served to set the building apart from its surroundings. In case that didn't make it distinctive enough, a large blue cross decorated each wall, proclaiming to all that this was a place of healing.

Olivia climbed out of the Jeep and stretched, enjoying the pleasant ache brought on by moving muscles that had been still for too long. She glanced over to find Logan doing the same thing and smiled. Due to his size the trip had probably been more uncomfortable for him, but he hadn't complained once. She appreciated his stoicism. Nothing made a long trip seem even more endless than a whiny travel companion. *Maybe I'll share that chocolate after all…*

A series of thumps made her turn, and she saw their driver was busy unloading their luggage onto the sidewalk. He appeared to be in a hurry, if his speed was anything to go by, and Olivia quickly walked over to intercede. Although she had mailed most of her supplies to the hospital well in advance, she had packed some things that were too fragile or too important to trust to the Colombian postal system. It would be a shame to make it here only to have them broken on the steps of the hospital.

She reached for a bag, grabbing it just before the

driver. He gestured for her to hand it over, but she shook her head, smiling to soften her refusal. "This one is very fragile," she explained.

He nodded. "As you wish." A moment later, the rest of the luggage was on the pavement. "Do you need help getting everything inside?" the driver asked, his hand already on the door handle of the Jeep. It was clear he had somewhere else he'd rather be, and Olivia couldn't help but wonder if he was one of the spies Carlos had mentioned. Was he running off to report they had arrived?

"No, thank you," she said, tipping him for his service.

"Perhaps he can help you," the man said, nodding his head at Logan. "He looks strong enough."

Logan snorted softly but otherwise gave no indication he'd understood. Olivia smiled politely. "Thank you. I'm sure we'll be fine."

The man climbed in and drove off without further comment, stirring up a faint cloud of dust in his wake. Olivia watched him go, frowning slightly.

"What's wrong?" Logan asked, his voice low and close.

She turned to find him standing next to her, his expression pleasant but his eyes intense. "I just think it's strange our driver was so quick to leave. In my experience, they're usually all too happy to offer additional assistance in the hopes of raising their tip. Do you think he might be on their payroll?" She didn't have to specify who "they" were—Logan knew the cartel was never far from her mind.

"It's possible," he said. "Or perhaps he had another fare to pick up."

"Maybe." But she couldn't shake the feeling the man was more than he had seemed. "I don't think we said anything revealing on the ride here…"

"We didn't." Logan's confidence washed over her and she felt her muscles relax a bit. "So even if the man does work for the bad guys, the only thing he can tell them is that we're here. Not exactly newsworthy, if you ask me."

"I suppose you're right." She offered him a half-hearted smile, feeling a little foolish for having over-reacted. "I guess I'm just being overly paranoid."

"That's not a bad thing to be right now." Logan squeezed her shoulder, triggering a wave of warmth down her arm. "Keep your eyes and ears open, but try not to let your vigilance get in the way of why you're really here." He nodded at the hospital. "You can't help people if you're afraid they're going to betray you at the first opportunity."

"That's true," she said, knowing he was right. She couldn't give her patients the attention they deserved if half her brain was busy worrying that they were spies for the cartel.

"Let me be the one to handle the nasty business. You've got more important work to do."

His offer was reassuring, and Olivia knew he meant what he said. Even though she hadn't known him long, something told her he was more than capable of following through on his words, a fact that was even more encouraging.

"I'll try to remember that," she said. It would be difficult to let go of her fears, but she had to trust Logan. Just because Scott had turned out to be a disappointment didn't mean all men were. Logan hadn't done anything to deserve her doubt—not yet anyway. She had to stop thinking of him as a man she was attracted to and remember that he was her lifeline. The two of them had to function as a team if they wanted to survive.

It was their only chance.

Chapter 8

Logan shifted his grip on the boxes, craning his head to see around them while he walked. Olivia led the way into the hospital, her arms similarly laden with their luggage. He didn't know what she'd packed, but if the weight of the parcels was any indication, she'd brought a lot of it.

"Almost there," she called back. He grunted in reply as she led him down a long hallway. The hospital hadn't looked very large from the outside, but now that he was carrying what felt like a metric ton of medical supplies the corridor seemed endless. On the bright side though, he was so distracted by the burning sensation in his arms and lower back he wasn't able to fully appreciate the view of Olivia's very fine backside. It was an unorthodox way of avoiding temptation, but it worked.

Kissing her in the Jeep had been a mistake. Even

though he'd only pressed his lips to the side of her head, once his mouth had made contact with her soft skin he'd immediately wanted more. He'd spent too much time wondering how her lips would feel against his and too little time paying attention to their surroundings. It was the kind of distraction that could ruin this operation, and he needed to shore up his self-control where she was concerned.

That was easier said than done, though, especially since the job required regular physical contact between them.

But only in public, he reminded himself. He didn't have any excuses to touch her when they were alone, and he'd do well to remember it.

They rounded a corner and a few feet later, Olivia ducked through a doorway. He followed and was rewarded by the sight of several chairs and a low table—a waiting area, he realized. She led him through a set of double doors and into a small room, where she set her bags down. He followed suit, letting out an involuntary sigh as he straightened back up.

She smiled at him sympathetically. "Thanks for carrying all that. I know it was really heavy, but I didn't want to risk making multiple trips. Things can disappear around here if you turn your back for even a moment." She tightened her grip on the strap of her backpack, which he noticed she hadn't set down. They had to find a safe location for the cartel's money—there was no way she could carry it around with her until it was time to make the exchange.

He opened his mouth to respond, but before he could speak a loud squeal of excitement rang in the air.

"Olivia!" A small dark-haired woman shot through

the doorway and grabbed Olivia, clinging to her like a human barnacle. The new arrival let out a stream of rapid-fire Spanish punctuated with smiles and the occasional laugh. Logan only managed to catch every third word or so, but it was clear this was one of the nurses and she was overjoyed to see Olivia.

The feeling was mutual, if Olivia's expression was anything to go by. A wide grin split her face, and she hugged the woman back with equal ferocity. The two chatted over each other in that curious way of women, each one apparently hearing and understanding the other even though they both spoke simultaneously. Finally, the nurse pulled back and Olivia gestured to Logan.

"This is Logan," she said, reaching out to pull him closer. "His company is thinking about investing in our work, and he's here to check out what we do."

The nurse eyed him up and down, her gaze zeroing in on their linked hands. "I see," she said in Spanish. "Is that the only reason he followed you?" Her tone was teasing, and twin spots of color appeared on Olivia's cheeks. Logan kept his expression neutral, pretending he hadn't understood.

"A lady never tells," Olivia replied, earning a belly laugh from her friend.

"This is Daniela," she said, this time in English.

Logan stuck out his hand and the smaller woman stared at it for a beat. "He's very direct," she murmured to Olivia. Then she placed her own hand in his.

"Nice to meet you," he said, making it a point to speak in a formal, stilted way that suggested limited fluency in Spanish. She returned his greeting politely and shot Olivia an amused glance.

"Where is everyone else?" Olivia asked. "I've brought gifts." She rummaged in her backpack and withdrew a small, brightly wrapped package, which she extended to Daniela. The other woman took it with a smile.

"You shouldn't have. You know the only gift we need is your presence." She examined the wrapping paper, tracing her finger over the scrolled print.

"I like to spoil you," Olivia said. A teasing note entered her voice. "Consider it a bribe."

Daniela laughed at that. "Working with you is all the reward we need. Stay here—I will find the others. It's been a slow day, so it shouldn't take me long." She nodded at Logan and left the room.

Olivia waited a few seconds, then turned to face him. "You did that on purpose, didn't you?"

"What?" he asked, pretending not to understand.

The corner of her mouth curved up. "You know it's not customary here for a man to initiate a handshake with a woman he's meeting for the first time."

"Really?" He tried to sound innocent. "I must have forgotten that."

Olivia laughed softly. "Hardly. You've only just met Daniela, and you've already got her convinced you're another one of those brash Americans. I'm sure she's telling the rest of the staff as we speak." She cocked her head to the side, a speculative gleam entering her eyes. "But that's what you wanted, isn't it?"

Logan inclined his head in a nod. "Like you said, if they think of me as a harmless presence they won't censor themselves. We might learn something."

Her delicate brows drew together in a small frown and she shuddered. He took a step closer and touched her arm. "Like I said before, let me worry about the unpleasant details. Just focus on your patients."

"I know." She pressed her lips together, clearly unhappy at the thought. "Still, I can't help but hope the nurses are innocent."

He hoped so, too, for her sake. It was bad enough the cartel was manipulating her like this. If she found out the people she'd worked with for years, whom she clearly considered friends, were also involved? It would hurt her deeply and cast a pall over her work here.

Logan wanted to reassure her that she had nothing to worry about, that the people she worked with and trusted were not doing business with the cartel. But he didn't know them and he couldn't bring himself to voice what might turn out to be a lie.

In any event, he was saved from having to make a reply by the sound of people moving closer. Olivia heard it, too, and her face brightened with anticipation. She straightened, and he could practically feel the vibration of excitement coming off her body. She moved toward the door and poked her head out into the hall, triggering a collective squeal of delight from the approaching group. In the next instant she was gone, stepping out into the hall with her arms spread wide.

Logan hung back, wanting to give her a moment to reunite with the group without worrying about making introductions. He leaned against the doorjamb and watched while Olivia was surrounded by women in brightly colored scrubs. They took turns embracing her, and he could tell by the look on her face she was genuinely happy to see them. They flitted around Olivia, each one talking over the next in their excitement. The swirls of color and chatter made him think of a flock of exotic birds, and he couldn't help but smile.

For her part, Olivia greeted each woman in turn, pausing to exchange words before turning to the next. It was obvious she cared for these people, and he marveled at the change in her. For a moment, the shadow of the cartel lifted from her face, and she relaxed in the presence of her friends. She was truly beautiful when she smiled, and he could feel the warmth in her gaze from here.

As the group continued to chatter, a young man approached from the opposite end of the hall. He was of medium height and build, and his dark hair was a little on the longish side. His face lit up when he saw Olivia, and he rushed forward, reaching through the crowd to touch her shoulder.

"Olivia!" he cried. "You made it!"

She turned and smiled. "Juan Pablo! So good to see you!" She enfolded him in a hug that the young man returned enthusiastically. When she moved to pull away, he kept his hands on her shoulders and leaned in, clearly intending to kiss her.

Logan pushed off the doorjamb and was halfway down the hall before he realized he was moving. He didn't know who Juan Pablo was, but he didn't like the way he looked at Olivia as if she was a tasty dessert he couldn't wait to sample.

Out of the corner of his eye, Logan saw Daniela nudge the nurse next to her, a knowing smile on her face. He realized he was acting like a jealous boyfriend, but wasn't that exactly who he was supposed to be?

"Care to introduce me to your friends, darling?"

Juan Pablo glanced past Olivia and frowned at him.

Good. He didn't want the young man getting any ideas where Olivia was concerned.

"Logan!" She reached for him and drew him into the circle, linking her arm with his. It was a definite signal, and as he glanced around the group he noticed the small smiles and murmurs that made it clear the women had understood. Olivia rattled off names and he did his best to memorize faces, but he knew it would take a few encounters before he learned who each person was.

Except for Juan Pablo. The young man was staring daggers at Logan, his dislike plain for all to see. "Who is he to you?" he asked in Spanish. "You are too good for him."

Olivia shot him a quelling look. "You go too far. It is not your concern."

Juan Pablo held up his hands in a conciliatory gesture. "I just worry about you," he said, his tone soothing. He flicked a glance at Logan before turning back to Olivia. "I don't want to see you get hurt."

Nice try, Logan thought. He wanted so badly to tell this guy off, but he wasn't about to compromise their mission over a jealous puppy of a man.

"You're a good friend," Olivia responded, putting a slight emphasis on the word *friend*. Logan almost smiled at the subtle reprimand, but kept his expression neutral.

Juan Pablo apparently decided not to press his point, but his pursed lips communicated his displeasure. Logan felt an immature spurt of satisfaction that he quickly tried to quash. He wasn't here to antagonize the nursing staff or complicate Olivia's friendships. Still, he couldn't help but feel a little smug over the fact that he'd gotten the girl.

Even though it was all an act.

"Why don't I take you to your apartment?" Daniela suggested, speaking English for Logan's benefit. "I'm sure we can get something set up for Logan, as well."

"That won't be necessary," he replied smoothly. "Olivia and I will share her apartment." *Take that, "friend."*

A shocked murmur rose from the group, and Juan Pablo sucked in an outraged breath. Daniela raised her eyebrows and looked at Olivia, silently asking if this was true.

Olivia's grip tightened on his arm, but she gave no other outward sign that she was surprised by his statement. She offered a shy smile, ducking her head slightly. "It's true," she said. "I should have mentioned it before, but I got so busy I forgot to say anything."

Daniela merely nodded. "Very well," she said. "Come with me and I'll show you both to the apartment."

Olivia quickly said goodbye to her friends, and Logan smiled and nodded his way through the farewells. The women were nice enough, although he did hear a few giggles as they walked away. Juan Pablo merely nodded once, his eyes bright with anger as he looked at Logan. When Olivia turned to acknowledge him, his expression shifted to one of concern and he opened his mouth, clearly intending to say something. But she didn't give him a chance, turning away before he could speak.

Logan linked hands with Olivia as they followed Daniela. What had he just done? His stomach churned as the implications sank in. He'd just made his job a hundred times harder, thanks to an impulsive declaration made in a fit of annoyance. Why had he let Juan Pablo's behavior get under his skin like that?

More important, could he really keep a professional distance from Olivia if they were living together?

He caught a whiff of her scent as she moved in front of him to pass through a door. Strawberries and cream. His mouth watered, and he found himself wondering if her skin would taste as sweet as it smelled.

Too bad he wasn't going to find out.

Olivia managed to keep smiling until the door closed behind Daniela. Then she whirled to face Logan.

"Are you crazy?" she hissed, careful to keep her voice down. The walls were thin, and she didn't want Daniela or anyone else to hear her.

Logan held up a finger and dug into his backpack, withdrawing a small black device she recognized as an electronic bug detector. He turned it on and moved through the small apartment, returning to stand in front of her.

"No," he said, turning off the detector and putting it back in his pack. "We're supposed to be dating, remember?"

"Dating, yes," she replied. "But this isn't the US. Colombian couples generally don't live together before they're married—it's considered scandalous."

"Sorry about that," he replied, his tone suggesting he was anything but apologetic. "But we need to stick together, and this seemed like the best way to ensure we weren't separated at night."

"I don't think there's any danger of that," she remarked drily, casting a meaningful look at the small bed in the corner of the room. He followed the direction of her gaze, and the tips of his ears turned pink.

"Ah. Well, don't worry. We don't have to stay *that* close."

She should have found his words reassuring, but a tiny spark of disappointment flared in her chest. "And where are you going to sleep?"

He glanced around the efficiency-size apartment, clearly looking for a sofa or recliner. When none appeared, he shrugged. "I'll bunk on the floor."

Olivia winced. "Not a good idea."

"Why?"

"You're close to the jungle. Bugs come out at night." When he didn't look impressed, she continued. "Big ones."

"I'm sure I'll be fine."

She shook her head. "No. If you sleep on the floor you'll be an all-you-can-eat buffet. It won't go well for you."

Logan cocked his head to the side and regarded her with a half smile. "If I didn't know better, I'd say you actually wanted me to share your bed." He took a step closer, and something dangerous glinted in his eyes. "Am I wrong?"

No, whispered a traitorous voice in her head. She swallowed hard, pushing aside an image of the two of them in the small bed, limbs tangled and skin flushed. What would it feel like to have his tall, powerful frame pressed against her body? To feel the strength of his arms as he held her?

She met his gaze, determined to keep things on a professional level. That was why they were here after all. Fantasizing about things that weren't going to happen

was a waste of time. "All I'm saying is that it's dangerous for you to sleep on the floor."

He frowned slightly. "What do you suggest I do then?
Can we have them bring in another bed?"

Olivia shook her head. "I don't think that's an option. There probably isn't one, and even if there were,
don't you think it would look a little strange? After all,
we're dating, right?" She couldn't resist teasing him just
a little, especially since it was his rash announcement
that had gotten them into this situation.

"I guess there's no help for it then," Logan said.
"We'll just have to share."

Olivia glanced at the small bed and then at his broad
shoulders. She bit her lip as a lesson from a long-ago
physics class echoed in her mind: *Two objects cannot
occupy the same space at the same time...*

Her skepticism must have shown on her face, because Logan grinned broadly. "Don't worry, it won't be
so bad. I sleep on my side. You'll have plenty of room."

Olivia let out a sigh, accepting her fate. "I hope you
don't snore."

He held up his right hand as if making a pledge. "You
won't even know I'm here."

She choked back a laugh. *Yeah, right.* It had been a
long time since she'd shared a bed with a man, especially for any length of time. And while she'd signed
on to play the role of the doting girlfriend, she hadn't
thought it would be necessary to stay in character behind closed doors.

Maybe that was the crux of the problem. She had to
act the part without reaping any of the benefits. Lying
next to Logan every night, hearing him breathe and

feeling the bed shift with his every movement—it was going to be pure torture.

There's always sleeping pills. Perhaps a little help was in order to ensure she wasn't spending the nights staring at the ceiling, trying to ignore the man next to her. But no, that wasn't a good solution. The few times she'd taken a sleeping pill, she'd woken groggy and it had taken hours to clear the mental fog from her brain. She couldn't afford to feel that way while she was here—too many people depended on her to help them, and she couldn't do that if her head felt like it was stuffed with cotton balls.

She was just going to have to suck it up. They were both adults after all. Surely they could share a bed without any problems.

Logan stretched out on the mattress and crossed his ankles. He was so tall his feet hung off the end, but that didn't seem to bother him. He patted the space next to him and grinned, looking every inch the smug, satisfied male. "Wanna break it in with me? I could use a nap."

It was going to be a long month.

Chapter 9

Logan was such an idiot.

He'd known, on an intellectual level at least, that sharing a bed with Olivia Sandoval was going to be difficult. But he figured he'd be able to grit his teeth and bear it, with the knowledge that their living arrangement wasn't going to last forever. In theory, it was a solid plan.

The problem was, the reality was so much harder than he'd anticipated.

No question about it, Olivia was a knockout. He'd been attracted to her from the start, when she'd moved in next door two years ago. Now that he was learning more about her, she was even more appealing. And given his lengthy dry spell, his body was quite interested in getting acquainted in a more personal way.

Unfortunately, their nocturnal proximity did not make things any easier on his wavering self-control.

The first week hadn't been so bad. They'd both fallen into bed exhausted, wrung out from working long days getting everything set up and preparing for Olivia to see patients. They'd been too tired for any awkwardness to set in, and sleep had claimed them quickly.

Tonight was different.

He was lying on his side, staring at the wall of the apartment, listening to Olivia's steady breaths. He could tell she was still awake, too. She always got a little hitch in her breathing right as she was dropping off to sleep. It was an intimate detail, the kind a lover would know. It felt a little strange, learning such a personal fact about her when their relationship was really more of a business interaction. But he was growing used to the odd dichotomy between them.

She sighed and shifted a bit, probably trying to find a more comfortable position. The mattress left a lot to be desired in terms of padding, but he'd seen the ones at the hospital and knew they were lucky. It was amazing how quickly his standards changed after being confronted with true poverty.

"Can't sleep?" He kept his voice low, barely above a whisper. He didn't want to disturb her if she was drifting off. But if they were both awake, they might as well pass the time together. His hormones proposed a few activities they could try to stave off boredom, but he ignored the predictable suggestions. Talking was a much safer choice.

She was quiet for a moment, making him wonder if she was going to respond. Then she sighed, the bed moving slightly as the breath left her body. "Yeah. Am I keeping you up?"

"Nope. I just don't feel tired. You?"

"I can't turn my brain off."

"That happen often?"

Her voice was wry. "Often enough."

Logan rolled to face the ceiling. It seemed rude somehow to carry on a conversation with his back to her, even though they couldn't see each other in the darkness. "Penny for your thoughts?"

She let out a soft laugh and the mattress bounced as she moved. He felt the brush of her shoulder against his own as she settled onto her back. The heat of her touch was like a warm coal from a dying fire, pleasant and welcome.

"I don't even know where to begin," she said, her voice closer now that they had both moved.

"I generally like to start at the beginning," he suggested. "But you do what you think is best."

"That's very helpful," she grumbled. But he heard the smile in her voice and knew she wasn't really upset.

He could guess what was bothering her, but it would be better if she told him herself. He didn't want to put words in her mouth. And while he'd never admit it out loud, a big part of him was hoping she trusted him enough to lower her guard and let him inside.

"I just can't stop thinking about my friends."

He searched his brain for their names. "Avery and Meredith?"

"Mallory," she corrected.

"Sorry."

"It's okay. You've never met them. You can't really be expected to remember their names."

"How long have you all been friends?" Female relationships fascinated and mystified him in equal measures. His sister, Amy, was only two years younger, so he'd had a front row seat to much of the drama of high school friendships. He'd never understood how women could go from best friends to mortal enemies in the space of a few hours, but what did he know?

"About ten years. We met in medical school and started studying together. We all got along so well we decided to move in together."

"Are they surgeons like you?"

"No. Avery works for the Centers for Disease Control and Prevention. She's part of their illness tracking team. And Mallory is a doctor on a cruise ship."

"Nice," he commented. "I wonder if there's a need for a resident DEA agent on a cruise ship."

She laughed. "Tell me about it. Sometimes I look at her life and think I've made all the wrong choices."

"Oh, I don't know about that. You seem to be doing pretty well for yourself."

"Thanks." There was an odd note to her voice and he hoped he hadn't made her more upset. He cleared his throat. "Can I ask you something?"

"Of course."

"Why is the cartel threatening these women? You're not geographically close to them, which means you can't see them all that often. Why aren't they going after your family?"

She took her time answering. "Because I don't have any."

Oh, man. His stomach dropped, and he could have kicked himself. *Way to make her feel worse.* "I'm so sorry. I didn't know." He'd noticed that she had left the getting-to-know-you questions pertaining to her family blank, but he had thought it was due to a wish for privacy. Never in a million years would he have imagined it was because she was alone in the world.

She shrugged and their shoulders touched again. "No reason why you should. I don't talk about it."

He searched his mind for something to say, for a safer topic that wouldn't cause her pain. But before he could come up with something, she spoke again.

"It was a car accident. Two years ago. They were airlifted to the hospital, but by the time I got there, they had both slipped into comas. My mother appeared to rally at one point, but it didn't last. They were in intensive care for several weeks, but it wasn't enough to save them."

Logan's heart broke for her. He couldn't imagine the pain of losing a parent, never mind losing both at the same time. He reached in the darkness and took her hand, unable to come up with the words to convey his sympathy.

"The worst part was I didn't really get to say goodbye. They never woke up."

He found his voice. "I'm sure they heard you nonetheless."

"That's what all the medical staff said. But a part of me still wonders if it's really true."

"I have to believe it is," he said, squeezing her hand gently. "I remember once when I was at college I woke up in the middle of the night with food poisoning. Ten minutes later my mom called me. Said she'd had a vivid dream that I was sick and needed to check on me. I think parents just know things, especially when it comes to their kids."

"I hope you're right."

"I know they'd be proud of the work you're doing here."

She laughed softly, but there was no humor in it. "I was supposed to be doing this kind of thing full-time. I had planned to join Doctors Without Borders after I finished my residency. Travel the world, help those who need it most. Real idealistic stuff."

"What changed?" he asked. She sounded bitter, which was unlike her. Even though he hadn't known her very long, he could tell she wasn't the kind of person to dwell on the negative parts of her past.

"I needed the money. My parents' medical bills were through the roof, and I also had a lot of debt from school."

"Your parents didn't have health insurance?"

He felt her shake her head. "Dad had lost his job a few weeks before the accident. They hadn't told me. I don't think they wanted me to worry."

"That sounds like solid parental reasoning to me."

"Yeah." He heard the smile in her voice and was glad her mood seemed to be improving. He was learning so much about her, more than the questionnaire could ever hope to tell him, but he didn't want to hear it if it caused her pain. "Anyway, when I got an offer to join a private practice, I took one look at the starting salary and couldn't really say no."

He stroked his finger across her knuckles, enjoying the rises and dips of her skin as he traced the bones. "You made a smart choice. You shouldn't beat yourself up for it."

"My practical side agrees with you. But there's still a small, idealistic part of me that thinks I sold out." She sighed softly. "But that's just life. It never really turns out like you expect, does it?"

"No," he said, his thoughts turning to Emma. His life would have been so different if he'd never found out about her cheating on him. They'd be married for sure, coming up on an anniversary, in fact. How long would it have taken him to discover her lies? He liked to think he was a good investigator, but he hadn't used those skills in his own personal life. If he hadn't walked in on her and Chris in bed together, would he have ever suspected anything? More important, would they have had children by now? His gut twisted at the thought. Not because he didn't want kids, but because he didn't want them with a woman who would treat her marriage vows as suggestions rather than words to live by.

After a few moments of silence, Olivia chuckled softly and shook her head.

"What's so funny?" he asked, eager for the distraction. He shoved thoughts of Emma back into the box where they belonged and focused on the woman next to him.

"I was just thinking. My mother would have loved you. You're just the kind of man she always hoped I'd bring home. But if she hadn't died, I never would have taken the job with my current practice and moved in next door. I'd probably be married to Scott, and we would never have met. It's strange the way things work out sometimes."

Logan's face warmed at the compliment, and his stomach did a little flip at the implication of her words. Neighbors didn't meet each other's parents. Did that mean she thought they had the potential to be something more?

"Oh, I don't know," he said, trying to sound casual. "I think if you're meant to be with someone, the universe will find a way to make it happen."

"Do you think we're meant to be together?" He heard a note of teasing in her voice, but there was something else there, too: interest.

His heart thumped hard against his ribs. How to answer that without sounding like a fool? He racked his brain, but came up empty. *Ah, to hell with it. Just be honest.* "I'm open to the possibility."

She was quiet for a moment, and he began to worry that she was reconsidering her decision to share the bed with him. Maybe he'd come on too strong—the last thing he wanted was to sound like a budding stalker. But he also didn't want to lie to her. She was the first woman he'd been drawn to in a long time, and he was curious to see where the attraction led him.

Apparently nowhere, if her ongoing silence was any indication.

Logan began to mentally prepare himself to sleep on the floor. Maybe he could spread some clothes around in a makeshift barrier to keep the bugs away while he slept... Just as he moved to pull his hand away and toss off the covers, Olivia's grip tightened.

"What would you think if I told you I'm open to the possibility, as well?"

Hallelujah! his body cried. But he tamped down the incipient celebration. It was nice to know his interest was reciprocated, but they still couldn't act on their feelings until they made it back to the US.

He swallowed hard to dislodge the lump in his throat. "It sounds like we have something to look forward to when we get home."

"I like that," she said. "Gives me something nice to focus on while we're here." She squeezed his hand and he smiled, feeling suddenly lighter. It was a boost to his ego to know she was interested in exploring the possibilities between them.

She shifted again, and this time her leg brushed against his. It was the barest whisper of a touch, but it lit up his nerve endings so intensely it might as well have been a kick. A tingling sensation raced outward from the spot, flooding his system and making his skin hypersensitive. He lay there in the dark, his breath trapped in his chest, waiting for another brush of skin against skin. His desire for contact warred with his recognition that another touch might make him lose his grip on his self-control. He didn't know which possibility was worse: not feeling her body again, or moving forward too quickly and losing sight of the dangers they faced here.

In the end, Olivia saved him by pulling her hand away from his. "I have to stop touching you," she said, her voice sounding a little strained. "If I don't, I'm going to forget all the reasons why we can't turn our fake relationship into reality while we're here."

He laughed, happy to know he affected her as much as she did him. "It's a good thing one of us has self-control."

But how long would it last?

A week later, Olivia pushed a wayward strand of hair out of her face and smiled at her next patient, a young boy with a cleft lip. He stared up at her with big brown eyes and gave her a shy smile before turning away and reaching for his mother's hand. The woman waddled in after him, hugely pregnant and clearly uncomfortable, if the grimace on her face was anything to go by. Logan immediately stood and pushed his chair over for her to use, and she sank down with a grateful smile in his direction.

"Hello, I'm Dr. Sandoval," she said in Spanish. "Can you tell me your name, please?"

The boy looked to his mother, who nodded. "Alejandro," he said, his voice barely above a whisper.

"It's nice to meet you," she responded, trying to sound soothing. It was clear little Alejandro didn't know what to make of her, and she didn't want to scare him. "Can you tell me why you're here today?" In her experience, it was better to ask the kids why they'd come rather than jumping in to the exam. They often found their confidence when explaining their condition to her.

He gestured to his mouth, the tip of his index finger tracing along the edges of the vee in his upper lip. "My lip is broken."

She smiled at his description. "Can I take a closer look?"

He hesitated a moment, then nodded. Olivia leaned forward and gently touched his face, angling it more toward the light. The cleft was on his right side, and extended up to his nostril.

"Will you open your mouth for me?"

The little boy obliged and Olivia clicked on her penlight, shining it into the darkness of his mouth. She did a mental fist pump when she saw the solid, unbroken surface of his palate. It was much easier to repair a simple cleft lip, and the recovery time was a lot faster, too.

"I have good news," she said, smiling as she leaned back. "I can fix your lip. Would you like that?"

Alejandro's eyes widened and he nodded in affirmation. Olivia patted his leg and turned to his mother. "When would you like me to do the operation?"

She winced and shifted on the chair. "As soon as possible," she replied, her voice tight.

Olivia frowned. Unless she missed her guess, Alejandro's mother was in pain. But she didn't know if it was the normal discomfort of advanced pregnancy or something more. "Are you all right?" she asked gently.

The woman nodded, but her mouth flattened and her eyes narrowed with strain. She let out a low moan and her hand moved to her belly.

"Logan," Olivia said, switching back to English. "Why don't you and Alejandro go play with the blocks in the waiting room?" She kept her eyes on the woman, assessing her condition.

"What's wrong with my mother?" the boy asked, his voice high with fear. Apparently he'd understood her tone, if not her words, and knew something was going on with his mother.

"Nothing, darling," the woman said. "But I think your brother is coming soon."

Alejandro darted to his mother's side and grabbed her hand. "I won't leave you," he promised solemnly.

"That's very sweet," she said, lifting her free hand to caress the side of his face. "But I need you to go and fetch your aunt. Will you do that for me?"

His delicate features twisted with indecision. "Go, my love," she said. "I need your aunt with me, and you are the only one I can trust to bring her."

The boy nodded slowly. "I'll be back soon." He turned to Olivia, suddenly looking much older than his six years. "Please take care of her."

"I will," she promised. The words had barely left her lips before he turned and ran out of the room, clearly on a mission.

Olivia turned to the woman. "How long have you been in labor?"

"Since this morning. The contractions woke me up."

"Has your water broken?"

She nodded. "A few hours ago. I thought I'd have more time, and I didn't want Alejandro to miss this appointment. We've been waiting for months to see you."

At least she had made it to the hospital. "Should I get a nurse?" Logan asked.

"Yes." Olivia hadn't delivered a baby since medical school, and she wasn't eager to do so now. The sooner she could get this woman to the labor and delivery floor, the better.

Just as Logan took a step toward the door, the woman let out another moan and doubled over. "I think he's coming!" she gasped.

Olivia cursed silently. "Help me get her to the bed," she ordered. They moved quickly, tugging her off the chair and half leading, half pushing her the few steps to the bed. The woman tried to help, but her contractions were coming fast and hard now and she was having trouble walking. Finally they were able to lift her up and she lay back with a great sigh.

"Get a nurse," Olivia ordered Logan. He wasted no time leaving the room. "What's your name?" she asked the woman. She was about to perform an intimate exam, and it only seemed fitting that she learned her patient's name first.

"Maria," the woman gritted out, her teeth clenched as another contraction hit.

"I'm going to examine you now, Maria," Olivia said, tugging on a disposable gown. "I need to see how quickly your labor is progressing."

She slipped on a pair of gloves and lifted the woman's skirt, holding her breath and hoping she didn't have to catch a baby. *Please, let the ob-gyn get here soon!*

Her stomach dropped as she made sense of the scene in front of her. Maria was in labor, all right. In fact, she was almost finished with it. The baby's head was visible and growing steadily larger as Maria's contractions pushed it farther down the birth canal.

Olivia took a deep breath and pushed aside her initial panic. She could to this. She had to do this—there wasn't anyone else in the room right now, and Maria needed her help. She closed her eyes and dug deep into her memories, recalling the motions she'd need to perform to safely deliver this child. What she wouldn't give for Mallory's help right now! Even though Mallory was a general practitioner, she'd had a lot more obstetric experience than Olivia. As if summoned, her friend's voice rang in her head: *You're still a doctor, Olivia. Take care of your patient.*

A sense of calm melted over her and she placed her hands on Maria. "You're almost there," she encouraged. "On the next contraction, I need you to push hard."

Maria grunted in acknowledgment and her body tensed. The baby's head moved closer, closer... Then suddenly, it was free!

"Good job!" Olivia encouraged. "Rest for a second, then give me another big push." She held the baby's head in her hand, wiping the fluids off its face. She glanced around wildly, looking for something she could use to suction its nose and mouth. Seeing nothing, she decided to yell for help. "I need suction!" she cried, hoping someone would hear her.

Maria's muscles clenched again, and the baby's body began to slide free. Olivia gently turned the little one to deliver first one shoulder, then the other. At that point, the rest of the baby's body slipped out in a warm rush.

Olivia rubbed the little one with Maria's skirt and patted its back to help expel the fluid from its lungs. Suddenly, a pair of hands entered her field of vision, and a suction bulb was used to clear the infant's airway. The baby let out a loud scream, and both she and Maria laughed in relief.

"Is he okay?" Maria asked, craning her neck to see her child.

Olivia finished clamping the umbilical cord and delivered the now-bundled baby into its mother's waiting arms. "Your baby is fine," she said. "But 'he' is actually a 'she.'"

Maria's eyes widened. "A girl?" she whispered. A smile spread slowly across her face as the news sank in. "My little princess," she crooned to the baby, running her fingertips along the infant's face, learning her baby's features by touch. She leaned in and pressed her nose to the little one's head. "My angel," she said softly.

Olivia looked away, feeling like an intruder on this private moment. She felt a touch on her shoulder and turned to find Daniela smiling up at her. "Dr. Moreno is on his way," she said.

Olivia nodded. "Good." Even though the baby was out, Maria still needed to be examined to make sure she didn't require further care. "What about the pediatrician?" The baby needed to be checked, too. Olivia hadn't noticed any issues during her brief exam, but she was not an expert in infant physiology. She'd feel much better knowing a specialist had seen to both mother and child.

"Also on the way."

Dr. Moreno slipped through the door, his cheeks flushed from the exertion of running. He took in the scene and turned to Olivia with one brow raised. "Are you trying to steal my patients?" he asked good-naturedly.

Olivia laughed and shook her head. "Believe me, that is the last thing I want. Too stressful." She moved aside so he could attend to Maria, relief washing over her now that the baby was here and the mother was in good hands. Her work was done.

She glanced up to find Logan in the doorway, his expression a mixture of pride and wonder. All at once, she was hit with the desire to go to him, to press herself against his strong chest and feel his arms around her. She prided herself on being a strong woman, but right now, as the adrenaline drained from her muscles, she needed his support, if only for a moment.

She took a step forward, but Maria grabbed her arm before she could get very far from the bed. Olivia glanced down, and the fiercely determined look on Maria's face made her stomach do a little flip. Something else was going on here, and Olivia had a pretty good idea that she wasn't going to like it.

The woman pulled her close, her baby momentarily forgotten as she focused on Olivia. "I have a message for you," she said, her voice barely above a whisper.

Olivia nodded slightly, holding her breath. This was it. She had almost managed to forget the cartel was watching and that she was going to have to collect the drugs. After she and Logan had shared that midnight conversation, she'd allowed herself to be distracted by thoughts of their future, of how they were going to explore their mutual attraction after this was all over. She hadn't spent too much time thinking about the interim and the things she'd have to do before they would get to that point. Now reality came crashing down on her head like a pitcher of ice-cold water. But she wasn't going to let her shock show—she didn't want word of her fear to get back to the cartel.

Maria glanced down at Dr. Moreno, who was busy with his exam. Apparently satisfied that no one was listening to them, she spoke again. "There is an old mining trail on the north end of the city—the entrance is just past the abandoned café. About two miles into the jungle there is a small clearing. They will meet you there, tomorrow at midday." She glanced in the direction of the door, then met Olivia's gaze again. "You must go alone," she said, squeezing Olivia's arm for emphasis.

Olivia nodded and tried not to let her emotions show on her face. She could feel Logan's eyes on her and knew he would be able to tell something had happened. And while she had every intention of sharing this news with him, she didn't want to have the conversation now, in the hospital where there were so many ears. Better for him to think Maria was thanking her for delivering the baby safely.

She pasted on a bright smile and patted the woman's shoulder. For her part, Maria looked almost apologetic, but it didn't take long for her to turn her focus back to the baby. "Good luck," Olivia said to the woman. She didn't blame her for carrying a message for the cartel. Poverty was a fact of life in this region, and Olivia was willing to bet Maria was just trying to survive.

Hopefully they had paid her well for her trouble and that would be the end of it. But it was possible the cartel had gotten its hooks into this family and was even now grooming Alejandro for the business. Olivia's heart ached at the thought of that bright-eyed, shy boy being exposed to such danger, but what could she do? She was just one woman against a seemingly endless number of narco-soldiers...

She stripped off the protective gear and made it to the door. Logan put his arm around her. "That was amazing!" he said, his voice filled with awe. "You did a fantastic job." She sagged against him, grateful for the casual strength of his body. He leaned down and pressed a kiss to her temple. "We can talk later," he whispered in her ear, confirming he had, in fact, noticed her little tête-à-tête with Maria.

Olivia nodded, warmth rising in her chest as they walked down the hall together. Of course he had seen her conversation. He never missed a thing, even though he often stayed in the background—a quiet, calm shadow that followed her everywhere.

She had to admit, being around Logan was just so *easy*. He seemed to fit her in a way no other man had before. She'd thought Scott had been the one for her, but looking back on their relationship she realized she'd never felt this kind of comfort even with him. Part of her worried that the amazing connection she felt with Logan was nothing more than his dedication to his job. After all, his mission was to stick to her like glue and make sure the drug exchange went off without a hitch. And given the awards and photos in his office, she knew he was very good at what he did. A sad, insecure voice in her head said she was reading too much into their fake relationship, and that she was only going to get her heart broken when they made it home and went their separate ways.

Maybe she would.

But she couldn't forget their conversation from the other night. He'd hinted very strongly that he found her attractive and wanted to get to know her better. Surely he wouldn't have done that if it wasn't the truth! He didn't seem to be the type of man who led a woman on, especially since she knew he'd been burned badly before. She was just going to have to have a little faith, and trust that he really did want to be with her once this was all over.

Either way, she couldn't spend too much time worrying about her relationship with Logan now. As Maria had reminded her, she had bigger problems to deal with.

And they had life-or-death consequences.

Chapter 10

"I'm not letting you go alone."

Olivia lifted one brow and gave him a flat stare that suggested he was an idiot. Maybe he was, but he couldn't let her go off into the jungle by herself to meet with a group of violent men. If she thought he was just going to sit back and twiddle his thumbs while he waited for her to return, she was sadly mistaken.

"I don't want to go alone," she said with exaggerated patience. "But what do you suggest? If you come with me, they'll know something is off. They'll probably shoot you on sight and then kill me after they get the money."

Logan shook his head. She was right, but that didn't mean he was going to give up so easily.

"I won't let myself be seen. I'll follow you and stay hidden. If things go wrong, I'll be there to pull you out of the fire."

Olivia chewed her thumbnail silently for a moment. "Okay," she said slowly. "But I don't think we can be seen leaving together. Maria said I was to come alone. If one of the cartel's spies sees us taking the path together, they can call ahead and warn the others. We'll have to go separately."

Logan nodded. He hadn't noticed anyone following them when they went out for a meal or an errand, but that didn't mean they weren't being watched. When dealing with an organization like Fantasmas, it was best to assume the worst.

"I'll set out in the morning. Before the sun is up. I'll hike up to the rendezvous point and find a spot nearby to hide. That way, I'll be in position before you leave, and before the men arrive." He made a mental note to fill his backpack with water before setting out. It was warm and humid in the jungle, and if he was going to sit outside all morning, he would need to stay hydrated.

"What will I tell people when you don't show up to the hospital with me? They'll wonder where you are."

"Tell them I'm sick," he suggested. "Nothing too terrible, since I'm going to recover quickly. Maybe food poisoning or something like that?"

"That could work," Olivia mused, tapping her finger against her chin. "Do you really think you'll be okay waiting by yourself in the jungle all morning? It's not like any forest you've ever hiked through before."

Logan shrugged. "I've done my fair share of camping. I'm not a total idiot when it comes to roughing it. I think I can handle myself for a few hours."

Olivia looked doubtful but she had the grace not to say anything. "I can't believe it's really happening," she muttered, shuddering slightly.

Logan closed the distance between them and drew her in, putting his arms around her in a loose embrace. His larger frame dwarfed hers by comparison, making her seem even more fragile. But he knew that under her delicate exterior lurked a core of steel. He'd caught a glimpse of it earlier when she'd delivered that baby. He had watched the emotions play across her face and had seen the exact moment she'd buried her fears and dug in her heels. It gave him goose bumps just to remember her fierce expression of determination and the way she'd forged ahead, her earlier doubts and worries banished. When Olivia Sandoval decided to do something, she followed through.

And even though she might not realize it now, this assignment was no different.

"I knew they weren't going to forget about me," she said softly. Her cheek rested against his chest, and her breath was warm through the fabric of his shirt. It was just the kind of close, personal contact that made his body sit up and take notice, and he pushed down the faint stirrings of desire to focus on her words. He was trying to comfort her, not put moves on her!

"I guess I just hoped if I ignored it long enough, it wouldn't happen. That maybe it wouldn't be real."

Logan ran a hand down the thick cascade of her dark hair. "I know," he said simply. "And I wish that was the case. But at least now we know what to expect."

She pulled back and met his gaze, her brown eyes sober. "Are you sure about that? They used a pregnant woman to deliver a message—hopefully she got paid to do it, rather than being forced or threatened." Her lips drew down in a frown at the thought. "I get the feeling these are not rational people, and that scares me more than anything."

Logan debated for a moment on how to respond. He didn't want to make her worry more, but neither did he want to deny her concerns. He'd seen enough of the aftermath of cartel violence to know that her instincts were correct.

"They're not rational," he said, deciding to give her the truth. "They're trigger-happy and quick to casual displays of violence. But they are motivated by money. If you do your part, they should leave you alone."

"I hope you're right."

"I am." He infused his voice with confidence, hoping it would reassure her. "Fear of Fantasmas runs deep. They have to know that crossing the organization would mean their death."

"I suppose that's good," she said, sounding a little steadier.

"Just promise me one thing." He touched the side of her face gently. "Don't turn your back on these men. They're like rattlesnakes. If they can find an opportunity to do harm without jeopardizing their deal as suppliers to Fantasmas, they will. Don't give them an opening."

Olivia's eyes widened and she sucked in a breath. "I'll do my best."

"I know you will." He leaned down and pressed a soft kiss to her forehead. It was a few inches north of where he really wanted to kiss her, but he had to keep things affectionate, not passionate. For now.

"I'll be there the whole time," he said, pulling her close again. "I won't let any harm come to you."

"I know," she said softly, wrapping her arms around

him and snuggling closer. Her simple declaration of trust hit him right in the gut, and he felt himself slip a little deeper under her spell. A tiny voice in the back of his mind warned that he was getting too close, too soon, but he ignored it. Now was not the time to worry about protecting his bruised heart. Not when Olivia's life was at stake.

Olivia pushed a strand of hair out of her face and adjusted the backpack, hoping in vain for a breeze. The air was thick and muggy, and the sounds of the jungle surrounded her, making her very aware of the fact that she was a lone human in a vast, untamed wilderness.

No, not alone. Logan was out there, waiting for her. The thought brought her some measure of comfort and she held on to the knowledge like a lucky penny, keeping it in the forefront of her mind.

A bright yellow spider rested on a wide green leaf and she shuddered, giving the arachnid a wide berth. How many creepy-crawlies were out there that she couldn't see? It was enough to trigger paranoia in even the staunchest of outdoorsmen. Her skin itched as she felt the imaginary sensation of thousands of tiny legs crawling up her neck, and she took a deep breath to dispel her rising disgust.

Poor Logan! He was sitting out there somewhere, probably making a fine meal for the many bloodsucking insects in the forest. *Oh, God, what if something venomous bit him?* It wasn't just insects that posed a threat—there were any number of snakes that could kill. And tree frogs too—all he had to do was inadvertently touch one, and...

Her heart pounded against her breastbone as her

mind raced with a thousand scenarios, each one ending with Logan dead or dying alone in the jungle. And it was all her fault. She should have never agreed to let him scout ahead. He had no knowledge of the wildlife in this area, no idea of what was safe and what was dangerous. How could she have thought this was a good idea? It was her own selfish need to feel safe that had led her to agree to his crazy plan. And now he was out there, facing a threat that was more immediate than the cartel. She had every confidence he could handle himself when it came to the dangers posed by humans, but did he know the first thing about surviving in the rain forest, even if only for a few hours?

She felt the sting of tears as her panic threatened to overwhelm her. It was all she could do to keep from running ahead, yelling out his name in the hopes he would respond. But that would be suicide. It was very nearly midday, and the men were probably already close by. If she gave in to her hysteria, they would know she had not followed instructions. Logan had told her they would look for any excuse to do violence, and she couldn't give them one. *Besides*, she told herself sternly. *He's a smart man. He's probably just fine.*

Right?

She stopped and took several deep breaths, forcing herself to calm down. If she walked into this meeting with her head filled with worries about Logan, she was as good as dead. He hadn't let her down yet. She simply had to trust that he was out there, safe and whole.

After a moment her heart began to slow its pounding, and the tightness in her chest eased. She wiped the sweat off her forehead and moved on, determined to get this over with. The sooner she and Logan were back in the safety of their apartment, the better.

Just as Maria had said, the trail opened up into a small clearing. Olivia stepped forward, feeling suddenly exposed after the relative claustrophobia of the dense foliage that had lined the trail. She scanned the tree line opposite her, but saw no movement other than the swaying branches at the top of the canopy. She glanced at her watch. Was she early?

She stood there for several moments, brushing away the questing insects that buzzed around her face. There was no sign of anyone else, and she began to worry. Was she supposed to give some sort of signal? Maria hadn't given her any kind of instructions on what to do once she arrived, but then again, the woman had just given birth unexpectedly. Perhaps she had forgotten some of the message in the heat of the moment.

Olivia turned slowly, scanning the clearing from one side to the other. Where was Logan? Hopefully someplace close. The vegetation was so thick it was impossible to see more than a few feet into the forest. He could be standing a few yards away and she wouldn't be able to see him. But then again, she wasn't used to this environment. Would the men who were meeting her find him through the jungle camouflage? One more worry added to the pile...

A particularly persistent mosquito kept flying around her face, seeking an undefended spot to land. The high-pitched buzz was an annoying distraction, and as the time passed with no sign of human activity, Olivia felt her fears gradually morph into annoyance. She wanted to get this over with, and the sooner the better.

Where are they?

* * *

Logan crouched in the shadows of a downed tree, his eyes glued to Olivia. She'd come charging into the clearing, her cheeks flushed and sweat-dampened tendrils of hair plastered to her neck and the side of her face. He'd caught her worried expression as she scanned the empty space, and he wanted so badly to signal her so that she would see him and know she wasn't alone. But he couldn't take the risk. The men could be anywhere, and he didn't want to blow his cover unless it was absolutely necessary.

He shifted a bit, trying to work out the kinks in his back. The hike in had been mostly flat and fairly easy, if hot. His shirt was soaked with sweat and plastered to his skin, but he didn't stink. Not yet anyway.

He poured a little water out onto the ground and used his finger to mix up some fresh mud. Moving slowly, he smeared it on his face and neck, patching over the exposed spots of skin left when his earlier application had dried and flaked off. It was an old trick he'd learned during his scouting days, and it was saving him from being eaten alive by bugs right now.

Olivia was not so lucky. She swatted the air around her head, clearly irritated. He glanced down at his watch. Twenty past the hour. Unless Olivia had misunderstood Maria's message—which was highly unlikely—these guys were late.

Logan frowned, considering. Were they trying to intimidate her by taking their time? Or had something happened to spook them and they weren't going to show? The politics in this region were fluid—it was possible the suppliers had decided to do business with a different cartel. If that was the case, he was going to have to come up with another plan quickly. He doubted Carlos would be very happy if Olivia came back without the drugs, even if it wasn't her fault the exchange hadn't taken place.

The minutes ticked by and Logan had to stop himself from fidgeting. Any extraneous movement on his part would draw the eye and give his position away. He hadn't spent hours camped here only to make such a rookie mistake at the very end. He wondered at what point Olivia was going to give up and go back to the hospital. Her absence would most definitely be noted if she stayed away for too much longer...

A movement at the tree line caught his eye and he lifted his gun to peer through the sight. Was that...? Yes, that was a person, walking slowly forward into the clearing.

Logan glanced over, but Olivia hadn't noticed the other man yet. A few seconds later, her body stiffened as she realized she wasn't alone. She watched the man approach with a wary eye, but her suspicion didn't seem to faze him.

Additional movement behind the newcomer revealed a group of men moving forward. They stepped into the clearing but made no move to come much closer—it was clear the first arrival was their leader.

Logan took a deep breath and settled into position, keeping the man in his sights. Adrenaline surged in his body, and his fingertips tingled as he watched the man approach Olivia. He was short and stocky, and the scars on his face and hands made it clear he'd been in his share of fights. "If you touch one hair on her head..." he muttered, his protective instincts roaring to the surface. Intellectually, he'd known Olivia would have to conduct this meeting. But he hadn't realized just how difficult it was going to be for him to watch her from afar while she put herself in danger.

Olivia stayed where she was and let the man come to her. *Smart move,* he thought approvingly. If things went bad, she was close to the tree line and could quickly dart back into the cover of the jungle. *But I won't let it get that far.*

The new arrival stopped a few feet away from Olivia and looked her over, clearly taking her measure. If he was surprised to see a woman there, he didn't show it. He took one final drag off his cigarette, then dropped it and ground out the embers with the toe of his boot.

Showtime.

Chapter 11

Olivia tried not to wince as the acrid stench of cigarette smoke burned the lining of her nose. She didn't want to let this man know he affected her in any way. There was something about his cold, flat gaze that told her a show of weakness, no matter how small, would be a dangerous mistake. He was a predator, plain and simple.

And she refused to be his prey.

"You have something for me?" She spoke the question in English, wanting him to think she had no fluency in Spanish. Let him be the one to underestimate her—it might be her only advantage.

He tilted his head to the side, openly studying her. She met his gaze, ignoring the ongoing insect harassment. A few bites were a small price to pay to make him think she wasn't intimidated, even though her insides were quivering like jelly.

After what seemed like an eternity, he spoke. "Where is the money?"

"Where is the product?"

He glanced at her shoulders where the straps of her backpack were plainly visible. His mouth twisted in a cruel smile. "I could just take it from you."

"You could," she agreed. His eyebrows shot up—he clearly hadn't expected her to display such sangfroid about the suggestion of assault. "But I think we both understand it would not be in your best interest to do so."

"What if you did not live to talk about it?" His voice was low and menacing and he took a half step forward. Olivia's heart shot up into her throat, but she stood her ground.

"Then you would not live long enough to spend it."

Hesitation flickered in his eyes, and she pressed her advantage. "They are expecting my call after I retrieve the product. If I do not contact them, well…" She let the suggestion hang in the air between them. In truth, she had no such arrangement with the cartel, but he didn't know that. Given the fearsome reputation of Fantasmas del Mal, she was only too happy to let his imagination run wild. The theoretical consequences he conjured up were likely much more frightening than anything she could say.

His lips flattened and he nodded once. "Very well." He raised his hand, and the three men who had walked into the clearing behind him moved forward.

They didn't speak while they waited for his cronies to join them, and Olivia deliberately kept her gaze on him and off the tree line. If he suspected for even a second she was looking for someone else… She mentally shuddered, not wanting to imagine the bloodbath that would result if Logan's presence was detected.

The men fanned out behind their leader and didn't speak, but they studied her with open curiosity. Olivia met their eyes and refused to flinch in the face of their speculative perusal. One of the men licked his lips and leered suggestively, but she merely raised a brow and stared at him until he looked away.

The leader held out his hand, and the man carrying a stained cloth bag withdrew a rectangular brown-wrapped package and passed it over.

The leader lifted his brow, plainly expecting Olivia to show him the money. Instead, she reached into her backpack and pulled out a penknife and a small vial of liquid. She almost laughed at the man's incredulous expression as she made a tiny incision in the package and used the blade to scoop out a bit of white powder, which she deposited in the vial.

"What are you doing?" he asked, caught between astonishment and annoyance at this delay in the proceedings. Olivia didn't respond as she used her finger to flick the vial, mixing the powder into the liquid. After a few seconds, she held the vial against a scrap of paper.

"I'm checking the purity of your product," she said finally, showing him the chart. Let him think the cartel was doing a bit of quality control. In reality, Logan had packed the tests before they'd set out, wanting her to confirm that she was actually receiving cocaine in exchange for the cartel's money. Otherwise, the bad guys could claim she had merely picked up a brick of baking powder and switched it out for the drugs later, to falsely incriminate them.

A murmur rose up from the men, and Olivia couldn't

tell if they were offended at her lack of trust or amazed the cartel would go to such lengths to ensure it was getting what it had paid for.

"Are you satisfied?" His tone was huffy, but there was uncertainty in his eyes.

She dug in the pack and tossed the stacks of bills at his feet. Then she held the bag open before her. "Put the rest in here," she instructed. *It's almost done*, she thought. Just a few more minutes and they'd be gone and she could give in to the shakes she was trying desperately to control.

One of the men who'd stepped forward glared at her, not bothering to disguise his hostility. "She needs to be taught a lesson," he said in Spanish. "No one treats us like this."

His compatriots grumbled in agreement, and another one spoke up. "This woman thinks she is in charge. She should learn the truth."

Olivia kept her gaze on their leader, who did not respond. As his men continued to complain, Olivia decided to take matters into her own hands. It was clear the idea of hurting her was starting to override their fear of the cartel, and if the balance tipped in the wrong direction, she wasn't going to get away unscathed.

"Are you really that stupid?" she said in Spanish. The men stopped talking and stared at her, their jaws hanging open in shock. She rolled her eyes at their surprise. "Did you honestly think I don't know your language? I know everything about you. Where you eat. Where you sleep. Where your families live. Fantasmas does not take chances." She let that sink in and looked at each man in turn. "And neither should you."

The men glanced at each other, chastened into silence. The one putting the drugs in her bag swallowed hard, his face now pale under his tan. He hurried to complete his task and then stepped back, clearly wanting to distance himself from her.

The leader gestured to one of the other men, who knelt down and scooped up the money. Olivia slung the bag over her shoulder and nodded. "Our business is finished. You can go now."

The three men didn't waste any time heading for the tree line, but the leader stayed behind a moment, glaring at her. Their tables had turned, and it was plain he didn't like being on this end of the deal.

Just go, she urged him silently. She wasn't going to leave until he did—it would be foolish of her to turn her back on him. She had won this round, but she wouldn't put it past him to go for a cheap shot if given the opportunity.

He muttered something under his breath, then turned and stomped off after his men. Olivia waited until they disappeared in the forest before releasing her breath in a gusty sigh. It was done. Now she just had to get back to the apartment and hide the drugs.

She waited a moment longer, just to be sure they weren't coming back. The normal forest sounds of birdsong and wind-rustled leaves filled her ears, and her heartbeat gradually slowed back to its normal speed. With one last look at the clearing, she turned and walked back into the forest.

She'd gone about thirty yards down the trail when Logan stepped out of the vegetation and onto the path in front of her. The shock of his sudden arrival made her freeze in place, and she emitted a startled yelp.

His frown eased as he realized he had scared her.

"Sorry," he muttered, taking her arm and tugging her farther along the path. "Don't stop here. We need to keep going."

She stared up at him, taking in his mud-caked skin and dirty clothes. "What happened to you?"

He cast her a puzzled glance, then seemed to remember his appearance. "Oh. That. It's bug repellant."

"I see." She bit back the urge to laugh, but was unable to stop a squeak from escaping. Logan frowned down at her and she quickly smoothed her features into an appropriately serious expression. She didn't let his display of grumpiness affect her, though. Relief had made her feel lighter than air, and she had the sudden, absurd thought that if Logan let go of her arm, she'd float away.

I did it, she thought, with no small amount of wonder. Somehow, she had stood up to those men and come out a winner, despite the fact that her confidence had been nothing more than an elaborate bluff. It was unlike anything she'd experienced before, and she felt simultaneously buoyed and drained by her success.

Logan tugged hard on her arm and she picked up her pace to keep up with him. "Where's the fire?" she asked, a little breathless. When he didn't reply, she dug in her heels and wrenched her arm free. "What is your problem?" He hadn't said a word, but she could practically feel the angry tension radiating off his body. Why was he so upset? Everything had gone according to plan.

Logan glanced around, then stepped off the path into the shadows of a small grove. Having no other choice, Olivia followed him.

He stood with his back to her, scrubbing furiously at the dried mud on his face. It flaked off in a shower of dust, but when he turned to face her, she could see his skin was still dark from the dirt left behind. The filth caked onto his skin gave his features a masklike quality, but his displeasure still came through loud and clear.

"You want to know what my problem is?" he said, practically hissing the words. "Do you have any idea how close you came to getting killed just now?"

His question popped the bubble of her relief, and she felt her own anger rising in response.

"What are you talking about? I thought that went about as well as it could have gone."

His eyes widened and she had the distinct impression he was reevaluating his estimation of her intelligence. "Those men were inches away from violence." He held his hand up, fingers almost touching in illustration. "If they had decided to hurt you—" He broke off, shaking his head.

"You would have stopped them," she said, placing her hand on his arm in the hopes of calming him.

"That's just it. I don't think I could have gotten to you in time." He was still upset, but now she heard a new dimension in his voice: fear.

Olivia rocked back on her heels, uncertain how to respond. She'd never considered the possibility that Logan might be afraid, as well. He'd always seemed so confident, so sure of himself and what they needed to do in order to get through this alive. His unflappable demeanor had comforted her on many occasions and reassured her that she was going to be okay.

The fact that he was scared, too, should have worried her, and for a brief second, it did. How was she going to survive if her protector was just as afraid as she was? But the concern passed before she took her next breath.

Logan's fears didn't make him any less reliable or any less capable. If anything, they made him more human.

The urge to comfort him rose in her chest, and she stepped forward and put her other hand on his shoulder. "It's okay," she said, pitching her voice low in the same tone she used to soothe an anxious patient. His muscles were tense under her fingertips and she squeezed gently, urging him to relax. "Nothing happened. You don't need to keep worrying about an outcome that didn't take place."

"You took too many risks," he said through clenched teeth. "You practically dared them to kill you."

"I did not!" She may have goaded them a little bit, it was true. But only because it was her best chance at keeping them at bay. Surely a man like Logan would understand that?

"I saw the expressions on their faces—you said something to make them angry. Did you forget you were outnumbered?"

"No." She glared up at him, indignation quickly replacing any remaining sympathy she felt for causing him undue stress. "Did it escape your notice that they *didn't* hurt me?"

He dismissed this point with a wave of his hand. "You don't get it. I—"

"No, *you* don't get it," she interrupted. "I did what I thought was best to complete the deal and get out. Maybe I didn't make the choices you wanted me to, but it worked and we have the drugs. Why are we standing here arguing when we should be celebrating?"

Logan simply stared at her a moment, emotions flickering across his face in rapid succession. Then he shook his head again. "Let's go," he muttered. "It's not safe for us to stay here. We need to get back to the apartment." He walked past her and stepped onto the trail, pausing for her to join him. As soon as she did he took off again, setting a punishing pace.

Olivia gritted her teeth and trotted behind him. She'd let this slide for now. But as soon as they were back at the apartment, she was going to find out what exactly was bothering Logan. It wasn't like him to act this way, and they couldn't work as an effective team if they didn't communicate.

"Get ready," she muttered to his back. "This isn't over."

Logan pushed a vine out of the way, remembering just in time to hold on to it so it wouldn't fall back and hit Olivia in the face. She probably wouldn't believe it after his behavior in the glen, but he hadn't meant to take his frustrations out on her.

How could he explain it, though? She'd think he was crazy, getting all worked up over seeing her in danger like that. He was the DEA agent after all. He was supposed to deal with this kind of thing all the time.

And he did. But a woman he was beginning to care for generally wasn't part of the mix.

As he'd learned the hard way, it was one thing to put a stranger in danger. Quite another to watch someone close to you risk themselves.

His heart had nearly stopped when she'd faced off with the four men. He'd been too far away to hear what they were saying, but their facial expressions spoke volumes. It was clear that, at least initially, they'd seen her as little more than a nuisance. Perhaps a plaything to be used up and discarded. He'd very nearly blown his cover when the man had leered at Olivia, but he'd stopped himself just in time.

For her part, Olivia had kept her cool. He still wasn't sure how she'd done it, but she'd shifted the balance of power in her favor and managed to hold on to her edge until the meeting was over. And it had ended just in time. The leader wasn't happy about the way things had gone, and if he'd stuck around much longer, his fear of Olivia probably would have given way to his anger.

Which was why they needed to get back to the apartment. He didn't think they were being followed, but the thick vegetation of the jungle had a muffling effect on noises, and it would be all too easy for the men to sneak up on them.

Olivia panted behind him but didn't speak. Maybe she was angry with him, or maybe she was just saving her breath for the hike. Either way, there would be time for talking once they were safely indoors.

If she was willing to listen.

He felt his face heat, and not from the exertion of the hike. He'd acted like a child, yelling at her when he should have been congratulating her. She'd gone into the lion's den and emerged unscathed, which was something to be proud of. She'd come a long way from the fragile, scared woman still shaking in the aftermath of Carlos's appearance at her home.

He pulled his hat down low on his face once they entered the village, not wanting to draw attention to his dirt-covered face. Fortunately the streets were fairly empty, as it was the hottest part of the day and most people were inside. They made their way quickly to the apartment building, and he led the way up the stairs to their second-floor unit.

The cool darkness of the apartment was a relief after his time in the jungle. He laid his pack on the ground, sighing in pleasure as the air hit the sweat-damp skin of his back for the first time in hours. He wanted nothing more than to lie on the floor and let the fan blow over him, but he had to make peace with Olivia first.

She carefully shut the door behind them, looking every bit as relieved to be inside as he felt. He watched her set her own backpack down, saw her features relax as she pulled the thick braid of her hair off the back of her neck to take advantage of the cooler air.

Words of apology crowded into his mouth, but he remained quiet for a moment, drinking in the sight of her. She truly was a remarkable woman, and she deserved to hear him say that. The last thing he wanted was for his earlier temper tantrum to crush her newfound sense of confidence with respect to this operation.

"Do you want to talk about what happened back there?" Her eyes were closed and her tone was mild, but he could tell from the remaining tension in her muscles that she was still annoyed with him.

"I overreacted," he said simply.

Her eyes popped open and he caught a flash of surprise in their brown depths. Olivia clearly hadn't expected him to admit fault so quickly, and her reaction stung a little bit. Did he really seem that arrogant?

"I'm sorry," he continued. "You were right—you did an outstanding job, and I shouldn't have given you a hard time about it."

She studied him a moment, weighing his words. "I'm sorry I scared you," she said finally. "I honestly didn't mean to."

He thrust a hand through his hair and looked down.

"I know. It's not your fault—I just let my emotions get the better of me. It won't happen again."

"Is that right?" He heard Olivia take a step and he looked up to find her standing only inches away. His muscles tensed in anticipation and his fingertips itched to touch her, but he forced his hands to remain by his sides.

She stared up at him, her dark eyes pulling him in. He couldn't look away, even if he'd wanted to. "Does that mean you care about me?" Her voice was soft, but there was no artifice in her tone. She wasn't asking because she wanted him to stroke her ego—she was asking because she genuinely wanted to know.

Might as well give her the truth. "You know I do." He unlocked his arm and brought his hand up to touch the side of her face. Just a brief caress, the slide of fingertips on skin. Enough to tide him over for a bit, until they could get out of this hellhole and back to a place where they could explore what was between them.

She closed her eyes and turned her face into his touch. His heart kicked against his ribs and he felt his breath hitch in his chest. They were standing on dangerous ground. He had to move away now, before he did something foolish.

Summoning all his self-control, Logan dropped his hand and took a step back. Disappointment flashed in Olivia's eyes and it took a lot of willpower to keep from reaching for her again. But it was important to maintain the separation between them. He couldn't think straight when he was touching her, and they were still in danger.

He cleared his throat. "We need to hide the drugs. It's not smart to have them in the open here."

Olivia nodded. "Did you have someplace in mind?"

"The mattress." It was a cliché, but it looked like the only viable option. The floor was tiled, which meant there were no loose boards to pull up. And the ceiling was a flat expanse of adobe with no nooks or crevices that would allow for concealment. The cupboards were too obvious, and the toilet tank wasn't large enough. That left the mattress. It wasn't perfect, but it was the best he could do at the moment.

They walked over to the bed and he flipped the mattress over, exposing its dingy yellow underbelly. Olivia brought her bag and knelt on the floor, then withdrew the plastic-wrapped packages.

"Are you sure we'll be able to get these back to the US?" she asked doubtfully. "Won't they be easy to detect?"

"Probably, but we have a baggage handler on the payroll," he explained. "He'll take the bag off the plane and bring it to Alan, bypassing customs and the drug dogs." He retrieved his pocketknife as he spoke and sliced through fabric. Fortunately the mattress was old and the stuffing crushed down, which meant he didn't have to pull any of it out to make room for the drugs. He inserted the packages, making sure they were flat. They did still have to sleep on this thing, after all. Then he sealed the slit in the mattress with a strip of duct tape and put the bed back together.

"Very tidy," Olivia observed drily.

"I'm glad you approve."

"I can't believe I'm actually going to sleep on a mattress full of drugs," she muttered, shaking her head. "How did my life get so messed up?"

"For what it's worth, I doubt you'll even feel it,"

Logan said, striving to lighten the moment. "Just try not to think about it."

A mischievous glint entered her eyes. "I can think of some ways you can distract me."

Heat flared in his chest, spreading down his limbs in a trail of sparks. He swallowed hard. "I can, too," he said, his voice suddenly raspy. "But we agreed to wait until we got back."

"Hmm…" She stepped closer and trailed her finger up his arm. Goose bumps rose on his skin and his mouth went dry. "We did say that. But what if I want to reconsider our arrangement?"

His body rejoiced and he reached for her before his brain could butt in and ruin things. She emitted a soft, breathy laugh as he pulled her hard against his chest. The sound warmed his blood and made his skin tingle with anticipation.

He threaded his hand through her hair, which was thick and damp with the sweat from her earlier exertions. A gentle tug brought her chin up and her lips into the perfect position.

"Are you sure about this?" he whispered. *Please say yes, please say yes, please say yes…*

Her breath was warm against his chin when she responded. "I've never been more sure in my life."

Chapter 12

"She has the packages."

Carlos picked idly at his salad, searching for a stray tomato. "You are certain?"

"Yes." But there was a slight hesitation to the word. Carlos remained silent, waiting for his informant to elaborate.

"I'm confident she has them. I saw her hike into the forest this morning, and she just now returned."

"Perhaps she was simply communing with nature," he suggested, feeling a perverse sort of satisfaction at antagonizing the caller.

"That's not like her."

"So you say."

The informant was silent for a moment. "I will search the apartment as soon as they leave to confirm she picked up the merchandise."

"They?" Carlos seized on the word. "You haven't dealt with him yet?"

"No."

Carlos dropped his fork and it clanged loudly against his plate. Heads swiveled, but he picked it up again, playing it off as a fumbling error. People quickly lost interest, but he waited a moment before speaking just to be sure.

"Were my instructions unclear?" He was careful to keep his voice level—it wouldn't do to draw attention to himself again.

"No—not at all. It's just—"

"Just what? You know how I feel about excuses."

"Yes, sir. I just haven't been able to get him alone. Yet," the informant tacked on, almost stammering with anxiety. "I will, though. Soon."

I doubt it. It seemed he was going to need to find another tool for this particular job. But whom could he trust?

"See that you do," he said, keeping his thoughts to himself. No sense in triggering panic—he might still have use for this one yet.

He blocked out the rapid-fire apologies and excuses ringing in his ear, trying to think. Dr. Sandoval was due to arrive back in ten days. That didn't leave much time for a plan B...

"Yes, yes, yes," he said impatiently, cutting the caller off. "Get back to me when you actually have news." He hung up mid-assurance and placed the phone on the table, next to the bread plate.

If Olivia Sandoval really did have the drugs, that was good news indeed. But it wasn't enough. The DEA agent had to be dealt with, and the sooner, the better.

El Jefe expected an update soon, and he wanted to have good news to share with the man when they next spoke.

If not, he wouldn't be speaking for very long.

Olivia had barely gotten the words out of her mouth before Logan's lips came down on hers. His arms banded around her torso, locking her in place against him.

Not that she wanted to move.

He kissed her fiercely, like a starving man who'd just found a meal. His passion was all-consuming, crashing over her in a wave that was almost overwhelming. She gasped for air and clung to him, fearing that if she let go she'd lose him forever.

Heat radiated off his body and she melted against him, feeling the edges of her body soften like warm candle wax. She tugged at the hem of his shirt, but their bodies were pressed too tightly together to move the fabric more than an inch or so. A groan of frustration escaped her mouth and Logan captured it in his own.

He obligingly moved back, keeping his mouth on hers while she pulled his shirt up. Only when the fabric bumped into his chin did he break the kiss, and then only for the split second it took to jerk the shirt over his head. It fell to the floor in a dirty heap and Olivia wasted no time putting her hands on his chest.

His skin was warm and dusted with dark hair that tickled her fingertips. He made a low sound in his throat, and the vibrations of his approval traveled down her arms and settled in her belly, creating a delicious sensation that complemented her own growing need. She slowly moved her hands up to the broad expanse of his shoulders, pausing here and there to trace the lines of his muscles, so different from her own.

Logan tugged on her shirt with a few hesitant jerks, silently asking her permission to remove the fabric that separated them. Not wanting to take her hands off him, she broke their kiss long enough to whisper, "Yes." In one smooth motion he pulled it off her body and she heard the rustle of fabric as it joined its fellow on the ground.

His hands were large but his touch was gentle when he reached for her. But just as his fingertips grazed her skin, he jerked back, almost as if burned.

"What's wrong?" Why was he taking a step back? Had he changed his mind? Oh, God, how was she going to get through the next ten days without dying of embarrassment if he pulled away now?

Logan held his hands out, fingers spread, and was staring at them as if he'd never seen them before. He turned them over and studied his knuckles, then ran his eyes up his arms. "I'm filthy," he said, his tone suggesting he was just now realizing this fact.

"Oh." Her brain scrambled to make sense of his words. Did this mean he wasn't about to explain why this was a bad idea? She had the sudden urge to laugh out loud, but she stopped herself, not wanting to seem like a crazy woman. "Is that all?" A little dirt never hurt anyone, and they had other, much more interesting things to focus on...

"I can't... Not like this." His cheeks went pink under the filth and he met her gaze, his green eyes distressed. "You deserve better."

Her heart turned over at his thoughtfulness and a

wave of affection came over her, washing away her earlier doubts. She smiled up at him. "You're very sweet."

He was already working the button of his pants and toeing off his shoes and socks. "Give me five minutes," he promised, his expression earnest. "I'll take the world's fastest shower and I'll be right back." He took a step back, bumped into the side table next to the bed and barely avoided falling down with his pants around his ankles. Wobbling slightly, he regained his balance and made it into the bathroom. He shut the door, then jerked it back open and poked his head out.

"Don't go anywhere," he said. The door shut again and the pipes groaned as he turned the shower on.

Olivia shook her head, smiling to herself. She'd never met anyone like Logan. He was the perfect combination of silly and serious, sweet and protective. He made her laugh and yet she felt so safe when he was around, like nothing bad could touch her. It was a strange feeling when her rational mind knew she was in the midst of terrible danger. But Logan insulated her from the worst of it, something she appreciated more than words could say.

She glanced down at her shirt, lying in a sweaty heap at her feet. She could do with some freshening up as well, and there didn't seem to be any point in waiting for him to vacate the bathroom. If they shared the shower, they'd be conserving water. It was the environmentally responsible thing to do…

Her mind made up, Olivia shucked off the rest of her clothes as she walked over to the bathroom door. She pushed it open, and Logan hollered from behind the curtain. "Almost done."

"Don't rush on my account."

"Just give me—" He stuck his head out and the words died in his throat when he caught sight of her. He swallowed hard. "Um."

Olivia raised a brow. "Cat got your tongue?"

He shook his head, his eyes glued to her body. "More like my brain just exploded."

She laughed, and a purely feminine part of her thrilled at his response. "Good thing I'm a doctor."

"Are you going to put me back together?"

"Something like that." She took a step forward. "Move over. I'm coming in."

Logan stepped to the side to make room for her, his muscles growing tense as she approached. She brushed past him and ducked under the warm spray, closing her eyes in bliss as the water cascaded down her body, washing away the feel of the jungle.

Logan made a low, strangled sound and she opened her eyes to find him staring at her, his gaze filled with desire and something close to reverence. His response made her feel both empowered and cherished, and she blinked back a sudden surge of tears. She hadn't connected with a man like this since Scott had left, and Logan's obvious appreciation gave her a sense of completion that she didn't realize she'd been missing until now.

She took a moment to look at him, to drink in the view of his strong, toned body, naked and willing. He was a glorious sight, made all the more appealing because she knew what lay beneath all that muscle and bone. Logan had the heart of a guardian, and she felt a little thrill at the knowledge that he had chosen to protect *her*.

She lifted her hand and reached out, stopping just before she touched him. He met her eyes and answered her silent question with a nod. She placed her palm over his heart, loving the feel of his pulse against her skin. Strong. Steady. So full of life.

He brushed his fingertips down her arm in a tentative caress that made her shiver. She stepped closer, pressing herself fully against him. His body was a study in textures, and she reveled in the different sensations. Soft skin. Coarse hair. Solid muscle. Her hypersensitive nerves cataloged each trait, and her need for him grew with every beat of her heart.

"I'm on the Pill," she blurted, knowing that in a few moments the part of her brain responsible for thought was going to shut down.

"Thank God," he murmured, his breath gusting out in a sigh of relief. "I'm clean. I was tested at my last check up a few months ago."

"Me, too," she said.

He grinned down at her, and the wicked spark in his eyes made her knees go weak.

"Then what are we waiting for?"

They moved together, exploring each other with hands, lips, and tongues. The warm water made her feel almost drugged, but the sensation of Logan's body against her own was a potent force that demanded her full attention.

He lifted her up and she wrapped her arms around his neck, his casual display of strength making her insides go liquid. The tile was cold against her back, but then Logan slipped inside her, and she forgot everything but the man in her arms and this perfect moment.

Logan stretched out on the bed, his body so relaxed he felt almost boneless. "That was, without a doubt, the best shower of my life."

Olivia put her hand on his stomach and traced a lazy

path up, up, up until she reached his breastbone. She pressed her palm to his heart and he put his own hand over hers, anchoring it in place. "I don't think I've ever been this clean before," she remarked.

"It was my job to get all the dirt off you. And I take my job very seriously." His blood warmed at the memory of his hands on her body, touching, caressing, gliding over skin slippery with soap.

She laughed, a contented, almost dreamy sound. "Let me be the first to compliment you on your…technique."

"I'm so glad you appreciated it."

"Indeed. It was just what the doctor ordered."

"Only for you," he said, pressing a soft kiss to the hollow of her shoulder. "I give very personalized attention."

"That's good to hear, because I don't like to share."

"I don't, either." A pang of memory pierced the bubble of his good mood and he frowned. *She's not Emma*, he told himself again. He took a deep, cleansing breath and pushed thoughts of his former fiancée out of his mind—there wasn't room in this bed for a third person.

"You know…" Olivia trailed off, sounding suddenly shy.

"Yes?"

She shifted until she could meet his eyes. "I don't hop into bed with every guy I meet."

"I'm glad to hear it," he assured her solemnly. She thumped him lightly on the arm and he grinned.

"You know what I'm trying to say," she said, sticking her tongue out at him.

He did, but it was fun to tease her. "Can't say that I do."

The mattress shifted as she flopped onto her back

and covered her eyes with the back of her hand. "You're impossible," she said, sighing dramatically.

Logan leaned over and pressed a kiss to the inside of her upper arm. "Tell me."

She eyed him narrowly. "I'm not sure I want to now." Her tone was serious but the corners of her mouth twitched, giving her away.

He rolled fully on top of her and began to tickle her, enjoying the way she squirmed against him. "Tell me," he repeated.

She giggled and intensified her struggles, creating some interesting friction between their bodies. Finally she cried out, "Uncle!" between laughs.

Logan stilled his hands and she went limp beneath him, the pace of her breathing gradually slowing as she relaxed. "I believe you were about to say something," he teased.

Olivia laughed again and grinned up at him. "If you must know," she said, sounding prim, "I was going to say that this was—*is*—special to me. That you…" She trailed off and looked away, her cheeks turning a lovely shade of pink.

"Go ahead," he said gently.

She took a deep breath. "I haven't done this in a long time."

"How long?" There was no judgment in his tone. After all, he was in the same boat, relationship-wise. Still, he was surprised she'd been alone…

"There was someone once… He left just after my parents died." She was silent for a moment, then cleared her throat. "So that's why this means so much to me."

Her words wrapped around his heart and he felt humbled by her admission. His throat tightened with emotion and he tried to clear it before speaking. "I feel the same way." It came out a little gruffer than he'd intended, but Olivia didn't seem bothered. She gave him an impossibly sweet smile and rolled toward him, seeking contact.

He folded her into his embrace, loving the feel of her body against his. She fit him perfectly—he could practically *feel* the broken, jagged pieces of his heart coming back together when she was with him. It was almost too good to believe, but if this was a dream, he never wanted to wake up.

Olivia let out a contented sigh and snuggled closer. "You know," she said, her breath warm on his chest. "You were right. I really can't feel the packages."

Her observation was innocent enough, but it made the hairs on the back of his arms rise. She was right, he realized, with a growing sense of horror. He couldn't feel them, either.

Logan sat up carefully so as not to knock Olivia off the bed. "What's wrong?" Alarm entered her voice. "Your muscles are locked tight enough to break a bone."

"I just want to double-check the mattress." He was probably being paranoid, but better to be safe than sorry.

Olivia obligingly hopped off the bed and helped him flip the mattress over. Logan peeled off the tape and stuck his hand into the stuffing. He groped blindly, his guts turning to water as he realized what he was feeling. Or rather, what he *wasn't* feeling.

The drugs were gone.

Chapter 13

Alejandro darted through the undergrowth, his breath coming fast as he ran along the forest path. His heart was still beating hard from adrenaline and there was a flat, metallic taste in his mouth. He wanted badly to stop for a drink of water, but he didn't dare take the time. The man was waiting for him, and he was not a patient person.

Part of him felt bad—the doctor had been really nice to him. She was the only person who had looked at him like he was normal, despite his broken lip. Everyone else stared at him at best, or laughed and pointed at worst. None of the other kids wanted to play with him, but that was okay because he had a job. A real, grown-up job, which was more than the other kids could say.

He was still impressed at the way the man had known exactly where he should look for the packages. It had taken a few minutes to figure out how he was going to get them—the mattress had been too heavy for him to lift by himself. But he'd fit under the bed easily, and after that, it hadn't taken long to get the wrapped bundles.

His stomach cramped as he relived his time under the bed, convinced the doctor was going to walk in the room at any moment. But then he'd heard the noises coming from the bathroom, and his fear was replaced by a sense of awkward embarrassment. He'd heard those sounds before and knew what they meant.

Still, he hadn't lingered. He'd shoved the bundles into his bag and crept out of the apartment, his guilt fading as he thought of how happy the man would be to see him. How much would he pay for this job? Enough for him to keep a little for himself, so he could buy a treat?

He didn't begrudge giving his earnings to Mama, especially now that his little sister was here. She was a tiny, pink little thing, but she took all of Mama's attention, which meant it was up to him to provide, at least for now. And he was proud to do it.

His lungs burned, but he was almost there. Just a few more yards…

Alejandro burst into the clearing and stopped, bending over to put his hands on his knees. He gulped air for a moment, then lifted his head and glanced around.

The man stepped out of the trees and beckoned him forward. Alejandro felt a flock of birds take flight in his stomach, but he marched forward, head held high. He knew better than to show fear in front of the boss.

"Do you have them?" The man puffed on a cigarette, the gray smoke curling up out of his lips when he spoke.

Alejandro nodded and pulled his bag off his shoulder, then opened it and withdrew the packages.

The boss nodded. "Good." He took the bag, but Alejandro didn't protest the loss. He could buy another with his earnings.

The man dug into his pocket and withdrew a thick fold of bills. Without really looking, he peeled several off the top and held them out. Alejandro reached for them, but the man didn't let go right away.

"You know the rules, yes?" He stared hard at Alejandro, and the boy fought the urge to squirm.

"I know nothing," he said.

It was the expected response, and the boss released his grip on the money. He reached out and ruffled his hand through Alejandro's hair. "Good work. Go home now. Tell your mother I will see her again soon."

Alejandro nodded and stuffed the bills into his pocket, next to the cell phone the boss had given him. Then he turned and ran, eager to get back to the safety of home.

"Dr. Sandoval?"

Olivia looked up to see Daniela hovering in the doorway, staring at her in concern. *Oh, God. What now?* She was barely holding it together today—one more crisis would put her over the edge.

"Is everything all right? I have been calling you for the past few minutes." Daniela took a step into the room, and Olivia was filled with the sudden, desperate urge to tell her everything. Maybe Daniela would have some flash of insight that had eluded her and Logan. After all, she knew this area better than anyone—perhaps she could tell them about the local players in the drug trade, give them some idea of who could possibly have stolen the packages. Someone, somewhere had to know *something*!

But Olivia knew it was a futile hope. Besides, she couldn't put another person in danger.

"I'm sorry," she replied, squelching her despair lest it show on her face. "I must have drifted off and didn't hear you."

"That's okay." Relief passed over Daniela's features as she accepted the excuse. "I only wanted to know if you were ready for a lunch break."

"That sounds nice. I'm almost done here."

Daniela nodded. "Very good. Should I bring something for your friend?" she asked delicately.

"Please do. He'll be along shortly." Right now, he was back at the apartment talking to the DEA, but Daniela didn't need to know that. "Logan had to make a few calls to his business partners this morning."

"Ah. Do you know if they are going to fund your trip next year?"

Olivia was taken aback by the question, and it took a moment for her to remember that was Logan's cover story for being with her. "I'm not certain," she stammered, turning back to her patient. "It would certainly be nice." She fumbled to apply a bandage, wishing Daniela would drop the subject. All the local staff was giddy at the prospect that Logan's company would donate money and supplies—they were practically counting the number of additional patients they could help. How was Olivia going to tell them that wasn't going to happen? It was just one more thing for her to worry about, and she felt like the lowest of the low for getting their hopes up in the first place.

The teenage boy in front of her squirmed uncomfortably, and Olivia realized she'd wrapped the bandage too tight. "I'm sorry," she apologized, unwrapping the gauze and starting over.

Daniela excused herself and Olivia waved absently in her direction. *Focus!* she chided herself. Her patients deserved her full and undivided attention, but try as she might, Olivia couldn't stop worrying. Where were the drugs? Who had taken them? More important, how could she get them back?

Her mind conjured up Avery and Mallory as she'd last seen them, relaxed and laughing as they enjoyed their girls' weekend. If she didn't bring home the drugs... A sudden, intense wave of nausea hit her and she swallowed hard to keep her earlier cup of coffee down. She didn't dare think about what the cartel would do to her friends. If she let her brain go down that path, she wouldn't be able to stop thinking about it, and no good could come of imagining the terrible price they would pay for her failure.

"All done," she said, attempting to smile at her patient. The young man's eyes widened a bit, and Olivia realized her smile was not as reassuring as she'd intended. He hopped off the bed with a muttered "Thanks" and made for the door, no doubt eager to get away from her. Not that she blamed him. In her present mood, she wasn't good company for anyone.

She began to clean up the wrappers and other detritus left behind. This room was running low on gauze and tape, two things that were in constant demand. There was a lull in patients right now, so she might as well take this opportunity to restock. No telling when she'd get another chance. Besides, it gave her something productive to do and would hopefully help keep her mind occupied.

It took only a few moments to make a list of all the supplies she needed to bring back. Olivia stepped into the hall, shutting the door quietly behind her. She didn't want to leave the remaining supplies unattended for long—staff from other floors of the hospital tended to raid these rooms when she was in town, wanting to use the materials she brought for their own benefit. She didn't blame them. This was a resource-poor area, so the people were quick to take advantage of any influx of new items.

The supply closet—it wasn't big enough to really call it a room—was located down the hall. Olivia fished the keys out of her pocket and stepped inside, grateful for the cool darkness of the windowless space. She took a deep breath and pressed her forehead against one of the metal shelves, closing her eyes. It was tempting, so tempting, to just shut the door and forget about the rest of the world. But Logan would be done with his calls soon and would wonder where she was. Hopefully he and the DEA had come up with a solution, or at least an idea of what they should do now. As long as they could keep Avery and Mallory safe... Her stomach cramped and she took another deep breath, trying to relax. Throwing up in here would not improve the space.

The surge of nausea passed quickly and she began to search the shelves for the items she needed. While she worked, her thoughts kept turning over in her mind as she sought answers to a seemingly endless number of questions.

Who had taken the drugs? It had to be someone who knew she had them, but who could that be? The only person Olivia had spoken to about them, aside from Logan, was Maria. She hadn't seen Maria since she'd delivered her baby, and it was highly unlikely the woman had found out where Olivia was staying, sneaked into the apartment and stolen the drugs herself. But she could have told someone else about the pickup...

What was the point, though? Logan had told her that the price of cocaine in Colombia was a fraction of what it was worth in the United States. Still, money was tight for a lot of people. Had someone stolen the drugs so they could sell them and keep the cash? It was possible. But she didn't know enough about the drug trade in town to have any guesses as to who might be guilty, and that wasn't exactly the kind of conversation she could have without raising a lot of suspicions.

One thing was clear—whoever had taken the drugs clearly hadn't meant her any harm. She and Logan had been sitting ducks in the shower. The thought made her face flush as she recalled exactly *what* they'd been doing there. Needless to say, they'd been totally oblivious to the outside world. Someone could have burst into the bathroom, guns blazing, and neither one of them would have been able to do anything about it. But that hadn't happened. Whoever had stolen the drugs had been careful to leave no signs of their presence. If she hadn't made the comment about not being able to feel the bundles, it was unlikely they would have realized the theft until much later. That meant whoever did this wanted it to be a secret. So should she pretend like nothing had happened, or should they search for the culprit?

Both options had merit, she mused, scanning the shelves for large gauze squares. Whoever took the drugs was bound to still be watching. If she acted like nothing was wrong, it might cause the thief to relax and make a mistake. If she and Logan were to respond, it would certainly blow his cover. That could mean all sorts of problems, and since they still had nine days to go before the end of the trip, it might make things difficult, to say the least.

But if they could somehow search quietly... Maybe it was possible for them to find out who had done this without being too obvious. Logan would have a better idea of just how to do that. Where was he? Why was it taking so long for him to talk to his fellow agents?

Footsteps sounded in the hallway, a steady, confident stride coming closer. That had to be him. Relief washed over her, and she poked her head into the hall to flag him down.

But it wasn't Logan headed her way. It was Juan Pablo, and his face broke out into a wide smile when he saw her. "Olivia!" He quickened his pace and took her hands in his own, then leaned forward to kiss her cheeks. "How are you?"

"I'm fine," she replied, dodging to the side to avoid his lips. She fought to keep the disappointment out of her voice and off her face. It wasn't Juan Pablo's fault that she wasn't in the mood to see him. On previous trips, they'd spent a lot of time together treating patients and hanging out with the other nurses after hours. But after her last visit, she'd gotten the impression Juan Pablo wanted more from her than just friendship. That feeling had intensified when she'd noticed the tension between him and Logan, and in an effort to defuse the situation, she'd kept her distance from Juan Pablo. She didn't want to hurt his feelings, but she also didn't want him to think there was a chance of anything romantic happening between them.

"I haven't seen you much," he chided. "Have you been avoiding me?"

Yes. She pasted on a smile. "Just very busy. I've been seeing lots of patients."

"I know—they all want to be treated by the best."

Please don't say nice things to me. She already felt bad enough at having to let him down—his heartfelt praise only made her feel worse. "That's very kind of you to say."

"Olivia." He waited for her to look at him, and when she did she felt a little shock. There was a gravity to his dark brown eyes that she'd never seen before. Juan Pablo was normally an easygoing guy. But his expression had shifted now into something quite serious.

"I am worried about you," he said, genuine concern in his voice. "You don't seem like yourself. You are quiet, more withdrawn. Is something wrong?"

She began to shake her head reflexively, the denial an automatic response. But he lifted his hand, forestalling her reply.

"Please. You know I consider you to be a friend. I hope you feel the same way about me. You can tell me if something is bothering you."

He was being so considerate, something she didn't deserve in light of the way she'd avoided him over the past few days. His worry for her brought tears to her eyes, and she blinked away the sting. He was truly her friend, but she couldn't tell him everything. A few hurt feelings were a small price to pay for keeping him off the cartel's radar.

"I'm fine," she said. His brown eyes filled with skepticism. "Truly, I am. I'm just worried."

He cocked his head to the side, inviting her confidence. The truth was on the tip of her tongue, but she settled for a little misdirection instead. "It's hard to come here and know that I can only help a few people, when there are so many in need."

Juan Pablo nodded in understanding. "I know. That is a frustration we all share." He took a step closer, and she felt the warmth radiating off his body. "But I think there is something more?"

She shifted uncomfortably, mentally cursing her inability to conceal her emotions. "It's nothing."

Juan Pablo studied her intently for a moment and she had to force herself to stand still under his scrutiny. Finally, he let out a disappointed sigh. "I will take your word for it. For now. But please, if you should change your mind…" He took another step forward, invading her personal space. Olivia leaned back, hitting one of the shelves. "I hope you know I am here for you. I care about you. Very much."

His eyelids lowered and he tilted his head. Olivia felt a brief surge of panic as she realized his intention, but she was trapped against the shelves, unable to move in the small space. She opened her mouth to tell him to stop, but his lips crashed down on hers and her protest came out as a muffled squeak.

Chapter 14

Logan stepped into the hospital and took the stairs on autopilot, his mind a million miles away. It had been good to talk to the guys back home—it always helped to bounce ideas off them and to find out if they'd heard anything through the usual channels. Unfortunately, they had no new information for him and were just as mystified as he was regarding the disappearance of the drugs. It didn't make sense for Fantasmas to steal them back, since they were counting on Olivia to bring them into the States. The most logical explanation was a rival organization making a play, but their intelligence had no news of any groups operating in this area.

There was also a third possibility, one that made the hairs on the back of his neck stand up. Someone may have deliberately targeted Olivia in an effort to sabotage her mission here. If she didn't make it back with the drugs, the cartel would kill her almost immediately. Whoever had stolen them had to know that, and perhaps that was their end goal. But who would want Olivia dead? And why?

From what he'd seen, the staff here loved her. They were friendly and respectful and seemed to genuinely like her and enjoy her company. But appearances could be deceiving, as he'd learned once the hard way. Maybe it was time he took a closer look at some of the hospital employees…

The door to Olivia's exam room was closed, meaning she was either with a patient or had stepped away. He pressed his ear to the door but heard nothing inside. *Where is she?* She wouldn't go far—they had agreed to meet here after his call, and he knew she was anxious to hear about it.

The soft susurrus of voices drifted down the hall, so he set off to see if anyone had seen Olivia. Maybe she was in the bathroom or had been called away to consult on a patient. The door to the supply room was open—hopefully he'd get lucky and would find her there.

A moment later, he had his answer. She was there, all right, along with Juan Pablo. Logan's hands bunched into fists at his side as he watched the man kiss her, anger flowing over him like hot lava.

Idiot! How could he have been fooled again? He'd thought Olivia was different, that what they had shared actually meant something to her. But it seemed she was no better than Emma. His stomach dropped as pain chased away his anger. At least he'd found out now, before truly losing his heart to her.

He turned to leave, not wanting to interrupt their moment. It wasn't his place—clearly, Olivia had made her choice and he was too proud to beg. But just as he moved, she made a faint sound of protest.

Logan turned back immediately and saw the situation with new eyes. Olivia had her hand on Juan Pablo's shoulder, her grip tight. But not with passion, he realized. She was trying to push him away.

Before he could think twice, Logan grabbed Juan Pablo by the nape of the neck and squeezed hard, tearing him away from Olivia. The man let out a startled cry and flung his arm out, trying to defend himself. Logan dragged him out of the supply room and pressed him against the wall of the hallway, the urge to do violence rising in him with a fierce intensity that nearly took his breath away.

"Logan!" Olivia stepped out and laid her hand on his shoulder.

"Are you okay?" he asked, keeping his gaze on Juan Pablo. The other man's anger was palpable, and Logan hoped he would lash out and give him an excuse to pound him into the ground.

"I'm fine. It was nothing. Just a misunderstanding."

"Did you ask him to kiss you?"

"No, of course not!"

"Then it seems to me like he was forcing himself on you." He punctuated this observation with a little shove that made Juan Pablo narrow his eyes.

"It's not like that—" Olivia began, but Juan Pablo cut her off.

"Who are you to interrupt us like this? We were having a private conversation."

Logan tilted his head to the side. "That didn't look like talking."

"What would you know about it?" Juan Pablo sneered.

Logan's fingers tightened on the man's shirt, but he willed himself to remain calm. "I think it's time for you to leave." He dropped his hand, and Juan Pablo made a show of straightening his shoulders and smoothing his shirt, removing the wrinkled evidence of Logan's grip. Then he looked up, defiance glittering brightly in his eyes.

"No."

Before Logan could respond, Olivia stepped in front of him. "Yes." Her voice was quiet but determined.

Juan Pablo's bluster slipped for a second, and Logan could tell Olivia's response had surprised him.

"But, Olivia—"

"You presume too much, Juan Pablo," she said, her voice cold. "We are friends, nothing more. You know this, and yet you tried to force affection from me."

He drew himself up, rebuilding his confident façade in the space between breaths. "I merely wanted to show you what you're missing." He flicked a dismissive glance at Logan, who didn't give him the satisfaction of a response. This was Olivia's show now, and he was content to let her run it.

Faster than a thought, Olivia slapped him. The loud smack seemed to echo through the empty hall, and all three of them sucked in a stunned breath. Juan Pablo paled considerably, making the red imprint of Olivia's hand stand out like a brand on his cheek.

Olivia was shaking with emotion, and Logan reached out and put his hand on her shoulder. He wanted to steady her, to let her know she wasn't alone. Her reaction was shocking in its intensity, and he began to wonder what else had happened before he'd come upon them…

She ignored his touch and leaned forward, unleashing a torrent of words in rapid-fire Spanish. Logan couldn't hear everything, nor could he keep up, but Juan Pablo visibly crumpled at the onslaught. Whatever she was saying definitely hit its mark.

"Go," she finished, the word low and lethal-sounding. "We are done here."

Juan Pablo straightened, hesitating a moment. It was clear his pride called for him to respond in some way, but evidently his common sense kicked in. He cast a final, hateful look at Logan and then started off down the hall, his steps measured and his pace regular.

Logan waited until Juan Pablo was out of sight before gently turning Olivia to face him. She seemed calmer— he no longer felt the fine tremblings of her muscles under his hand, and her features had relaxed somewhat. But her eyes turned to the empty hall and it was clear she was still upset.

"Want to tell me what that was about?" he asked quietly.

She didn't answer right away. Her chest rose as she took a deep breath, then she let it out, deflating before his eyes. She glanced up, looking so small and defeated that he was struck with the urge to gather her in his arms and wrap his body around her. His hands twitched, moving of their own volition to do just that. But he stopped himself in the nick of time. She'd just been pawed by one man. She didn't need another offering of unwanted physical contact, even if his intentions were good.

"I snapped," she said simply. Her voice was flat, as if

she was too exhausted to express any emotion. "It was wrong of me, I know. But in that moment, I couldn't stop myself." She shook her head and tucked a strand of hair behind her ear. "I am just so tired of feeling out of control. With everything going on—" She stopped and glanced around, then took a step closer and lowered her voice. "With all that's happening, I feel like I no longer have any say in my own life. And when he forced himself on me like that…" She shuddered, and Logan felt a renewed surge of anger. "I took all my frustrations out on him."

"Understandable," he said. His throat was still tight with emotion and he tried to relax his jaw before speaking again. "I'm sorry I didn't get here sooner."

"I'm just glad you got here when you did." She was quiet for a moment, then shook her head. "Why did he do it?"

Logan opened his mouth to respond, but it was clear she wasn't looking for an answer. She lifted her hand to cut him off. "We've always been friends. Why did he have to go and ruin that now?"

"I don't know," Logan said. It was poor comfort, but it was all he could offer her at this point. "Maybe he didn't think your friendship was enough."

"Maybe not," she said, her voice low. "But that's all I can give him."

And what about me? The question was on the tip of his tongue, but he didn't say it. Olivia had been through enough already—she didn't need him trying to define what was between them, especially not now. Better to focus on getting home. The rest could wait.

"Dr. Sandoval?"

They both turned to see Daniela standing at the end

of the hall. She held up a paper bag with a smile. "Ready for lunch?"

Olivia smiled and nodded. "We'll be right there. Thank you."

She turned and met his eyes, determination settling over her face. "Let's go get something to eat. You can tell me about your conversation later. I could use a distraction now."

A few days later, Olivia and Logan shared a meal at a small restaurant. Olivia took a bite of fish and glanced around, checking to make sure no one was eavesdropping. Then she leaned forward and caught Logan's eye.

"Do you think we should tell Carlos the drugs were stolen?"

He lifted one brow and took a sip of *guarapo*, a ubiquitous fruit juice concoction served with most meals. He appeared to consider the question. "Why would you want to do that?"

She shrugged. "I just thought if they knew about the theft, they might have some of their people look into it. I can't imagine they'd take too kindly to the loss of their property."

"They don't," he confirmed, cutting off another bite of tamale. "But you have to remember, the only thing keeping you and your friends alive right now is the fact they think you have their merchandise. If you let them know that's no longer the case, they won't hesitate to kill the three of you as they're tying up loose ends."

Olivia's shoulders slumped. "I suspected as much. But I had hoped they'd be so busy trying to track down their stuff they would forget all about me."

Logan gave her a sympathetic smile. "I'm afraid it doesn't work that way."

She took another bite, but the meal had lost its flavor. "What are our options now? I don't have their stuff, which they will discover as soon as we get home. How am I going to get them away from Avery and Mallory when I can't deliver on the one thing they wanted?"

Logan polished off his tamale and eyed her plate. She shoved it forward without a word, and he shot her a grateful smile.

"We're going to do a little switcheroo," he said, digging into the remains of her dinner. "My colleagues and I have access to a lot of product, given the nature of our work."

"And you're going to give me some of it, to deliver as promised," she finished, nodding as the pieces fell into place.

"Basically," Logan confirmed. "This fish is fantastic," he said, closing his eyes in pleasure.

Olivia couldn't help but smile. "I'm glad you like it," she murmured. "But back to the matter at hand. Is that even legal?"

He dismissed this concern with a wave of his hand. "We do it all the time. Besides, we're going to take it back right after the exchange when we move in to arrest everyone."

"I see." It was a straightforward plan, one that should be easy enough to execute. The knots that had been in her stomach ever since they'd discovered the drugs were gone started to unravel, and for the first time in days she felt like she could breathe easier.

"So we just have to pretend like everything is fine until we get back?"

Logan nodded, scraping the plate with the edge of his fork. "Exactly. So try to relax and enjoy the last few days you have here."

She laughed softly. "I'd love to, but I still can't figure out who broke into the apartment."

Logan's eyes narrowed briefly. "You let me worry about that." He stretched his arm across the table, palm up in invitation. She slid her hand into his and was rewarded by a gentle squeeze. "I said I'd keep you safe, remember?"

She nodded. "I do."

"I meant it."

Her stomach fluttered at his words and a warm pulse spread from their joined hands, flowing up her arm and settling in her chest. "I know."

Chapter 15

The next few days seemed almost normal as Olivia settled back into a routine of seeing patients and conducting surgeries. Logan walked her to the hospital every morning in time for her first appointment of the day and was waiting for her when she wrapped things up for lunch. According to Daniela, while Olivia conducted surgery, Logan hadn't hesitated to step up and volunteer for all the small, menial tasks that mounted up in the department, earning him the admiration and gratitude of the nursing staff.

"He is quite nice to have around," Daniela confessed one morning during surgical prep. "He doesn't mind changing sheets, taking out the trash or cleaning. It's remarkable!"

Olivia smiled, happy to hear that Logan had fit in so well with the rest of the team. His willingness to help with the traditionally "female" chores had earned him a place in Daniela's good books, which was a coveted spot. "I'm glad he's making himself useful."

"Oh, yes," Daniela said. "We will be sad to see him go."

"I'll miss you, too," Olivia teased.

Daniela laughed. "You know what I mean. I had my doubts about him when you first arrived, but I am glad to be proven wrong."

"I understand." And she did. There was something about Logan that made the people around him feel comfortable. She had felt her own resistance start to crumble as she spent more time with him, and she was beginning to question all her reasons for keeping him at arm's length. Maybe he was worth the risk to her heart after all...

She pulled off her scrub cap and stepped into the hall, glancing around for Logan. She had finished up surgery a little early today, so he might not be here yet... No, there he was, standing at the end of the hall. She started for him, anticipation building as she approached. Spending time with him was the best part of her day, and she intended to enjoy it as long as she could.

She opened her mouth to call out to him, but before she could say anything, his whole body stiffened in shock. That was odd. Maybe he'd been stung by something? She didn't see any bugs, but the hospital had its fair share of insects, being so close to the forest.

In the next instant, Logan started walking, his steps jerky and reluctant. He glanced down the hall and his eyes widened when he saw her. His expression shifted to one of horror, and he mouthed the word *No!*

Olivia froze, her stomach cramping as she realized

that something was terribly wrong. She ducked into a doorway and waited a beat, then poked her head out in time to see Logan disappear, a shorter dark-haired man close on his heels. It looked like Juan Pablo, but why would he be going anywhere with Logan?

She stood there for a few seconds, indecision paralyzing her muscles. Whatever was going on, Logan plainly wanted her to stay out of it. But if he was in danger, could she really leave him to face it alone?

No, she decided firmly. After all he'd done for her, she wasn't about to turn her head and hope for the best. He wasn't going to like it, but she was going after him.

Her mind made up, she slipped out of the doorway and moved down the hall, then turned and followed the men.

Logan gritted his teeth as Juan Pablo herded him out of the hospital and down the sidewalk, keeping the gun pressed to his side. They made it to the end of the block before Logan decided to try to get some answers. There was more going on here than Juan Pablo's bruised pride, and he wanted to know what he was up against.

"What's your plan?" Logan kept his voice level and his movements easy, tamping down the urge to fight back. He didn't want to startle Juan Pablo, not while the man was pointing a gun at him. It was clear from the way Juan Pablo held the weapon that he wasn't comfortable with it, and the last thing Logan wanted was to get shot by accident.

"I'm getting rid of you," Juan Pablo said, his voice oozing with satisfaction.

"How do you figure that? Are you just going to take me into the forest and shoot me?" They were approaching the entrance to the trail he and Olivia had used earlier, and his brain came up with a hastily concocted plan: he'd wait until they were a few feet into the forest, away from innocent bystanders, and then he'd take Juan Pablo down. His muscles tensed in anticipation as they got closer to the tree line. Just a few more steps...

Juan Pablo let out a short laugh. "Nothing so predictable. Violence is not my specialty."

"I suppose you prefer forcing yourself on unwilling women?"

That earned him a sharp poke in the back with the muzzle of the gun. The unexpected pain caught Logan off guard and he let out a grunt, which made Juan Pablo laugh again.

"Bastard," Logan muttered. He was going to enjoy turning the tables on this guy.

They entered the forest, stepping into the shade of the canopy. Logan stopped walking and set his feet, preparing himself to attack. He left his arms loose at his sides, not wanting to telegraph his intentions. He was confident he could handle Juan Pablo, but he didn't want to give the other man any advantage.

Juan Pablo moved to stand next to him, but remained just out of arm's reach. No matter. Logan would have the gun out of the other man's hand and slam him on the forest floor before he knew what hit him.

Logan braced himself, adrenaline flooding his system. It was now or never. He started forward...

"Here he is. As promised."

A sound from the undergrowth drew his attention and Logan converted his movement toward Juan Pablo, twisting to the side so he could see this new threat.

Three men appeared on the path, their faces grim

and their hands gripping guns. Logan realized with a small shock they were part of the group that had met Olivia before to hand over the drugs. Had Juan Pablo been the thief all along? But why?

"Excellent." The leader eyed him with undisguised malice. "We will have some fun with this one."

"No, you won't," Logan muttered. It was clear these men wanted to kill him, but he wasn't going down without a fight. Better to die on his feet here than at the hands of these men.

Before anyone could make a move, Logan darted to the side and grabbed Juan Pablo. He shoved the other man in front of him and wrenched the gun from his hand, then pressed it to his temple.

"Stay back," he said, keeping his arm around Juan Pablo's neck to lock him in place. Juan Pablo clawed at his arm, his nails raking into Logan's skin in painful drags. Ignoring this, Logan took a step back, pulling his human shield along with him.

The leader's mouth curved up in a cruel smile. "Do you really think he will protect you?"

"Maybe. Or maybe the threat of Fantasmas will. I work for them. If you kill me, you will face their wrath."

To his surprise, the leader laughed. "I doubt it, since they're the ones who want you dead. Mr. DEA Agent," he finished, his eyes lighting with glee.

Logan's mind went blank as the man's taunt registered. His cover had been blown. But how? They'd been so careful…

In the next instant, his questions were dwarfed by a sudden, horrible realization: Olivia. If they knew he was a DEA agent, she was in danger. He had to get back to her before it was too late.

"You're not even going to deny it?"

"Would you believe me if I did?" he replied, taking another step back. Three against one wasn't great odds, but if he could increase the distance between them, he might have a chance. He could squeeze off a few shots, then duck into the forest and lose them in the vegetation.

The leader shrugged. "Not really. Besides, Fantasmas wants you dead. That's good enough for us."

Logan tightened his grip on Juan Pablo. "You'll have to go through him first."

"Very well." The leader made a quick gesture with his hand, and one of the men shot Juan Pablo. The man crumpled in his arms just as Logan felt a searing flash along his ribs.

Logan dropped Juan Pablo and fired in the direction of the men, not taking the time to aim. There was a split second of stunned silence, as if the men couldn't believe he'd shot at them. A short, sharp cry told him at least one of his bullets had found its mark, but he didn't stick around to view the damage.

The men opened fire, but Logan had already ducked into the forest, and the dense growth shielded him from view. He kept his head down and moved quickly, trying to get out of the path of the bullets. Loud, solid thunks sounded as nearby tree trunks were hit, and the near misses spurred him on. He ignored the burning pain in his side—if he stopped now, he was as good as dead.

Someone barked out a loud command and the shooting stopped. The sudden silence was almost as deafening as the gunshots and Logan slowed his pace. If he went crashing through the jungle, he'd lead them right to him, something he figured the men were counting on. His body screamed at him to go faster, to run, but he forced himself to creep along, trying to keep his sounds to a minimum. He had a head start and a few bullets left, but he wasn't naive. The men who were chasing him knew this forest, probably lived in it. It was only a matter of time until they found him.

But maybe, just maybe, he could get back to the village before that happened. They weren't that deep in the forest—at least, they hadn't been when they'd stood on the path. Now that he'd wandered off, though, who could say? There were no landmarks here, no helpful signs to point him in the right direction. He was lost.

Or was he? He glanced up at the sky, searching for the position of the sun. He knew the village was to the east of the forest. If he could find the sun, he could orient himself and start heading in the right direction.

Dappled light shone all around him, but it was almost impossible to see the sky, thanks to the thick canopy of branches that loomed overhead. Panic knotted his lungs as he searched for a break in the cover, to no avail. Dammit, now what?

He started moving again, careful to keep his steps soft. The spongy forest floor helped absorb sounds, but he didn't want to give the men chasing him any clues. He had to find some way to get back to the village. He stepped over an old, rotten tree trunk, slippery with moss. The sight of it tugged at something in his memory, and he frowned.

Moss on tree trunks... He closed his eyes briefly, trying to grab hold of the memory. Camping with his dad and grandpa, lying out under the stars...

"You can always tell direction by looking at the trees," his grandpa had said. "Moss usually grows on the north side of the trunk."

Logan opened his eyes and stared at the tree. *Moss usually grows on the north side...* Was that true here, as well? Or was it the opposite, since he was below the equator?

"I've got a fifty-fifty shot of getting this right," he muttered. He did a mental coin-flip and made his choice, then turned and set off again. His side protested every step, but he ignored the pain. If the wound was really serious, he'd be dead by now. Since he wasn't, it could obviously wait.

He had to get to Olivia.

Chapter 16

Olivia hurried forward, her heart in her throat. Once she'd realized the men were headed into the forest, she'd hung back a little, letting them get far ahead of her. But now that they were out of sight her nerves took over. What if they loaded Logan into a vehicle and took off into the jungle? She'd never find him again. And even though she had no idea how she could help him, she still wanted to keep an eye on him. It was silly, she knew, but part of her thought that as long as she could see Logan he would be okay.

She picked up the pace, anxiety propelling her forward. A series of sharp pops split the air, and her heart jumped into her throat.

Gunshots.

She moved to the edge of the path, uncertain of how to proceed. If she just waltzed up with no warning, she was likely to get shot for her troubles. But she didn't want to let anyone know she was here, either. Maybe she could creep ahead and get a view of what was happening, then go for help. That was probably the best thing to do, even though her mind screamed at her to rush in and make sure Logan was okay.

"You can't help him if you're dead," she muttered to herself.

Moving cautiously, she inched forward. The gunshots had stopped, and based on the loud crashing sounds now drifting back, someone—or *someones*— had headed into the jungle. *Please be Logan.* Let him be alive still!

An eerie stillness fell over the rain forest, and Olivia got the sense that the path ahead was deserted. Had the men headed into the vegetation for a deadly game of hide-and-seek?

Feeling brave, she sped up a bit and came to a bend in the path. She stepped into the trees and used a large trunk for cover, peering around it to see what was ahead.

Two men were on the ground, their blood staining the leaves on the forest path. Her first instinct was to rush forward to see if she could help, but she held the urge in check, glancing around to make sure they were truly alone. No one else was on the path, and the lush greenery surrounding them didn't stir. Evidently, they all had run into the forest.

She jumped back on the path and scurried forward, her nerves jumping at the exposure. If someone came back, they'd see her right away… But she couldn't just leave these men. They were clearly injured, and she took her oath as a doctor seriously. It was her duty to try to help them, if she could.

She knelt down by the closest man and recognized him as one of the group who had been at the exchange. Unfortunately, he was beyond saving. The bullet had hit him in the head, and he'd likely died immediately. Olivia shifted to go to the second man but something on the ground caught her eye. It was a gun, and it had probably belonged to the dead man. She reached for it and tucked it into the waistband of her scrubs. She didn't really know how to handle a gun, but just having it close made her feel better.

It was a few steps to the other man, and as she lowered herself next to him she caught a glimpse of his face. Shock hit her like a bolt of lightning as she realized it was Juan Pablo.

Tears burned her eyes as she assessed his injury. He'd taken a bullet to the chest, and while he was still alive, his breathing was shallow and his color was pale, indicating he'd lost a lot of blood.

"Why did you do this?" She pressed hard on the entrance wound, her grief building. Bad enough she'd lost his friendship. How could he have betrayed her like this? Never in a million years would she have thought him capable of trying to hurt someone else, much less lure Logan into the woods to meet his death.

He let out a soft moan and moved sluggishly, lifting a hand to try to brush her away. "Wake up," she said. "Talk to me."

His eyelids fluttered and then opened, his gaze unfocused. "Stay with me," she ordered.

He glanced around wildly and then saw her face. "Olivia," he whispered, his voice cracking.

"We're going to get you out of here," she said, trying to sound confident.

"No," he mumbled. "You need to leave. They're coming back."

"Who's coming back?" She glanced over her shoulder automatically, but no one was there.

"The producers. They're going to kill Logan."

"Why?" She had to know what had made Juan Pablo turn against her like this. There had to be an explanation.

"Carlos knows he's DEA. He told me to get rid of him."

The name washed over her like a bucket of ice water, and Olivia's breath caught in her chest. "What did you say?"

Juan Pablo frowned, clearly confused by the question. He was growing weaker by the minute, so she had to act fast.

"Who wants Logan dead?"

"Carlos."

She swallowed hard. "From Fantasmas?"

Juan Pablo's eyes widened. "Don't say their name." He tried to lift his head but lacked the strength. "Don't call them here!"

So it was the same Carlos. How had he discovered Logan's identity?

Then another thought struck her—since he knew the truth about Logan, was Carlos going to kill Avery and Mallory? Were her friends already dead?

The idea filled her with terror, and she leaned over and vomited in the dirt. Logan was gone, and her two best friends were probably being targeted at this very moment. Was she destined to lose everyone she cared about in one fell swoop?

"Leave, Olivia," Juan Pablo said. He reached up to grip her hand. "You have to get out of here. I don't want you hurt."

"Too late for that." She pressed harder on his wound and he let out a small cry of pain. "I'm not going to leave you here to die alone."

His eyelids fluttered. "I don't deserve your help."

"That's true," she agreed. "But you're going to get it anyway."

Juan Pablo pressed his lips shut, stifling another moan. Satisfied she'd done all she could to stop the bleeding, Olivia rocked back on her heels and glanced around. They were still alone, but for how much longer? Could she leave Juan Pablo here while she searched for Logan, or should she try to get help first and come back with reinforcements? She hated the idea of leaving without Logan, but Juan Pablo wasn't exactly stable. The longer he was spread out on the jungle floor, the more likely it was he would die.

There was no help for it—she had to tend to the patient in front of her and hope that Logan had evaded the men chasing him. He'd already shown himself to be resourceful in the jungle—hopefully his luck was holding.

"I will find you," she said softly. Logan couldn't hear her, but just saying the words out loud made her feel a little better about leaving.

She bent at the waist and hooked her hands under Juan Pablo's armpits. Moving slowly, she began to drag him along the path, taking care not to jostle him more than necessary. It wasn't ideal to move him before his condition was fully stable, but she had no other choice.

If she left him alone, he might die before she could bring back help. The muscles of her arms and legs burned and her lower back cramped in protest, but she stayed hunched over, her anger fueling her efforts. He had to survive so she could question him and find out exactly how he was involved with Fantasmas and who he had sent after Logan.

Inch by torturous inch, she moved back toward the town. At this rate, it would take a while to return to civilization, but she refused to give up. Logan wouldn't abandon her—she wasn't going to leave him, either.

She took another step back, and her foot landed on something hard. Probably a rock or branch in the path. She kicked out to displace the obstacle, but her foot struck something large and unmoving. She glanced behind her shoulder to try to see what was blocking her way, and her heart skipped a beat.

A man stood behind her, tall and unyielding. But not just any man, she realized with a sick sense of dread. It was the leader from her earlier drug swap.

Recognition flared in his eyes and his mouth curved in a wide smile. "*Hola*, Senorita Doctor. We meet again."

The voice carried on the wind, an eerie, disembodied sound that seemed to come from everywhere and nowhere at the same time.

"Mr. DEA Agent, I have something you want."

Logan paused, trying to determine the taunt's source. The voice was audible but not too loud, which meant the men chasing him were a good distance away.

Or at least one of them was. There was no telling

where the second man had gone—perhaps he was waiting for Logan to make a mistake and reveal himself.

Too bad he wasn't going to give them the satisfaction.

He moved on, stepping carefully, trying to avoid rustling the vegetation too much. But the voice followed him.

"Don't you want to speak to her?"

That brought him up short and his mind started to race. The *her* could only be Olivia. But she was safe in the hospital.

Wasn't she?

Yes, he told himself firmly. *This is nothing but a ploy.* The man was clearly trying to goad him into revealing his position. But a small voice of doubt piped up in his mind. How did the man know he was connected to Olivia? He hadn't seen them together before, so unless Juan Pablo had said something about her, how would the man know to use her as bait?

"Say hello," the voice continued. A split second later a feminine cry rang out, startling a flock of birds nearby.

Olivia!

Logan's heart flip-flopped in his chest and fear slammed down on him with all the force of an avalanche. He had barely managed to get away from these guys on his own—how the hell was he going to rescue Olivia?

"Come join us," the man taunted. "She's dying to see you."

Another cry of pain echoed through the trees. Then Olivia yelled, "Don't listen to him, Logan! Stay aw—" Her voice cut off abruptly, and Logan's stomach dropped. What had they done to her?

"I'm coming!" he yelled. There was no other choice. It was possible she was already dead, but he couldn't leave her without knowing for sure. "Don't hurt her!"

"You have five minutes," the man replied. "Then she dies."

Logan began walking in the direction of the man's voice, making no effort to hide his movements. He still wasn't sure quite where they were, but hopefully the second man would find him and bring him in. He briefly wondered if they were going to shoot him on sight but dismissed the thought almost as soon as it had formed. They wanted to torture him first.

"I'm coming!" he yelled again. His muscles burned as he picked up the pace, and sweat ran into his eyes, blurring his vision. Where was the damn path? Had he really gone that far?

He got his answer a moment later when he spotted a small gap in the vegetation. Ducking through this, he found himself back on the dirt trail. But which direction should he take?

"One minute," the man said, his voice much closer now.

Logan turned and ran, his feet digging into the dark, loamy earth of the forest floor. It felt a bit like running in a thin layer of sand, but he pushed harder, refusing to let it slow him down.

He skidded and slipped around a bend in the path and caught sight of three figures up ahead. "Here," he yelled, as loudly as his lungs would let him. *Please don't let me be too late...*

Logan slid to a halt and took in the scene, his heart pounding from exertion and worry over Olivia. Was she still alive? Yes! There she was, kneeling on the ground next to Juan Pablo's body. He saw the marks on the ground and figured she had come across the injured man and had been trying to drag him back to town when the group had found them. It was just like her to put herself in danger to save someone else, and he wanted to simultaneously kiss her and strangle her for it.

The leader turned to face him but kept his hand on Olivia's shoulder. Logan ran his gaze over her body, looking for signs of injury. There were no visible marks, but as he watched she cradled her left arm. The bastard must have twisted it pretty hard to make her scream, and Logan vowed silently that he would make the man pay for hurting her.

"I'm here," Logan said. "You can let her go now."

The man raised a brow. "I could. But you killed one of my men. You owe me a life." He jerked Olivia to her feet, shoving her in front of him. "Maybe I should take this one as payment?"

"No!" Logan stepped forward but drew up short as the second man pointed his weapon at him. "No," he said, more calmly this time. "I know you're going to kill me. That is your payment. She had nothing to do with it."

"That is true." The man looked from Logan to Olivia and back again, speculation bright in his eyes. "But your life doesn't mean that much to me. I think I will take you both. I have questions for you," he said, looking at Logan. "And my men are lonely." He used the barrel of his gun to flip Olivia's ponytail over her shoulder. She didn't move, but Logan saw her lips press tightly together in disgust. His fists clenched and he rocked forward onto the balls of his feet, wanting to pull her out of reach. But the second man lifted his gun, the threat clear. Logan forced his body to relax—he couldn't help Olivia if he was dead.

The leader smiled as he watched Logan's reaction, as if it had confirmed something he'd suspected. In that instant, Logan realized his mistake. By making his feelings for Olivia clear, he had put her in even more danger.

"Time to go," the man announced. He gestured to his partner, then poked Olivia in the back.

"Wait," she protested, digging her heels into the dirt. "We can't just leave him here. He needs medical attention."

Oh, no. Logan knew what was going to happen next, and he wished more than anything he could spare her the sight. He tried to catch her eye, to distract her, but she was focused on her patient and didn't look at him.

The man glanced down at the prone figure of Juan Pablo, pale and limp on the ground. He shrugged, then took aim and fired.

The shot sounded like a cannon in the otherwise quiet space, and Olivia jumped. She stared at Juan Pablo, her eyes wide and her mouth opening and closing in shock.

"Move," the man told her, poking her in the ribs with the muzzle of his gun. "Or I'll do the same to you."

Chapter 17

Olivia huddled on the floor and stared at the door of the small shack. She was exhausted, but she didn't want to close her eyes. Every time she did, she relived Juan Pablo's death over and over again until she thought she'd go mad.

It's my fault. If only she hadn't drawn attention to him! They would have left and he might have been able to crawl to safety, or someone may have come across him while hiking on the trail. Either way, he would have stood a chance at survival.

Instead, he'd died in the dirt at her feet.

The men hadn't missed a beat. After shooting Juan Pablo, the leader had grabbed her by the arm and yanked her after him, while the other man forced Logan to follow. She wasn't sure how long they walked, but before they came to the clearing where she'd met them earlier, they veered off the trail at a small break in the vegetation. She tripped and stumbled down the rocky path and saw the men growing more impatient by the minute. Finally, after what seemed like an eternity, they came to a Jeep and she was shoved unceremoniously into the backseat.

Logan landed next to her, but before he could say anything, the leader turned to face them both from the front seat. "If either of you speaks a word, I will torture the other. Slowly." He grinned in a way that suggested he hoped they would test him.

Olivia shuddered and looked out the window. She couldn't meet Logan's eyes or she would start sobbing, and the man was sadistic enough that he'd probably count that as talking.

She lost track of time as they bounced along, the scenery passing by in a blur thanks to the tears in her eyes. This was it—she had failed. Not only would Avery and Mallory lose their lives due to her actions, but Logan was going to die, too, and in a painfully brutal way. The thought of it was overwhelming, and her body started to go numb—first her toes and fingers, then her ankles and wrists, the loss of sensation proceeding inward until she felt frozen over. A detached, clinical part of her brain recognized that she was going into shock, but there wasn't anything she could do about it. She actually welcomed the reaction, since feeling nothing was preferable to the crippling weight of guilt.

The next thing she registered was being pulled out of the Jeep and dragged across a dirt yard. They'd thrown her into this small shack and left her, and she hadn't seen them since.

Someone had brought food earlier—was it time

for another meal? She shook her head, uncertain. The shack had a small opening near the roof that passed for a window, but the forest growth was so dense it was hard to tell if the low light illuminating the space was early morning or dusk. She was half tempted to try to open the door, but it wasn't worth the risk. They hadn't chained her up, and she didn't want to give them a reason to. At least not yet.

Her stomach growled and she focused on her hunger, grateful for the distraction. Had anyone at the hospital missed her yet? Probably so, but it didn't matter. They wouldn't have any idea of what had happened or where to start looking. She was on her own.

And where was Logan? She had caught one final glimpse of him before they'd shut the door of the hut. He'd been standing in the middle of the yard, a gun to his head, men streaming out from the other buildings that lined the yard. He'd met her eyes for a brief instant, and she'd been struck by his defiance even in the face of such an onslaught. She'd fought to keep him in her sights, but the door had slammed shut, cutting them apart. And so she'd paced the confines of the shack, breath held, waiting to hear the shot that would signal the end of his life.

But it never came.

What was worse? she mused now, staring hard at the door. Dying outright, or being kept alive only to suffer?

And just why were they keeping her alive? She'd been puzzling over that little mystery since they'd brought her food ages ago. She wasn't exactly in a hurry to die, but she did wonder why they were bothering to feed her. She had no value to them as a prisoner. If they knew Logan was a DEA agent, surely they knew she'd been bluffing about the strength of her connection to Fantasmas. It didn't make sense for them to keep her around, unless... She shuddered, the leader's words echoing in her ears.

My men are lonely.

Revulsion made her skin crawl and she rubbed her arms absently. If what he'd said was true, they'd just have to stay that way. Their arrival had clearly triggered interest among the men of this camp, but so far, their excitement had not turned to speculation. If it did, though...

I'll fight.

She touched the solid weight of the gun, still tucked into the waistband of her scrubs. Fortunately, the top she wore fit her like a tent and had concealed the telltale bulge of the weapon. Even luckier, the men had underestimated her and hadn't thought to search her before shoving her into the Jeep or into the shack. No one knew she was armed, but her advantage would only last as long as the gun remained undetected. She wanted to pull it out and examine it but didn't dare. She didn't know the first thing about guns and had no idea how to check if it was even loaded. With her luck, she'd accidentally fire the thing and alert the whole camp. No, better to keep it hidden for now.

If she could just figure out a way to get it to Logan, he'd know what to do. The thought of him gave her strength, and some of the numbness started to fade. He must still be alive—they would have come back for her otherwise. But how could she find him?

Her musings were interrupted by a commotion outside. Men started shouting and she heard the pounding of running feet in the yard. What was going on?

She walked to the door and pressed her face up to the seam between the door and the frame, but she couldn't make out much. Snatches of words came to her, but not enough for her to determine what had happened.

Please don't let Logan be dead. She repeated the thought over and over again, chanting it silently as the noise eventually died down. *He can't be,* she thought, trying to reassure herself. Killing a DEA agent would have been cause for celebration in this camp, and that had sounded like something closer to distress. Whatever had happened, it probably hadn't involved Logan.

Right?

She started pacing again, the steady movement both a distraction and a way to help focus her thoughts. Maybe she could contrive some way to get outside the shack, so she could get another view of the camp. She needed to find out exactly how many huts there were and, if possible, what function they served. Were they homes? Used for storage? Jail cells? Torture chambers?

They would probably bring her food again. Maybe she could get whoever delivered it to talk.

As soon as the thought formed in her mind, the sound of footsteps reached her ears. Someone was running and coming toward her, if the noises were to be believed.

Olivia backed away from the door, uncertainty making her stomach churn. Who was coming? What did they want with her?

The door opened with a slam, flooding the shack with light. She squinted against the brightness and made out a dark shape in the doorway.

"Come with me. Now." His voice was urgent, and he stepped forward, clearly intending to grab her.

She stepped to the side and tucked her arms in close.

"Why?" He could easily force her to go, but hopefully he would talk before resorting to that option.

"A man is injured. You are a doctor, yes?" Impatience crept into his tone and he made another reach for her.

"Yes," she said, allowing him to take her by the arm. "But I don't have any supplies."

"We do." He led her out of the shack and into the yard, pulling her toward another hut. She glanced around quickly, trying to count the number of huts. Five, six…no eight total, at least that she could see. She couldn't tell if there were any behind her, but she'd be able to find out when they brought her back.

Which one held Logan?

Each hut looked like the others—small, worn, anonymous. There were no guards standing outside any of the doors, so it wasn't immediately obvious which one was doubling as Logan's prison.

"Come on," the man said, pulling harder. They reached one of the larger buildings and he opened the door, pushing her in front of him.

Inside was a wall of bodies, men crammed shoulder to shoulder as they craned their necks and strained to see.

"Move!" her escort ordered. "I've brought the doctor."

Somehow, the crowd was able to make enough space for her to squeeze through, and as she popped out at the other end of the wall, she saw what they'd been staring at.

A man was laid out on a bed, moaning softly. He was covered in black soot from head to toe, his ailment not immediately obvious under all the grime. But as Olivia got closer, she realized he wasn't dirty.

He was *burned*.

The smell hit her then and she swallowed hard against a rising tide of bile. *Oh, God.*

She knelt next to the bed, glancing over him and wondering where to start. His face, his arms—every inch of exposed skin was charred black. To make matters worse, his clothes had melted, fusing with his body. There was no way she could remove them without causing him unbearable pain, but she couldn't leave them either—it would only invite infection.

Does it really matter? she asked herself. The majority of his body had suffered third-degree burns. Even if he was in a top-notch hospital, his prognosis would be grim. Here, in the middle of the jungle? He would almost certainly die.

And when he did, what then? Would they blame her for failing to save him? Would they hurt Logan even more to punish her?

Her mind raced as she tried to figure out a way to help this man. There wasn't much she could do for him, but perhaps she could ease his pain.

She opened her mouth to rattle off a list of supplies, but before she could get a word out, a woman burst into the room. She took one look at the man on the bed and fell to the floor, sobbing hysterically. She reached up and made to grab his hands, but Olivia stopped her before she could touch him.

"You can't," she said, feeling sorry for the woman. "It will only hurt him more."

She didn't know if the woman heard her, but she stopped trying to touch him. Instead, she gripped Olivia's hands so hard she could feel her bones grind together. "Please, you have to save him." She looked up and Olivia caught her first glimpse of the woman's tear-stained face.

It was Maria.

Logan lowered his foot to the ground, gradually putting more weight on as he tested the joint. They'd smashed his ankle with a tire iron to keep him hobbled, and he hadn't had a chance to stand on it yet. The joint felt huge and it throbbed in time with his heartbeat, but he had to know if it would support some of his weight. He'd jump out of here on one foot if he had to, but it would be a lot easier if he could limp.

He bit his lip to stifle a groan as his ankle protested. Pain shot up his leg and for a moment, he thought his ankle was going to give out altogether. But it held. Barely.

It would have to do. Once he found Olivia, she could help support him while they escaped.

Never mind that he didn't know where she was being held or if she was okay. Never mind that he didn't know how they were going to get out of here. His plan consisted of two steps: find Olivia and steal the Jeep. He hadn't had the time or the energy to work out the finer details yet.

But he was going to find a way.

He glanced around the hut, but there wasn't much to see. A small wooden table sat against the opposite wall. A thin gray mattress was on the floor to his right, a ceramic pot next to it. And that was it—just the barest necessities.

Dark stains on the floor testified to the history of this place. Clearly, these men had tortured people before. They seemed to enjoy it, too, if their attitude was any indication. They'd practically danced with glee when they'd brought in a large bag, its contents clinking. The leader had placed it on the table and had taken great pleasure in removing lethal-looking instruments one at a time, spreading them out so Logan could see what was in store for him.

His gut had cramped, but he hadn't given them the satisfaction of showing fear. The leader hadn't liked that. His eyes had narrowed with displeasure, but before he could start the torture session, a commotion outside had distracted him. There had been a knock at the door and another man had come inside, whispering a message into the leader's ear. The leader had gone pale under his tan and practically run from the shack, leaving his minion behind to scoop up the instruments on his way out the door.

Logan glanced that way now, wondering if they'd left any guards outside his door. If the whole camp was distracted, this would be the perfect time to mount an escape.

He took a cautious step forward, and as he moved, the light glinted off something on the floor. He made his way over to the table and nearly laughed out loud.

A knife lay on the ground, its blade mostly covered by the fine dirt of the floor. It was one of the torture implements, and the minion must have dropped it in his haste to get out of the shack.

"Thanks, buddy," Logan muttered as he knelt to retrieve the weapon. It wasn't very big, but he tested the blade on the pad of his thumb and was pleased to find it was sharp.

He stepped to the door and pressed his ear against the wood, straining to hear the noises outside. Breathing, voices, the shuffling of feet—anything to indicate if there were guards stationed at the door. But he heard nothing. Holding his breath, he eased the door open and peered out.

The yard was deserted, but he could see the men clustered around a hut on the other side of the camp. *So that's where all the action is.* He glanced around, trying to see if he could find where Olivia was located. But all the buildings were depressingly alike, yielding no clues as to their contents. He'd have to check out each one to find her.

So be it.

He eyed the closest shack, deciding to start there first. But before he could make a move, a man came out of the crowd and hurried across the yard, zeroing in on one of the shacks with the focus of a cruise missile. He flung open the door and stepped inside, and a moment later he popped out again, dragging Olivia by the arm.

Logan's breath caught in his chest, and he forced down the urge to shout her name. He wanted to run out into the yard and grab her, but as he shifted his weight, his ankle reminded him why that wasn't possible. Not only was he in no condition to run, he'd be vastly outnumbered. The crowd of men was still turned away, but it wouldn't take much to gain their attention, and he couldn't take on that many people.

He clenched his jaw as he watched the man pull her toward the crowd and a split second later, she disappeared into the mass of humanity. What was going on? *Probably something medical*, he mused. They knew Olivia was a doctor, which meant they likely needed her to treat someone. But who? And how long would it take?

Hopefully a while. If the men of the camp were tied up with some kind of emergency, they weren't torturing him. And if his reprieve lasted until dark, he could make his move once night fell.

Logan carefully shut the door and hobbled back to the chair in the middle of the room. There was nothing to do now but wait.

Chapter 18

"She's gone."

"What?" Carlos tightened his grip on the phone, as if a show of force could change the words he was hearing. "What do you mean?"

"She finished surgery this morning and I haven't seen her since. She's vanished."

His mind whirred with possibilities. "Maybe she snuck out for a moment alone with her friend."

"I don't think so. Someone saw him leaving earlier with Juan Pablo."

Ah, so his instructions had been obeyed. That was good to know.

"Is it possible she is resting or otherwise not feeling well?" Even as he suggested the possibility, he knew it wasn't true.

"I checked her apartment," Daniela assured him.

"When she didn't answer, I used my key. She's not there."

Carlos had a sinking feeling he knew exactly where she was. Damn interfering woman. She'd probably seen Logan leaving with Juan Pablo and had followed them, only to get caught up in the same trap he'd set for the DEA agent.

"I'm not sure what to do," the woman confessed. She sounded scared now, as if she was afraid he would blame her for this turn of events.

"Do nothing," he said shortly. "I will take care of this."

"Thank y—"

He hung up, cutting her off. Then he let out a string of curses. This was not how he had imagined events would unfold. He had told Juan Pablo to remove the DEA agent discreetly, but it would appear the man had failed in that respect.

Was Dr. Sandoval with the gang? His hand clenched on the arm of his chair. He hoped not, because his plan depended on her. She was the perfect conduit for drugs, and El Jefe had made it clear he wanted her on the payroll permanently. Carlos had given her a small job to start with, partly to see if she could handle it but also as a means of trapping her. Once she'd gotten her hands dirty, he could use it as leverage to force her to make bigger hauls in the future.

But then she'd gotten involved with the DEA agent. It had proved to be a minor complication, all things considered, and one that he had handled. She'd have to be punished for it, of course, but he didn't mind waiting until she was back in the US before killing her friends. Perhaps he'd make her watch, he mused, enjoying the thought. She reminded him of a horse that refused to be broken—too much defiance for her own good. It would be amusing to watch that spirit fade away as she saw the lifeblood drain from her friends.

But first, he had to make sure she returned.

He glanced at his watch and cursed again. They'd had her for hours—plenty of time to do real damage, even kill her if they were so inclined. She was such a troublesome woman he wouldn't be surprised if they did decide to get rid of her.

He picked up the phone and thumbed through the list of contacts. He had one shot to fix this, and he had to make it count.

Hopefully it wasn't too late.

"If he dies, you die."

The words echoed in Olivia's mind, playing on an endless loop as she stared at the burned man's chest, watching it rise and fall in a labored rhythm. She'd thought the camp leader, the man who'd so callously shot Juan Pablo, was indifferent to human suffering. But he'd taken one look at the man on the bed and his knees had given out, causing him to land with a solid thump next to her.

He'd stayed there for a moment, his eyes wide and face pale. Then he'd shaken himself free of whatever emotions gripped him. "Bring her whatever she needs to help him," he'd ordered. Then he'd turned to face her, his expression once again cruel. "If he dies, you die," he promised.

They'd had a surprising amount of medical supplies, most likely stolen from the hospital. She'd covered the man's skin in cool, wet cloths and had carefully, painstakingly peeled his burned garments off his body. He'd screamed until his voice gave out and had fortunately lost consciousness soon after. Olivia hadn't dared sedate him—he was too unstable, and with no resuscitation equipment to hand it was too much of a risk.

He was still unconscious and to her great surprise, he was still breathing. There wasn't much for her to do now but monitor him and hope he lived through the night.

She cast a quick look across the bed at the other occupant of the room. Maria sat silently, her face lined with anguish as she stared down at the man, his features now almost unrecognizable. Who was he to her? A husband? Brother?

Maria glanced up and noticed Olivia's attention. "He's Alejandro's father," she whispered, anticipating the question. "And the baby's."

"How is your daughter?" It felt strange to ask something so normal in this situation, but Olivia didn't know what else to say.

"She's fine. She's with my sister. I left the children with her so I could come visit him. I only get to see him once a month." Her eyes never left him and she lifted her hand, clearly wanting to touch him. Olivia opened her mouth to stop her, but really, did it matter? The man was going to die—it was just a question of when. Perhaps Maria's touch would bring him some small measure of comfort and let him know he wasn't alone.

Maria laid her hand on the bed, her fingertips barely touching the gauze bandage on his upper arm. But even that tenuous connection seemed to calm her, and her muscles visibly relaxed.

"We're getting married next month," she whispered.

Then she shook her head. "Not now, though." Her eyes welled with tears and she stroked the bandage.

"I'm so sorry," Olivia said. She wanted to reach over the bed and touch Maria, but the other woman likely wouldn't welcome the contact right now. She was focused on her lover, and Olivia didn't want to distract her.

They sat in silence for a few moments. Now that things had calmed down, Olivia began to worry about Logan again. Where was he? Was he still alive? She had no idea where the camp leader had gone after he'd left—had he taken his distress out on Logan? She hadn't heard any gunshots, but there were other ways to kill...

"He's going to die, isn't he?"

Maria's voice was soft, barely audible over the sound of the man's labored breathing. Olivia debated lying to her, but one look at Maria's face changed her mind. This woman deserved to know the truth.

"Yes. I'm so sorry."

Maria nodded, as if Olivia had confirmed her suspicion. She bowed her head, her lips moving in a silent prayer, or perhaps simply a goodbye. When she lifted her head again, Olivia was surprised to see her eyes were clear and determined.

"You need to leave."

"Do you want some time alone with him?"

Maria shook her head. "No, I mean you need to get out of here now while you still can."

Goose bumps broke out on Olivia's arms and she glanced around, paranoid that a guard had overheard. "What do you mean?"

"Raúl took most of his men and left to go deal with the situation at the processing camp. This is your only chance to get away. If you don't do it now, you'll never be able to."

Was she telling the truth? Or was this a setup, designed to test Olivia? Olivia wanted desperately to believe her, but she couldn't quite bring herself to trust the other woman.

Apparently Maria sensed her hesitation. "I'm not lying." She reached across the bed and grabbed Olivia's hand, squeezing hard. "I swear on my children's lives, this is your only chance."

She seemed so sincere Olivia couldn't help but feel a spark of hope. Could she really escape? But what about Logan?

"I can't go," she said. Maria looked at her like she was crazy. "Do you remember the man who was in the room when I examined Alejandro?"

Maria nodded, understanding dawning. "He is here, too?"

"Yes. And I won't go without him."

Maria cast a glance at the man on the bed, her face softening. "I understand."

"Do you know where they might be keeping him?"

"There's a shack across the yard—it has a yellow door. That's usually where Raúl does his work." This was said with a faint tinge of disgust, as if Maria didn't approve of the man or his actions. Perhaps that was why she was trying to help now.

Olivia's mind raced with possibilities. She could sneak out of here, then circle around to the back end of the shack and somehow free Logan. She'd give him the gun, and they could head into the forest.

And then what? Neither one of them possessed an extensive set of survival skills, and they were miles away from any kind of civilization. Plus, Logan could be hurt badly. How exactly were they going to get far enough away from this camp that Raúl and his men couldn't find them again?

Her heart began to pound as her worries mounted, and Olivia took a deep breath, forcing the doubts away. One thing at a time. Logan might have a plan of his own to get them out of here. But first, she had to find him.

"What are you going to do?" she asked Maria. Olivia wanted desperately to escape this hell, but she didn't want Maria to be punished for her disappearance. The woman had two young children depending on her for their survival. "Won't Raúl know you helped me?"

Maria lifted one shoulder in a casual shrug, as if the possibility didn't bother her overmuch. "I will pretend to be asleep when he returns. I'll say you must have snuck out while I slept. He won't be able to prove otherwise."

"If you're sure…" Olivia said slowly. She glanced around the room, looking for anything that might be useful as a weapon. Maria followed her gaze. "Here." She leaned over and picked something off the floor, then rose up to present a belt with a large-bladed knife, the kind used to hack through the jungle. "This was Jaime's—he used it in the forest. He won't need it anymore."

"Thanks," Olivia replied. She wrapped the belt around her waist, cinching it tightly. The idea of using the knife on someone was just as unappealing as the thought of shooting them, but hopefully it wouldn't come to that.

"Before you go," Maria said. Olivia turned to look at

her, tamping down her impatience to leave. This woman was saving her life—she could give her a moment more.

"Yes?"

Maria looked down at the man on the bed—Jaime, she'd said. "Is he in pain?"

Olivia bit her lip. How to answer that? The burns were extensive and deep and most likely excruciating. But he was unconscious and hopefully feeling no pain. Still, if he were in a hospital he'd be receiving pain relief.

"I don't think he's feeling anything now," she said carefully. "But if he wakes up, it will be bad."

Maria nodded, but Olivia didn't think she was done asking questions. "Is there anything you can do to make sure he doesn't wake up?"

Olivia sucked in a breath, the question hitting her like a slap. She opened her mouth, her first instinct to refuse Maria's request. She was a doctor—she'd taken an oath to do no harm.

But Jamie's labored, rattled breathing filled the silence and Olivia began to wonder if keeping him alive was doing more harm than good. Surely saving this man from untold agony was the better choice?

Olivia reached into the bag of supplies one of the men had brought her and removed a few vials and a syringe. "This is morphine." She set the supplies on the table next to the bed. "Do you know how to use a syringe?"

Maria nodded, her eyes wide and serious.

"If you think he is in pain, inject some of this into the muscle of his thigh."

She nodded again and blinked back tears. "Thank you." Her voice was equal parts gratitude and sadness, and Olivia's heart broke a little for this woman and the life she led.

"Maria…" What could she say? How could she thank her for helping her escape? That she was sorry for the loss of her man, that she hoped things would get better for her and her children?

The woman gave her a sad smile tinged with understanding. "Good luck, Doctor."

"Thank you," Olivia whispered. She took one last look at Maria, sitting vigil by Jaime's bed. Then she slipped out the door and started down the hall, careful to keep her steps light.

It was time to find Logan.

Logan eased the door open and peered out into the yard, searching for signs of life. It had been curiously quiet in the camp all afternoon, and now that the sun was going down, the emerging shadows made the place look eerily deserted, like a ghost town suddenly abandoned in the wake of a disaster.

He slid through the opening and moved to the corner of the shack, keeping his back pressed against the wall. There was no movement from the yard, no cry of alarm or angry shout at his presence. *Where is everyone?*

The building where they'd taken Olivia stood across the yard, a soft glow emanating from under the door. He could hear the faint rumble of a generator, but other than that the place was silent. Even the forest creatures seemed to be holding their breath, waiting for something.

Logan hobbled around the shack until he met the edge of the forest. It would be easier and faster to cut across the yard to get to Olivia, but he didn't want to risk the exposure. He hadn't seen anyone, but that didn't mean they weren't there, waiting in the shadows to cut him down when he revealed himself.

He started moving, careful to stay just inside the tree line. It made for slower going, but the vegetation gave him a little extra cover and made him feel more secure. He stopped every few feet and listened, straining hard to detect any noise that might reveal the presence of a sentry. But he heard nothing unusual.

This feels too easy. Where were the guards? The camp leader had been all set to torture him to death a few hours ago—why had that changed? It must have been something big for the man to forget about him so quickly. And to not even leave a guard… It just didn't feel right.

Maybe it was a trap. But to what end? They already had him in captivity. What more harm could they do if they caught him trying to free Olivia? *You could only kill a man once*, he mused.

Nevertheless, he wasn't going to pass up an opportunity to escape. Especially not if it meant getting Olivia out of here, too. He hadn't heard any vehicle engines start in the aftermath of the earlier excitement—hopefully they were still parked on the edge of the camp. He'd grab Olivia, make a run for the Jeep and hot-wire it. Then he'd floor it and get them the hell out of here.

The sound of a twig snapping jerked him out of his thoughts. He froze, holding his breath. Was it some forest creature, out for an evening stroll? Or something more dangerous?

He had his answer soon enough, as the crackle of footsteps met his ears. Someone was coming toward him, and they weren't bothering to be quiet about it.

Logan took a step back, entering farther into the forest and its cover of darkness. The sound grew louder, and he watched as a small dark figure came into view.

He frowned, watching the way the stranger moved. There was something familiar about that walk...

The newcomer walked past him and bumped into a bush, startling a bird. The creature took to the air with a squawk of annoyance, and the interloper ducked, letting out a small cry of alarm.

A very *feminine* cry.

Logan stepped out of the woods and crept up behind the figure, hardly daring to believe his luck. Had Olivia escaped on her own? Or was this a wife or girlfriend of one of the camp residents?

Time to find out. He grabbed the woman, banding an arm around her torso and clapping his hand over her mouth. She screamed and kicked out, clawing at his hold, but he tightened his grip and hauled her back against his chest. He bent his head to put his mouth next to her ear. "Olivia?"

She stilled immediately, but the tension remained in her body. "It's me. Are you all right?"

Apparently recognizing his voice, her muscles relaxed and she sagged against him in relief. She nodded, and he realized he still had his hand over her mouth. He released her and she spun around and threw her arms around his neck, squeezing him tightly.

"Logan! What are you doing here? I was coming to find you."

He wrapped his arms around her, enjoying the feel of her body pressed against his. She was safe. That was all that mattered at the moment. He dipped his head to press his nose into her hair, inhaling the sweet strawberry scent of her shampoo. Everything else faded as he focused on the woman in his arms, his worries and anxieties drowned out by the sound of her voice in his ears.

"Are you hurt? What did they do to you?"

She pulled away and he reluctantly loosened his grip. Her eyes were wide and luminous in the moonlight, and in another time, another place, he would have pulled her in for a kiss under the stars.

"I'm fine," he said quietly. "But we need to get out of here."

"How?"

"The Jeep. I think it's still parked where they left it earlier."

"Oh." She bit her lip, considering. "It's worth a shot."

Logan grabbed her hand. "Let's go. And try to be quiet. I don't know if anyone else is out here."

Olivia nodded. "I have something for you," she whispered. She fumbled at her waist and for a second, he had the absurd notion she was going to take off her pants. *Down, boy*, he told himself. Now was not the time to engage in ridiculous fantasies.

Olivia passed two objects to him, and as his fingers curled around them he realized she'd given him a machete and a gun. "Where—" he began, then shook his head. She could explain it all to him later, in the Jeep.

They made their way around until they came to a small clearing that served as the parking lot for the camp. Just as he'd hoped, the Jeep that had ferried them here was parked, dark and solid in the night.

He glanced around but saw no sign of a guard. Just to be on the safe side, he picked up a branch and tossed it into the clearing. Nothing moved.

Behind him, Olivia let out a sigh of relief, one that echoed in his mind. It looked like they were in the clear…

They stepped out of the cover of the trees and headed toward the vehicle. Too late, he saw a shadow detach itself from a tree trunk. Logan flung an arm out to stop Olivia and lifted the machete as a man stopped a few feet away.

He eyed them both dispassionately, then tossed something at Olivia's feet. Keys, if the metallic jingle was anything to go by. He jerked his chin at the Jeep. "Get going. Raúl will be back soon."

Logan heard Olivia gather up the keys, but he didn't take his eyes off their mysterious savior. Nothing about this made any sense. Who was this stranger? Why was he coming to their rescue now?

Apparently Olivia felt the same way. "Why are you helping us?" she asked.

The man merely shrugged. "I have my orders. You have to make it out of here alive."

"What about me?" Logan said, his stomach sinking as the implication of the man's words became clear. He took a step back, but it was too late.

The man lifted his arm and a deafening sound pierced the stillness of the night as he fired his gun. The bullet hit Logan in the chest, pushing him back with the force of a battering ram. He landed flat on his back, dazed and shaken. He tried to gasp for air, but he'd apparently forgotten how to breathe.

The man's face entered his field of vision, blocking out the stars. "She survives. You don't."

Logan opened his mouth to respond, but he couldn't

get his tongue to work. A loud cry filled his ears, and he realized Olivia was screaming. Then the stars winked out, and the darkness consumed him.

Chapter 19

It was happening again. Someone she loved was dying, and there wasn't a damn thing she could do to stop it.

"Logan. Logan, please wake up! Talk to me!"

Olivia glanced over at his still form as she tore down the bumpy track that passed for a road in this part of the country. Was he even still breathing? Could she risk stopping to check?

She looked in the rearview mirror, but it was blessedly empty. How long until Raúl returned and realized they were gone? She didn't know how much of a head start they had—she was so focused on Logan everything else was a blur.

Panic and adrenaline had given her the strength to heft his body into the passenger seat of the Jeep. She'd paused for a moment to apply a quick bandage to the entry wound and then had stomped on the gas, wanting to put as much distance between them and the camp as possible. She didn't know why they were being allowed to escape, but it wouldn't happen a second time.

The Jeep hit a particularly deep rut and Logan moaned. Her heart lifted at the sound—he was still alive!

"Talk to me," she pleaded. "We're almost to the hospital."

"No." The word was soft and sluggish, but she heard him loud and clear. "No hospital."

"You need medical attention!" God only knew how severe his injury was—it had been too dark for her to really take stock of the entrance wound, and in the rush to leave, she hadn't been able to tend to him as much as she wanted to. The sooner he got to a hospital, the better.

"Can't...trust...them."

His words froze her blood and her grip on the steering wheel slipped a bit. *He was right*, she realized grimly. She'd been so focused on the medical aspects of the situation she hadn't stopped to think about their safety. Juan Pablo hadn't hesitated to sell Logan out to Raúl and his gang. Who else worked for them or was sympathetic to their cause? Could they really risk stopping there, knowing Raúl was steps behind them?

Olivia bit her lip and looked at Logan. Even in the darkness, she could tell he'd grown pale. How much blood had he lost already? Would he survive if she didn't stop at the hospital?

As if he felt her gaze on him, his eyes opened a crack. "Go to the embassy," he gritted out through clenched teeth.

They had made it back to the village now, and she approached the turn that would lead them either to the hospital or the main road out. She tapped the brakes, unsure of the best choice. If they left the village they'd be safe, but Logan might die. If she stopped at the hospital, he could get the care he needed but they might both die if Raúl found them.

Panic urged her to take the road out of the village, to put as much distance between them and Raúl as possible. But if Logan died, she'd never be able to forgive herself...

"The embassy," he repeated, a little louder this time.

"It's at least an hour away," she said softly.

"I know."

"Logan, what if—"

"I said I'd protect you, Olivia. I'm going to make sure you get home safely if it's the last thing I do."

She blinked hard to clear the tears from her eyes. Stubborn fool—he was gambling his life in a bid to keep her safe. It was almost enough to make her turn in the direction of the hospital, but the thought of Raúl gave her pause. At least if she kept driving they had a chance.

Swallowing hard, she wrenched the wheel to the right and took the road that led out of town. *Please let us get there in time...*

"Good girl."

She shot him a glare, which he ignored. "Don't you dare die on me, Logan Murray."

He closed his eyes and leaned his head back, his body going limp again. Talking must have taken more effort than he'd let on, and Olivia's stomach cramped at the realization he was doing worse than before.

"I'm not planning on it," he murmured, then fell silent.

"Logan?" He didn't respond, and her heart began to

pound hard against her breastbone. Should she rouse him and force him to talk or let him conserve his energy? But what if he lapsed into a coma and she didn't realize it until it was too late?

There were no easy answers here, and her brain kept supplying awful possibilities, each one more terrible than the last. She gripped the wheel hard, feeling like the contact was the only thing keeping her sane. *Just keep driving.*

She let the tears fall now, not bothering to wipe them away. "Please, Logan," she muttered. "Don't leave me now."

Logan came awake slowly, cautiously feeling his way up through the murky depths. He opened his eyes to a bright world of white—white ceiling, white walls, white light streaming in from somewhere. Then he blinked, and colors began to emerge as his eyes adjusted to the light.

"Look who's back."

He turned his head to see Alan sitting in a chair next to his bed. His friend leaned forward, tossing aside his crossword puzzle to grab Logan's arm. "Man, it's good to see you awake."

"Where am I?" His throat was scratchy and sore and he glanced around, hoping to see some kind of liquid close to hand.

Alan correctly interpreted his actions and reached for a bottle of water on the table next to his chair. "Here you go, buddy," he said, unscrewing the lid and handing Logan the bottle.

Logan took a careful sip, the water a cool, refreshing relief for his parched tissues. It felt so good he took a healthy gulp, which made his throat ache a little as he swallowed.

Alan watched him drink, his eyes widening a little as Logan tipped up the bottle to drain it. "Take it easy. You don't want to overdo it."

Logan waved away his concern. "Where am I?" he repeated. Obviously he was in some kind of hospital, but where?

"Bogotá."

He felt a rush of pride in Olivia. It couldn't have been easy for her to get here with the threat of Raúl and his goons following her the whole way, but she had done it. She had saved them both.

"Where's Olivia?" He was mildly concerned by her absence, but if Alan was here, the other guys were probably nearby, as well. Surely one of them was keeping an eye on her.

Alan confirmed this suspicion. "She's being debriefed at the embassy as we speak. Keith and Joseph had to practically drag her away from your side."

"So she's okay?"

Alan nodded. "Seems to be. Bruised, battered and shaken up, but otherwise fine."

Logan leaned back against the pillow and closed his eyes. "She's a hell of a woman."

"How well do you think you know her?" Alan asked casually. *Too* casually…

Logan cracked one eye open and stared at his friend. "Well enough." No way was he going to share what had happened between them in the village. That was their special moment, one that he held close in his heart.

But Alan wasn't interested in locker room tales. There was something else on his mind, something

Logan suspected he wasn't going to like. "What are you really asking me?"

Alan lifted one shoulder in a shrug, trying to play it cool. "Cut the crap," Logan said, letting an edge creep into his voice. "What's going on here?"

His friend sighed and ran a hand through his hair. "Olivia said some guy named Juan Pablo sold you out to the local nasties."

"He did."

"We've picked up some chatter indicating they knew you were a DEA agent and targeted you because of it."

"That's true," Logan said, his mind drifting back to the encounter with Raúl in the forest. The man had taken great pleasure in telling him Fantasmas wanted him dead and that they knew who he worked for.

Alan gave him a meaningful look. "How did they know who you are?"

"I'm not sure," Logan replied slowly. It was a question that had been in the back of his mind ever since he and Olivia had been taken prisoner. Who had blown his cover? No one had known his true identity, except for...

"Olivia," he whispered, the pieces clicking into place.

Alan nodded, his expression rueful. "It has to be her. She's the only one who knew."

Logan immediately rejected the notion, unable and unwilling to believe she would betray him like that. "But why would she do such a thing? It doesn't make sense."

"Are you sure?" Alan raised a brow. "Think about it. You came along to keep her safe but also to follow the money and drugs and learn more about the cartel operations. What if she's not as innocent as we originally thought? What if this whole thing had been a setup from the start? She's been going to Colombia for years. How do we know she hasn't been on the cartel's payroll all that time? What better way to kill a DEA agent than to lure him to Colombia where he can get 'lost' in the jungle?"

Logan frowned, considering his friend's words. "That's going to a lot of trouble to kill one man."

"True," Alan conceded. "But what a signal it would send."

Logan was silent for a moment, digesting the possibility.

"Think about it," Alan urged. "Did she come to you after Carlos approached her with this deal? Or did you only find out because you pushed and pushed until she had no option but to tell you?"

He was right, Logan realized. Olivia hadn't wanted to tell him about the cartel's offer. At the time, he'd chalked it up to her fear for the lives of her friends, but what if that was just a cover? What if she hadn't wanted to tell him because she was in on the deal the whole time?

"Once you knew and brought the DEA in on the operation, she had no choice but to play along. Any other reaction would have been too suspicious. So she lures you here, away from any kind of support. Then she stages the abduction to get rid of you. Just like that, she's got a believable sob story to explain your death and deflect suspicion off her so she can go on working with the cartel."

Logan's stomach knotted as he listened to Alan. He wanted to deny it, but his friend's version of events made a sick kind of sense.

Had Olivia even been coming to find him, or had

she been headed for the Jeep to make her escape, leaving him to the mercy of Raúl? Perhaps that goon had been some kind of insurance policy, to make sure she got out of there unmolested.

I have my orders. She survives. You don't.

"But then why did she try to save me?" he muttered to himself.

Alan cocked his head to the side. "Say again?"

"I got shot while we were escaping the camp." He touched his chest absently, the movement triggering a stinging pain as it pulled on his stitches. "I remember lying on the forest floor, looking up. Then I passed out. When I came to, I was in the Jeep and she was driving. Why bother putting me in the vehicle if she just wanted me to die?"

Alan shrugged. "Plausible deniability? If she makes it look like she tried everything to save you, she comes off as innocent."

"I suppose." It *did* sound reasonable, unfortunately.

"Why not just drop me off at the village hospital and let Raúl take me again?"

Alan gave him a pitying look. "Better for you to die on the drive to Bogotá," he said quietly. "That way, we have a body to bury and she can pretend to be the hero."

Logan took a deep breath, ignoring the pain of his wound and the ache in his heart. He didn't want to believe Olivia was capable of such deceptions. But Alan was right—she had been evasive from the beginning, and as much as he wanted to trust her, this version of events was highly plausible. Besides, could he really trust his own judgment? Somewhere along the way, he'd fallen hard for Olivia Sandoval. And she knew it. He'd foolishly thought his feelings were returned, but what if it had all been an act on her part? It certainly wouldn't be the first time he'd been betrayed by a woman he loved...

"I'm sorry, man." Alan rested his hand on Logan's shoulder and gave a gentle squeeze. "I didn't want it to be like this."

Logan swallowed hard, the muscles of his throat tight with emotion. He didn't want Alan to see how much Olivia's lies had affected him. Better for his friend to think he was simply upset at being targeted by the cartel, nothing more.

"What happens now?"

"We let her back into the US and monitor her. She's supposed to contact Carlos to set up a meet. We'll be watching."

"Do you think she has the drugs?"

"Not that we've found. But it might not matter. The theft—if it really was one—may have been a ruse to draw you out. It's likely she and Carlos will consider this a practice run, and he'll have her bring back product another time when they think we're not watching."

Logan nodded. "Sounds like you have it all figured out."

Alan studied him for a moment. "Why don't you get some rest? I know Joseph and Keith will want to see you when they're done talking to Olivia."

"Does she know?"

"Of course not. We can't have her warning Carlos before we get the trap in place."

"So I'll have to see her again."

"Yes. But we won't leave you alone with her."

"Good." Logan didn't think he could handle seeing her again, at least not right now. He needed some time to process everything Alan had said. How was he going to pretend as if everything was fine, when in reality his world had just been turned upside down?

And the worst part was, he hadn't seen it coming.

He'd thought Olivia was so different from Emma. That she was honest and good and *real*. But she'd proved to be no better than his ex-fiancée. *Worse, even*, he thought with a mental snort. At least Emma had never tried to kill him.

"Need something to help you sleep?" Alan asked. "I can call in a nurse for you."

Logan shook his head. "No, thanks. I've got a lot of thinking to do."

Alan nodded. "I'll leave you to it. I'm going to grab a cup of coffee. I'll be in the waiting room if you need anything."

"Thanks, man."

He waited until Alan shut the door behind him before letting out a huge sigh. Once again, he'd let a woman take advantage of him. How did this keep happening? What was wrong with him that he let himself get played over and over again?

The initial shock was wearing off now and his anger was building, a slow, steady pressure in his chest. He welcomed the emotion, knowing it would serve him well in the days to come. Olivia probably thought she was so clever, that she had pulled one over on him and the DEA. She deserved an award for her performance as the innocent victim. But she wasn't the only one capable of keeping secrets.

Logan pushed aside his hurt and betrayal and focused on the job at hand. He'd pretend like everything was still fine, that he didn't know she'd sold him out to the cartel's lackeys. Keep her close, so they would know the perfect moment to spring the trap. He'd tear down her lies one by one, using them against her to build his case.

And then he'd walk away and try to repair his shattered heart.

Chapter 20

Olivia forced herself to walk, matching the pace of Keith and Joseph as they led her down the hospital corridor. They were on their way to visit Logan, and the anticipation of seeing him again made her feel a little light-headed.

They had been separated soon after arriving in Bogotá. She'd driven straight to the hospital, not even bothering to turn off the engine of the Jeep before jumping out and grabbing the closest person to help her get Logan inside. Only after he'd been surrounded by medical personnel did she call the US Embassy and explain the situation. The doctors had taken Logan away for surgery, and soon after, an embassy representative had appeared and stayed by her side as she paced a hole in the floor and counted down the minutes until his operation was over.

She'd spent the night at his bedside, hyperattuned to his every small noise and movement. His coworkers had arrived the next morning, and Keith and Joseph had escorted her to the embassy. She hadn't wanted to leave Logan, but the events of the last few days had caught up to her and her body had cried out for rest. Alan had promised to stay by Logan's side and the other men had led her from the room, offering her a bed and a shower. She hadn't had the energy to put up much of a fight.

Now though, she wanted to see him again. *Needed* to see him, in fact. Even though she knew Alan was there helping him and keeping him safe, Olivia had to see Logan with her own eyes to believe he was really okay. The memory of him, pale and unconscious, was too fresh in her mind. She needed to replace it with a vision of him awake and healthy, to chase away the cold fear that still lingered when she thought of losing him.

His brush with death had shaken his coworkers, as well. All of the men on his team had been reserved and subdued around her, their reaction a testament to how much Logan meant to everyone who knew him.

They slowed as they approached the door, and Joseph rapped lightly on the frame to announce their arrival. He pushed open the door and stepped inside, and Olivia and Keith followed.

"Hey, there," Joseph said, walking forward to approach the bed. His body blocked Olivia's view of Logan and she bit her lip to contain a sigh of impatience. Logan hadn't seen his friends in weeks—he deserved a moment with them.

"Hey, yourself," she heard him say. His voice was a little scratchy, probably from the intubation during his surgery. How's his pain? she wondered. Were they taking good care of him here? Did he need anything? Her fingers itched for something to do, wanting to make him more comfortable in any way possible.

Joseph stepped to the side and Olivia got her first glimpse of Logan. She was relieved to see he was sitting up in the bed, which meant he was likely feeling pretty good. His color was much better, and the tightness around her heart eased as the knowledge that he was going to be okay sank in.

She swallowed hard, feeling suddenly shy. "Hi," she said softly.

His gaze found her then, and something flashed in his green eyes. "Hello." There was a coolness to his tone that hadn't been there before, and Olivia felt a tremor of uncertainty in her belly. Was he angry with her? Did he blame her for his injuries?

"How are you feeling?"

He shrugged, then winced slightly. "Pretty good, as long as I don't forget and move the wrong way." He smiled ruefully and the awkward tension between them eased a bit.

"I'm so sorry about what happened," she began, but he lifted a hand to forestall her words.

"Don't worry—it wasn't your fault," he assured her. He glanced at his friends and the corner of his mouth quirked up. "Part of the job, am I right, guys?"

The men's soft laughter was like the rumble of distant thunder, a sound that should have been comforting. But Olivia couldn't shake the feeling that something was just a little bit off.

Keith said something that made Logan laugh, but it wasn't the deep, booming noise she'd heard him make before. It seemed slightly forced, as if he were simply humoring his friend.

Maybe he's in more pain than he's letting on, she mused. It was possible Logan was trying to play it cool in front of his coworkers. Before they'd come to Colombia she had seen the way the men all joked around with each other. Perhaps Logan felt like he needed to act tough, to avoid getting teased about this later. But would they really give him a hard time about needing painkillers after a major surgery? She frowned slightly, able to picture it all too well. The male ego was a mystifying creature, one she would probably never fully understand.

"I'm going to go grab some food for us," Alan said, rising from the chair and stretching his hands over his head. "Help me carry the stuff, Keith?"

"Sure thing," the other man said.

"I'll hold down the fort," Joseph said with a smile. "Be sure to bring me back something good."

Alan punched him lightly on the arm as he walked by. "Oh, I'll be sure to find something special just for you."

The teasing continued as the men left the room. "Do you know where the bathrooms are?" Joseph asked.

"Down the hall and to your left," Olivia said. He nodded thanks and stepped out.

She turned back to face Logan, the atmosphere in the room lighter now that his friends had left. The men were nice enough, but she wanted to be alone with Logan. She'd grown used to his constant company over the past few weeks, and it was amazing how much she'd missed his presence after only a few hours apart.

"I missed you last night," she said, trying to keep

her tone light. "I've gotten so used to the sound of your snoring it was hard to sleep in a silent room."

He lifted a brow and gave her an arch stare. "I could say the same about you," he replied drily.

She smiled and crossed over to his bed. "Are you feeling all right? You seem a little off today."

"I did just have surgery," he pointed out.

"True. But it just seems like you're holding something back, or that something isn't quite right with you."

A look of shock passed over his face, but it was gone so quickly she might have imagined it. "I'm fine."

"Are you in pain?" Maybe he would admit it to her, now that they were alone.

"A little."

"And you don't want to say it in front of your friends?"

He shifted on the bed a bit, as if the question made him uncomfortable. "They'd never let me live it down," he confessed, confirming her earlier suspicion.

Men. She mentally shook her head. "Do you want me to call a nurse? She can bring something for you before any of them get back."

"No need. They gave me something before you got here. It's starting to kick in."

"Okay." She eyed him doubtfully, but didn't press the issue. It seemed he would rather suffer now than deal with the teasing of his coworkers, and she wasn't going to be able to convince him otherwise.

Joseph returned, and he and Logan fell into the easy banter of old friends. Olivia was content to sit and listen to them chat, but she couldn't shake the feeling that Logan was keeping something from her.

But what?

She needed to get him alone, away from his coworkers. Whatever was bothering him, he wasn't going to talk about it in front of them. Maybe the men would head back to the embassy after lunch and she could stay and talk to Logan. There was so much she wanted to say to him, and she didn't want an audience for their conversation.

His injury had made her aware that her feelings for Logan went beyond a simple attraction. She had fallen for him, despite all the reasons why she shouldn't. It seemed her heart was immune to the logic of her mind.

Did he feel the same way? She watched him quietly, happy to see him alive and whole. The thin hospital sheets did nothing to hide the long, graceful lines of his body, and she was struck by the memory of touching him, feeling him next to her, reveling in his heat. Her skin warmed at the memory and she glanced away, hoping neither he nor Joseph would notice her reaction.

Maybe he regretted what they'd done. After all, they'd been caught up in the emotion of the moment. It was easy to lose yourself in passion when you were far from home, away from all the reminders of normal life. It was possible this hint of awkwardness between them was nothing more than Logan trying to distance himself from her so he could let her down easily once they returned. And it made sense he wouldn't want his colleagues to know how the nature of their relationship had changed in Colombia—it hadn't been terribly professional of either of them. Still, she held on to the hope that her feelings for him weren't all one-sided.

Losing her parents had been devastating. If she lost Logan, too...

She wasn't sure her heart could take it.

* * *

Logan took a deep breath, steeling himself to get through the next few hours. It was going to be difficult, but he didn't have any other choice.

He took his seat next to Olivia and attempted a normal smile. She frowned slightly but gave him a shy smile, then returned to her magazine.

She was far more perceptive than he wanted to admit, and it was clear from the puzzled looks she'd been giving him that she knew something was up. Of course, his acting skills weren't anything to write home about, so it was no wonder she'd picked up on his distress.

After the plane took off, Olivia shut her magazine with a sigh and shoved it into the seat pocket in front of her. Then she turned to face him, wearing a determined expression that made his stomach flip.

"Can we talk?" She kept her voice low, presumably so the guys couldn't overhear. They were seated across the aisle and chatting with each other like this was just another trip. As far as he could tell, Olivia didn't realize that *she* was now the focus of the investigation.

"Sure." He tried to sound casual. "What's on your mind?"

"I'm just wondering if everything is okay. You've been distant lately. Ever since the hospital."

"I'm sorry," he said. "I've had a lot on my mind."

Olivia nodded. "I get that. And I figured you wouldn't want your coworkers to know how things developed between us."

"That's part of it." Bad enough he'd fallen for another liar. If the guys knew, they'd look at him with pity and forever question his judgment. He didn't deserve any better, but he wanted to keep this secret as long as possible.

She placed her hand on his and squeezed gently. "I understand. But I want you to know that I treasure the time we had together. I don't want to lose you after all this is over."

She sounded so sincere, and her dark brown eyes were large and inviting. Despite everything Alan had said and all the evidence of her deceit, Logan found himself drawn to her, wanting to trust her. His brain knew she was trouble, but his heart refused to get the message.

"I feel the same way," he said, almost choking on the words.

If she noticed his trouble, she didn't show it. "I was worried you were angry with me," she went on. "Because of your injury. I still don't know who that man was, or why he gave us the keys to the Jeep."

Logan lifted his shoulder, being careful not to pull on the stitches. "We'll probably never know."

"It doesn't make any sense!" There was distress in her eyes now, and his traitorous body wanted to fold her in his arms and comfort her.

"You can't obsess over it," he told her. It was advice he should heed himself. No matter how much he wondered, he'd never understand how he'd fallen for another beautiful liar. He'd go mad trying to figure it out.

"I know. But I hate that you got hurt." She shook her head and strands of her hair fell forward to frame her face. "I was so scared that night. I thought I was going to lose you…" She trailed off and Logan frowned, hearing an echo of her voice in his mind.

Please, Logan. Don't leave me now.

Where had that come from? Had he imagined it, or was it something she'd actually said?

Help me, please. You have to save him!

He shook his head to clear it of the disjointed thoughts. Alan's explanation of events was logical and made sense. But sitting next to Olivia now, hearing the memory of her words, he began to wonder...

If she really had wanted him dead, why bother rushing to Bogotá? He'd been mostly out of it during the drive, but he remembered the beating his body had taken as Olivia hit every divot and ditch in the road at full speed. It would have been much easier for her to let him bleed out on the way and claim she hadn't made it in time...

And what about the things she'd said? It was starting to come back to him now, and he could hear her muttered voice chanting "stay with me" over and over like some kind of mantra. Not exactly the words of a woman who wanted him dead...

Was it possible Alan was wrong? The facts were compelling enough, but maybe they had misinterpreted things.

Or maybe, his cynical side said, *you just don't want to be wrong about another woman.*

"Do you think Avery and Mallory are still safe?" The question jerked him out of his thoughts and he glanced over to find Olivia's features twisted with worry.

Logan nodded. This was something he did know for sure. "We've still got people watching them. They're fine." And apparently totally unaware of Olivia's entanglement with the cartel.

Relief shone brightly in her eyes. "I'd never forgive

myself if something happened to them. I can't wait for this ordeal to be over so my life can go back to normal."

Normal. Now there was a thought. Would things ever be normal for him again? Was it possible for his life to go back to the way it was before he'd met Olivia? He wasn't sure what was worse: getting shot or finding out about her betrayal. Both wounds hurt badly, and he'd carry their scars for the rest of his life.

"Soon," he promised. "We'll have you set up the meet with Carlos once we get back. You'll be done before you know it." The thought should have given him pleasure, but instead he felt hollow inside. This was the worst op he'd ever been on, and it was all his fault. He'd let his emotions rule his behavior and he'd gotten attached to Olivia when he should have kept his distance. Was it any wonder he felt like he was falling apart inside?

He glanced over at the guys who were talking quietly. Alan caught his eye and gave him a thumbs-up, and Logan nodded in return. They'd decided that since Logan lived next door to Olivia, he'd keep an eye on her until she met with Carlos. They didn't want to risk putting her under surveillance and having her get suspicious, especially at such a critical juncture in the investigation. If she realized she was now under the microscope, she might warn off Carlos and they'd lose their chance to get him.

Logan had agreed to the plan but he still felt torn. Part of him saw it as a way to atone for the mistakes he'd made in Colombia. But another part of him still questioned Olivia's role in this play. Was she really capable of such deception? They'd practically lived in each other's pockets for the past few weeks, and he'd been by her side constantly. Hell, they'd even shared a bed. During all that time, he'd seen the compassion and skill she brought to her patients and her intense dedication to her job. There had been many days she'd seen patients from sunup to sundown and she hadn't complained once about being tired or wanting a break. That wasn't the kind of attitude a person could fake, at least not for so long. It seemed wrong to him that a genuinely dedicated physician like Olivia could also be working for the cartel.

But she does have a lot of debt. Money was a powerful motivator, and she'd said herself she had loans to pay both from her education and her parents' medical bills. It was possible she had been bought, but the more he thought about it, the more it just didn't ring true.

He closed his eyes and feigned sleep, wanting more time to think. This whole situation seemed like a Gordian knot, impossible to understand. But Logan wasn't going to give up so easily. If he kept at it, he'd find some way to untangle the problem, to separate the truth from the lies and misunderstandings.

The guys were closing in, getting ready to arrest Olivia and present their case in court. If she was guilty, then she deserved to go to prison. But if she was innocent...

He shook off the distraction. He would figure out what had really happened and who was truly to blame.

Before it was too late.

Chapter 21

"I can't believe you took some guy you barely know to Colombia! I wanted to go."

Olivia smiled despite the disbelief in Avery's voice. "You couldn't get off of work," she reminded her friend. It was such a relief to talk to her, to hear her voice and know that she was okay! Logan and his coworkers had assured her that Avery and Mallory were fine, but a small part of her had still worried about them. As soon as they'd given her the all clear, she'd called Avery to check on her. They hadn't been talking long, but Olivia already felt so much better.

"How did you meet him anyway?"

Olivia bit her bottom lip. "His company was interested in investing in my trip and they wanted him to come along and see firsthand what I do there." She hated lying to her friend, but it was for the best. She couldn't risk tipping off Carlos before Logan and his men were able to arrest him.

She'd already called the man, and the memory of it made her shudder. Even though she'd only spoken to him long enough to set up their meeting, just hearing his voice in her ear had sent waves of revulsion through her body. It had taken all her self-control not to gag.

"Is he cute?"

Olivia laughed, thoughts of Carlos dimming as she called up Logan's face. "No," she said, warmth kindling to life in her belly as she pictured him. "He's definitely not cute—that's a description for a boy. Logan is all man, and he's very handsome."

"Ooh," Avery squealed. "I want details! What happened? Are you two an item now? Start from the beginning!" Olivia heard the protest of springs and knew her friend had just plopped down on her ancient sofa. "Don't leave anything out," Avery commanded.

Olivia hesitated a moment, debating on what to say. Should she play it cool and pretend like nothing had happened? Or confess everything and get her friend's take on things? Even though Logan claimed he was feeling better, he still seemed a little off and she couldn't shake the impression that he'd taken a step back from her ever since his surgery in Bogotá. It reminded her of the way Scott had distanced himself before finally leaving her, and her stomach ached at the thought of Logan doing the same thing. Maybe talking it over with Avery would help her understand what was going on and if there was anything she could do to make him see that she still cared for him.

She opened her mouth, preparing to spill it all. But

just then the doorbell rang, distracting her. "Hang on," she told her friend.

Avery groaned in frustration. "Not fair! I haven't been on a date in ages—I'm living vicariously through you!"

"What makes you think I have anything good to share?" Olivia teased as she made her way to the door.

"You said he was 'all man' and 'very handsome,'" Avery reminded her. "Those aren't the words of a woman who kept her professional distance."

"Guilty as charged." Olivia laughed. "Just let me get the door."

She opened it to find Logan standing on the stoop, his hands in his pockets. "Hi," she said, genuinely pleased to see him.

"Hello," he replied. "Mind if I come in?"

"Of course not," she said, stepping aside so he could enter. She caught a whiff of his soap as he passed by, and the now-familiar scent lit a spark of excitement in her chest. "Avery, I'm going to have to call you back."

"That's him, isn't it?" her friend asked. "Never mind, I can tell it is. He sounds sexy."

Olivia stifled a laugh. "I'll talk to you later, okay?"

"Yeah, yeah. Forget about me. I'm just the friend. Go be with your guy."

"I will call you back," Olivia promised, following Logan into the kitchen. "I still haven't heard about your trip to Kansas."

"There's not much to tell," Avery said. "I'll talk to you later."

Olivia hung up and gave Logan a smile. "Sorry about that—I was catching up with Avery."

"Everything okay?"

"Yes. It's so good to hear her voice." She let out a sigh and set the phone on the kitchen counter. "I left a message with Mallory and I hope to hear back from her soon. I know the DEA is looking after them both, but I feel better after talking to Avery."

Logan studied her for a moment and she fought the urge to blush. "You look better," he commented. "You seem more relaxed now that you're home."

"I feel that way, too," she said. "Want something to drink?"

He shook his head. "I'm just here for a quick visit."

She tamped down a flare of disappointment. "That's too bad. We haven't seen much of each other lately." She was surprised by how lonely she'd felt over the past few days. Did he feel the same way?

If he did, he didn't show it. He looked amazing, especially for a man who'd recently had emergency surgery. His color was good and he didn't appear to be in any pain. He seemed to be recovering quite nicely, and she knew most of that was due to his sheer determination to get well as soon as possible.

He gave her an apologetic smile that sent zings of sensation through her limbs. "They're keeping me busy at the office," he said. "But I wanted to stop by and make sure you're all set for tomorrow's meeting."

The reminder chased away Olivia's lingering enjoyment from her conversation with Avery. "I suppose," she said. "There's really nothing new to it, is there?"

Logan shook his head. "Not really. We'll have the same setup—you in your office, surveillance teams on the street and in the waiting room. Only this time, once he's inside your office, we're going to move in."

That was the part that made her nervous—she'd

never been involved in something like this before. "Are you sure the other people in my office will be safe?" What if Carlos had a gun and started shooting? What if one of her coworkers or a patient was injured? She'd never forgive herself if more people were hurt because of her.

Logan dismissed her concerns with a wave of his hand. "We've cleared your schedule. It won't be an issue."

"If you're sure," Olivia said. She crossed to the fridge and opened it to retrieve a bottle of water. "I don't mean to question your plan. It just worries me, that's all."

Logan moved to stand next to her. "I understand. And it's natural for you to feel anxious about it. But I told you once I'd keep you safe. I've kept my promise."

She met his eyes, trapped by his deep green gaze. "Yes, you have," she murmured.

"Trust me to see you through tomorrow safely, as well."

"I do," she said honestly. His proximity was almost intoxicating, and Olivia wanted nothing more than to throw her arms around him, bury her nose in the hollow of his throat and stay there for days. He had become her addiction, and she wanted more.

He nodded and glanced away, as if preparing to leave. She felt a sudden bolt of panic at the thought— he'd just arrived! Surely he could stay a little longer? Just a few more minutes, then she could let him go…

"Logan," she blurted out. He turned back to give her a questioning look. "Ah, can you stay for a bit? Just to catch up?"

He lifted one brow in amusement. "It's only been two days," he pointed out.

"I know, but I miss you." She bit her lip, wishing she had the gift of eloquence. Instead, she sounded like a desperate woman.

His eyes softened and he nodded his head. "All right. Just let me call the guys and tell them I'll be late getting back." He pulled his phone from his pocket. "Mind if I step into the other room for a moment?"

Olivia shook her head, unable to stop the smile from taking over her face. "No problem. Want me to make some coffee?"

"That sounds nice." He ran his hand down her arm on his way out of the room, and her insides quivered in response to his touch. How long would he have this effect on her? Would she ever be able to see him and not want to be near him? Could they ever go back to being just neighbors again?

No, she decided. That wasn't an option. Like it or not, she'd fallen for Logan Murray. Her heart saw him as her future. Now she just had to find out how he felt about her.

"She doesn't suspect anything." Logan ran a hand through his hair and started to pace, careful to stay on the rug so his steps would be muffled.

"Notice anything suspicious?" Alan asked. They had agreed to give Olivia details about the meeting tomorrow as a test—would she contact Carlos and warn him? Alan had asked for authorization to set up a wiretap, but the judge had said they didn't have enough evidence to justify it. All they could do now was wait and watch...

"No. She seemed happy to see me." His heart tightened a bit at the memory of her face when she'd opened the door and seen him standing there. She'd looked both thrilled and relieved, a combination that mirrored his own emotions. The more he thought about her and her actions in Colombia, the bigger his doubts grew. The Olivia he knew could not willingly be involved in this mess. He just had to figure out how to prove it.

"That's good," Alan said. "Hopefully she just thinks you're there on a social call."

"I'm staying for coffee." He hoped Alan didn't ask why. He didn't want to explain his thoughts on the matter, or the way his heart rate had jumped when Olivia had confessed she missed him. He felt the same way, but he didn't want to admit it just yet. There was still a vanishingly small chance things were not as they seemed, and he didn't want to surrender to his feelings until he knew for sure Olivia was innocent. Bad enough that he'd fallen for her. If she was guilty, at least he'd still have his pride intact.

"Glad to hear it," Alan replied. "Keep your eyes and ears open and let me know if you notice anything."

The faint chime of the doorbell drifted into the room and he frowned. Was she expecting someone? "Will do," he said distractedly. He hung up before Alan could reply and slipped the phone back into his pocket. Then he moved to the doorway and stood to the side, out of sight. He was being paranoid, he knew, but Olivia hadn't mentioned another visitor.

He heard her steps as she walked to the door, and the click of the lock as she flipped it open. He was starting to feel a little foolish listening in, but something kept him glued in place...

She opened the door and gasped, then there was a solid thud as the door met something hard, probably a foot or a hand.

"Dr. Sandoval, is that any way to greet an old friend?"

"You are not my friend. What are you doing here?" Her voice was heavy with fear and Logan's heart sank as he realized he'd been played for a fool.

Carlos was here, ahead of schedule and in the wrong location. Olivia must have been expecting him, but at a later time. No wonder she sounded scared—she'd just been caught in a lie.

Betrayal burned hot and bright in his chest, making it hard to breathe. Logan pushed aside the hurt and glanced around the room, looking for a way out. He could climb through the window and into her backyard, but then he'd miss hearing valuable information they needed to make the arrest.

In the end, his desire for justice trumped his concerns for his own safety.

He removed his phone and sent a quick text to Alan. Carlos is here. Come now. Then he slipped the phone back into his pocket and took a deep breath, focusing his thoughts on the job ahead. Later he'd take the time to agonize over his misplaced trust. Now he needed to block out his emotions and do what was necessary to end this once and for all.

Chapter 22

Carlos waltzed into her home like he owned the place, trailed by his silent, menacing bodyguard. His smug confidence sucked up all the oxygen in the room—or at least it felt that way to Olivia. She put a hand to her chest, struggling to breathe in the wake of his appearance. Why was he here?

Her next thought was of Logan, still in the other room. Had he heard the doorbell? *Please stay away.* If he were to walk out now, there was no telling what Carlos or his henchman might do.

"Why are you here, Carlos?" she asked, a little loudly. Maybe Logan would hear her and could text for help before things got out of hand. The thought made her feel a little better and helped steady her nerves. Logan would do his job. She just had to distract Carlos until the DEA arrived.

"I'm here for my merchandise." Carlos raised a brow, his expression clearly indicating that he found her question ridiculous. "Did you think I had forgotten?"

Olivia shook her head and fought the urge to look at the door of her study, where Logan had gone to make his call. "No. But we had agreed to meet tomorrow."

Carlos smiled, a thin, cruel slant of his mouth. "We had. But I do not trust you." He took a step forward, and his bodyguard followed suit. They were trying to intimidate her, and Olivia was ashamed to admit it was working.

She swallowed, trying to stall. "I've given you no reason to doubt me," she said, her voice only a little shaky.

Carlos tilted his head to the side, studying her the way a cat might a mouse. The look in his dark eyes made her stomach twist and she felt the burn of bile in the back of her throat.

"Where is your friend?" he asked softly.

Olivia held her ground and met his gaze. "Which one?"

He snorted softly, apparently amused by her response. "Let us not play games. I know your potential financier is not who you claimed."

His words made her blood run cold. *He knew.* Somehow, Carlos had discovered the truth about Logan's identity.

Her denial was automatic. If she admitted the truth, Carlos would likely kill her on the spot. She thrust her chin up and took a step forward, determined to sell her bluff. "I don't know what you're talking about."

Now he laughed outright. "I don't know if you're brave or merely stupid." When she didn't respond,

Carlos grabbed her arm and squeezed hard. Olivia tried to wriggle out of his grasp, but he pulled her up to him and shoved his face in hers.

"Logan Marshall is really Logan Murray, a DEA agent. Did you honestly think I would not discover your deception?" His breath was hot on her cheeks and Olivia closed her eyes, drawing deep for strength.

She had two choices: admit the truth and hope Carlos didn't kill her outright, or continue to play dumb and pretend to be shocked.

Carlos gave her a little shake, apparently annoyed by her silence. In that moment, Olivia made up her mind. She was tired of letting this man terrorize her, tired of feeling at his mercy. He had hurt the man she loved, threatened her friends and almost ruined her life. She was done letting her fear of him rule her actions. It was time to take back her life.

Even if it only lasted a few moments longer.

She opened her eyes and glared at him. "I told you," she said, her voice low and threatening. "I don't know what you're talking about." She yanked hard against Carlos's hold and took a step back. He released her but didn't take his eyes off her face.

"You're lying." But there was a thread of doubt in his voice.

"Why would I lie? You threatened the lives of my friends, the people I love most in this world. Why would I do anything to jeopardize their safety?"

He studied her for a moment, clearly considering her words. She stared him down, knowing that if she looked away now he'd see through her bluff.

Finally, he nodded once. "Very well. We will move on. For now."

Olivia sighed silently, some of the tension leaving her body. He had bought her story and hopefully the DEA would arrive before he figured out the truth.

"I'll give you the drugs and then I want you to leave."

Carlos's eyes widened a bit, as if he was shocked by her boldness. "You dare to tell me what to do? You forget you have no power here. I am in control."

A flash of movement caught Olivia's attention and she saw Logan creeping out of the study. He moved silently, tracking Carlos's bodyguard, clearly intending to take the man down. Her heart thumped double-time as a mixture of relief and fear swirled through her. She no longer had to face Carlos alone, but what if Logan got hurt again while attacking the other man?

She returned her focus to Carlos, hoping her temporary distraction hadn't clued him in to what was happening behind him. "Forgive me," she said, almost choking on the words. "I just want to conclude our business."

"As do I." He turned to gesture to his associate just as Logan reached the bodyguard. Carlos let out a cry of alarm, but it was too late. Logan hooked his arm around the man's neck and pressed his gun to his temple. "Drop your weapon," he instructed calmly.

The man did as he was told, but Olivia could tell by the flash of fire in his eyes that he hadn't truly surrendered. If Logan gave even an inch, he would jump into action...

Logan eyed Carlos over his henchman's shoulder. "Have a seat," he said. "You might as well get comfortable while we wait for my friends to arrive."

Carlos sighed and shook his head. "I think not." Before Olivia realized what was happening, Carlos snaked his arm out and grabbed her, pulling her roughly to stand in front of him. She felt a sudden pressure on her neck, cold and flat. The detached part of her brain realized Carlos must have drawn his own gun, but before she had time to process what was happening, his voice filled her ear.

"Your move, Agent Murray," he said coldly.

Logan cursed silently and tightened his grip on the man he held hostage. He should have gotten Olivia out of the way before making his move, but there hadn't been time. He'd meant to take this guy out while Carlos had his back turned and then go after Carlos, but he'd been forced to act when Carlos had turned around. Now he was in a classic standoff, and his enemy wore the flat, calculating look of a man with nothing left to lose.

He shook his head slightly, trying to clear his mind. His emotions were all over the map, a maelstrom that threatened to drag him down. He'd gone from trusting Olivia to feeling betrayed so fast it had given him whiplash. After overhearing her conversation with Carlos, he realized she'd been innocent all along. She'd had several opportunities to sell him out in the last few minutes alone, and every time she'd protected him, buying him time to organize a response. A heavy surge of guilt washed over him—how could he have ever doubted her?

He met her eyes, wanting to apologize for this, for Colombia, for everything. He expected to see her brows drawn down in anger since he had failed to protect her from Carlos. Instead, she wore a look of total and absolute trust, her brown eyes steady and warm. Her faith in him shone brightly on her face, and it nearly brought him to his knees. After the way he'd questioned her integrity, the last thing he deserved was her unwavering loyalty. She was too good for the likes of him.

He was going to have to work hard to be a man worthy of her confidence.

"It doesn't have to be like this," he said, darting his eyes from Carlos to the door. The guys should be getting here any minute, and he didn't want the surprise of their arrival to spook him into shooting Olivia. There had to be some way he could convince Carlos to let her go...

"You're right," Carlos said. "It doesn't. Put down your gun."

"Why do you care?" Logan asked. "The cartel has never been concerned with the lives of its underlings."

A flash of anger sparked in Carlos's eyes, and Logan realized with a shock that the man he held hostage was no ordinary cartel employee.

"Who is he to you? Your brother? Your son?"

Carlos didn't respond, but Logan saw his jaw clench and knew he'd hit upon the truth.

In light of this information, Logan mentally reviewed his options. He could stand here and argue with Carlos, trying to stall the man until Alan and the rest of his backup arrived. It was the easy choice, but there was no guarantee Carlos would cooperate. He was a smart man and would probably see through the tactic. And Logan knew Carlos wouldn't hesitate to shoot Olivia if he thought it would help him escape.

That left another option: he could surrender. Carlos wasn't expecting him to give up so easily, but it was the only way he could see to protect Olivia. If Logan gave up his weapon and released Carlos's relative, Carlos would have no reason to hold Olivia hostage. And if he let her go, she'd be out of danger when the guys arrived, which they were likely to do any minute.

Of course, there was nothing to stop Carlos from shooting him the moment he surrendered, but Logan would have to take that chance. Olivia's safety was more important to him than anything else.

"If I drop my gun, will you let her go?"

He saw the flash of surprise in Carlos's eyes. "Naturally."

It was a lie and they both knew it, but Logan nodded, pretending to accept his word.

"Logan, don't—" Carlos jerked his arm up, choking Olivia. She blinked hard, her eyes watering, and Logan felt his blood begin to boil. He tightened his grip on the man in front of him, digging his fingers into the side of the man's neck. He felt the pulse of blood thrum under his fingers and squeezed, keeping his eyes locked on Carlos. The man began to go limp in his arms, and he loosened his grip just enough to keep him conscious.

"Play nice," he warned Carlos. "If you hurt her, I hurt him."

For a terrible moment, he thought Carlos was going to strangle Olivia in front of him. A calculating look flashed across the man's face and his arm tightened around her neck. She emitted a soft choking sound but didn't move, as if sensing any kind of struggle would give him the excuse he wanted to kill her. After what seemed like an eternity, he loosened his arm and Olivia drew in a full breath.

"Very well," Carlos said. "We seem to have arrived at an understanding. I believe you were going to drop your gun?"

Logan tossed his weapon on the sofa but maintained his grip on the man in front of him. "Your turn."

"I never said I'd drop my gun," Carlos replied.

"No, but you did say you'd release her."

Carlos cocked his head to the side. "True. But I neglected to mention what her condition would be." His smile was pure evil as he cocked his gun and lifted it to Olivia's temple.

Logan reacted on instinct. He shoved his hostage forward, ramming him into Olivia and knocking both her and Carlos off balance. The bodyguard rolled off his boss and lunged to the side, clearly going for Logan's discarded gun. But Logan didn't care. He pushed Olivia out of the way and threw himself on top of Carlos, scrabbling for the man's hand before he could bring his gun up to fire.

Carlos was a lot stronger than he looked, and he put up a decent fight. He landed a glancing blow across Logan's chin and a spike of pain radiated through his jaw, distracting him.

There were the sounds of a scuffle behind him, and Olivia let out a muffled cry. Then the sound of a gunshot ripped through the air, and both Logan and Carlos froze.

"Olivia?" Logan turned, half-afraid of what he might find. Had she been shot? Was she lying dead on the floor? *Please, no…*

She stood a few feet away wearing a shocked expression as she stared down at the body of Carlos's relative. Logan saw at a glance that his gun was in her hand, and he felt a fierce surge of pride and relief at seeing she was safe.

He turned back to Carlos with renewed determination, but the other man had managed to regroup during the distraction. He swung for Logan's head, and Logan realized too late that Carlos had picked up a bowl that had been knocked over during the scrimmage.

He heard a terrible crack as the bowl struck home, and his vision wavered as pain swamped his consciousness. He keeled over and curled up on the floor, clutching his head in a vain attempt to stop the ringing in his ears.

His brain cried for him to get up, some part of him knowing that Carlos must be rising to his feet, gun in hand to shoot him. But his body wouldn't cooperate. He was as helpless as a newborn, and any second now, Carlos was going to kill him.

Logan managed to open his eyes. The room swam around him and black spots danced in his field of view. He squinted to try to clear them, but it didn't work. No matter. As long as he could still see Olivia. He wanted to see her face one last time before he died.

He moved his head slightly and gagged as his stomach revolted. Blinking hard to clear the tears from his eyes, he saw her, still standing a few feet away. There were two of her now, and they both turned to face him.

He tried to speak, but his tongue was thick and heavy in his mouth. He wanted to tell her he was sorry for letting her down, for leaving her like this. He'd promised to protect her and he'd failed. Hopefully Alan and the rest of the team could make up for his shortcomings.

Olivia and her twin moved as one, lifting their arms in his direction. Two loud booms rang out, and a sudden, heavy weight fell on Logan. He struggled to breathe against the unexpected pressure and tried to move away, but he couldn't coordinate his limbs and wound up flailing helplessly.

Then Olivia was there, her arms pulling him free and cradling his head in her lap. "Don't move," she said, her hands on either side of his face.

He stopped struggling and gazed up at her, trying to decide which one of her faces to focus on. They wore identical expressions of concern, but it was too difficult to tell which one was Olivia and which one was her twin. He gave up, closing his eyes to block out the confusing sight.

"Open your eyes," she said urgently. "You can't go to sleep here."

"Wasn't gonna," he mumbled. But in truth, he was suddenly very tired. His body felt heavy and sluggish, and his brain struggled to process the reasons why he should stay awake. He'd just take a quick nap and when he woke up things would make more sense.

He dimly heard Olivia's voice, growing more panicked as she continued to talk. Logan felt bad for worrying her, but he'd explain it all when he woke up. There was a loud crash from somewhere far away, and then something grabbed at him, pulling and prodding. The sensation reminded him of fishing with his grandpa, the way the pole would vibrate when he'd managed to hook a fish. His grandfather's face flashed in his vision, smiling and proud, and Logan drifted off with him, eager to cast the next line.

Chapter 23

Two days later

"I have a confession to make."

Olivia glanced up from her plate to find Logan watching her, the emotion in his green eyes unreadable. Nerves jangled to life in her stomach, making her suddenly nauseated. Ever since they'd returned from Colombia, she'd been worried that Logan was going to tell her he didn't want to be a part of her life anymore. Since she'd caused him a lot of trouble, she understood the reasons why, but the thought of his absence still drove a spike of pain through her chest. He was the first person she'd let into her heart since her parents had died and Scott had left. Losing him now was going to hurt.

"Sounds serious," she remarked, reaching for the pitcher to top off her glass of iced tea. She gestured to Logan's glass and at his nod filled it up, as well.

"I suppose." He looked down and started tracing the tines of his fork on his plate, making idle patterns in the sauce that remained.

"Let me guess," she said, trying to keep her tone light. "You don't really like my homemade lasagna." It was obvious she was trying to delay the conversation, but she needed a moment to marshal her emotions, to brace herself for the coming blow so she didn't do something silly like beg him to stay.

He smiled, which eased the tightness in her chest somewhat. "No. It's fabulous."

"What is it then?" Might as well get it over with. He'd break the news and go home, and she could have a good cry and nurse her broken heart in peace.

"I doubted you. In Colombia."

"What?" She shook her head, unsure of what she'd just heard. What was he talking about?

Logan shifted in his chair, clearly uncomfortable. "I thought you were involved with Carlos and the cartel. That you were really working with them, and you had betrayed me to get me out of the picture."

Shock flowed over her like ice water and Olivia sat frozen to her chair for a moment, unable to speak. Finally, her brain came back online again. "Why on earth did you think that?" She wasn't angry—not yet anyway. Just curious to hear how he'd formed such a mistaken impression.

The tips of his ears turned pink, signaling his embarrassment. It was clear he was ashamed of what he was about to say, but he took a deep breath and told her what Alan had said and the explanations he'd proposed to explain what had happened in Colombia.

"I see," she said after he finished. They sat in silence

for a few moments, each lost in introspection. Olivia thought back over more recent events, and the pieces started to click into place. "So that's why you seemed upset with me in the hospital."

Logan nodded. "I thought you had betrayed me."

Like his former fiancée, she realized. No wonder he'd been distant and reserved.

"What changed your mind?"

"I overheard you talking to Carlos when he showed up. At first, I thought it was proof that you'd been lying to us all. But when I listened to what you said to him, I realized that wasn't the case. I heard you lying to him to protect me, and I knew I'd been wrong to doubt you."

She nodded again but didn't say anything. It was a lot to process, and part of her was stung by the fact he'd thought her capable of such deception. But as she studied his face and saw the guilt he carried with him in the depths of his eyes, her anger softened. He'd been burned before. Was it any wonder he'd had trouble trusting her, especially when Alan had told him such a convincing story?

"I guess I'm lucky they didn't shoot me on sight then," she said, referring to Alan and Keith's arrival after she'd shot Carlos. They'd kicked down the door of her home, taken one look at the carnage on the ground and immediately rushed to help. Fortunately, they'd been able to rouse Logan long enough for him to explain what had happened, and the men had stopped looking at Olivia like she was the devil incarnate.

"They are professionals," Logan said, with the ghost of a smile.

"And a good thing, too," she replied. "Otherwise, I wouldn't have been able to hold off Carlos and his man for much longer." She shuddered just thinking about it. Her shots had both hit their marks but hadn't proved fatal. If anything, the injuries had only served to make the men angrier, and if Alan and Keith hadn't shown up when they did, Olivia had no doubt both she and Logan would be dead.

"You were amazing," Logan said. He placed his hand on the table and tentatively extended it, as if asking permission to touch her. Olivia reached across and grabbed it, threading their fingers together. It was a relief to feel his skin again, to know that things were all right between them.

"Only because you were with me."

He snorted at that and she squeezed his hand. "It's true, Logan. Your presence gave me the confidence to stand up to that monster. Without you, I don't know what would have happened."

"I guess we make a pretty good team." His words flew into her heart, making it swell with love and hope. Against all odds, despite her fears and the trouble they'd faced, they'd survived.

Together.

"I think so."

Logan smiled shyly. "What can I do to make this up to you? I feel terrible."

Olivia cocked her head to the side, pretending to consider her options. "Do you trust me now?"

"Yes." He said it immediately and without reservation.

"Then that's enough."

"But—"

She held up a hand, cutting him off. "Logan, I know why you doubted me. Honestly, I probably would have done the same if the shoe had been on the other foot. I can't blame you, especially knowing what I do about your ex."

A shadow passed over his eyes. "I hate that she's still affecting my life."

She took a deep breath. Confession time. "If it makes you feel any better, I'm still haunted by the deaths of my parents."

His face softened with understanding. "Is that why you've wanted me around so much lately?"

Olivia felt her face heat but nodded. "I've been afraid you were going to dump me now that we're back. Like Scott."

Logan leaned forward and grabbed her other hand. "Never. But do you still want me, after what I did?"

"You didn't *do* anything," she pointed out. "You had some questions, and now you know the truth. As far as I'm concerned, there's nothing to forgive."

His green eyes shimmered and he blinked hard. "I am so lucky," he murmured.

She smiled, touched by his reaction. "We both are. But as long as we're being honest with each other, I have a confession of my own to make."

Logan swallowed and nodded. "Hit me. I deserve it."

"I didn't actually cook this lasagna."

He was quiet for a moment, then a slow smile spread across his face. "You didn't?"

Olivia shook her head. "Nope. Bought it from a little Italian place by my office. It's good though, right?"

"Very. But why tell me? I would never question your cooking skills."

"I don't want any lies between us, Logan. Even silly

little white lies about nothing. If we're going to do this, we have to be able to trust each other."

He nodded. "I won't leave you, Olivia."

"And I won't lie to you, Logan."

The look in his eyes grew heated, and Olivia felt an answering tingle deep in her belly. Logan rose from the table and extended his hand. "Come on. We need to celebrate properly."

Olivia stood, anticipation thrumming in her blood. "But what about your head? The doctor said no strenuous activity for at least a week."

The look he shot her was positively sinful. "Don't worry. I have faith in your healing skills. I've seen you in action, remember?"

She laughed, feeling genuinely happy for the first time in months. "I'm not a miracle worker."

He pressed a kiss to her temple. "You're *my* miracle worker," he whispered.

She wrapped her arms around him. "And you're mine," she said.

"Let's go find out what it's like to make love on a bed." He sounded almost giddy at the prospect.

"Are you sure you can handle it?" she teased. "What about your head?"

He smiled, and she felt the warmth in his eyes like the touch of the sun. "As long as you're with me, I can handle anything."

* * * * *

#1907 THE PREGNANT COLTON BRIDE
The Coltons of Texas • by Marie Ferrarella

When scandal rears its ugly head, rancher Zane Colton offers to marry his pregnant secretary to give her baby his surname and quell the vicious rumors *someone* is emailing to the entire company. All the while, the disappearance of the Colton family patriarch is being investigated...and Zane is a suspect!

#1908 BEAUTY AND THE BODYGUARD
Bachelor Bodyguards • by Lisa Childs

Gage Huxton was tortured for six months after being captured behind enemy lines. But that torment was nothing compared to watching the woman he loves become another man's bride. When gunmen storm the wedding, can Gage keep the woman he loves safe...and convince her she's the only one for him?

#1909 KILLER COUNTDOWN
Man on a Mission • by Amelia Autin

Both Senator Shane Jones and investigative reporter Carly Edwards have loved and lost before. But when an assassin targeting Shane over a controversial vote in Congress puts both of them in danger, they must rescue each other from mortal peril and learn to risk everything for love.

#1910 COVERT ALLIANCE
by Linda O. Johnston

Kelly Ladd and Alan Correy are both undercover due to the same murder. Kelly needs protection from the murderer she implicated in the death of her sister, and Alan is looking for enough evidence for a conviction. A fake relationship might help them apprehend her brother-in-law, but it won't remain pretend for very long... _____

REQUEST YOUR FREE BOOKS!
2 FREE NOVELS PLUS 2 FREE GIFTS!

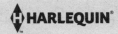

ROMANTIC suspense

Sparked by danger, fueled by passion

YES! Please send me 2 FREE Harlequin® Romantic Suspense novels and my 2 FREE gifts (gifts are worth about $10). After receiving them, if I don't wish to receive any more books, I can return the shipping statement marked "cancel." If I don't cancel, I will receive 4 brand-new novels every month and be billed just $4.74 per book in the U.S. or $5.49 per book in Canada. That's a savings of at least 12% off the cover price! It's quite a bargain! Shipping and handling is just 50¢ per book in the U.S. and 75¢ per book in Canada.* I understand that accepting the 2 free books and gifts places me under no obligation to buy anything. I can always return a shipment and cancel at any time. Even if I never buy another book, the two free books and gifts are mine to keep forever.

240/340 HDN GH3P

Name	(PLEASE PRINT)
Address	Apt. #
City	State/Prov.	Zip/Postal Code

Signature (if under 18, a parent or guardian must sign)

Mail to the **Reader Service:**
IN U.S.A.: P.O. Box 1867, Buffalo, NY 14240-1867
IN CANADA: P.O. Box 609, Fort Erie, Ontario L2A 5X3

Want to try two free books from another line?
Call 1-800-873-8635 or visit www.ReaderService.com.

* Terms and prices subject to change without notice. Prices do not include applicable taxes. Sales tax applicable in N.Y. Canadian residents will be charged applicable taxes. Offer not valid in Quebec. This offer is limited to one order per household. Not valid for current subscribers to Harlequin Romantic Suspense books. All orders subject to credit approval. Credit or debit balances in a customer's account(s) may be offset by any other outstanding balance owed by or to the customer. Please allow 4 to 6 weeks for delivery. Offer available while quantities last.

Your Privacy—The Reader Service is committed to protecting your privacy. Our Privacy Policy is available online at www.ReaderService.com or upon request from the Reader Service.

We make a portion of our mailing list available to reputable third parties that offer products we believe may interest you. If you prefer that we not exchange your name with third parties, or if you wish to clarify or modify your communication preferences, please visit us at www.ReaderService.com/consumerschoice or write to us at Reader Service Preference Service, P.O. Box 9062, Buffalo, NY 14240-9062. Include your complete name and address.

HRS15

SPECIAL EXCERPT FROM

⊞ HARLEQUIN®

ROMANTIC suspense

*Suspicion surrounds Zane Colton's possible
involvement in his stepfather's disappearance, but
another scandal might be just what he needs to find love
with his pregnant assistant, Mirabella Freeman.*

*Read on for a sneak preview of
THE PREGNANT COLTON BRIDE,
the next book in **THE COLTONS OF TEXAS**
continuity by* USA TODAY *bestselling
author Marie Ferrarella.*

Her voice sounded oddly hollow. "Something wrong?"
he asked, doubling back.

Mirabella turned the monitor so he could see the
screen more readily. The anonymous email sender was
back. He glanced at the time stamp and saw the email had
been sent out early this morning. It was the first thing she
had seen when she'd opened her computer.

"What new bridegroom is getting away with murder?"
the first line read. "Better be careful and watch your back,
Mirabella, or you might be next on his list."

Anger spiked within him. Zane bit back a number of
choice words. Cursing at the sender, or at her computer,
would accomplish exactly nothing. He needed to take
some kind of effective action, not merely rail impotently
at shadows.

Zane put his hand on her shoulder in a protective
gesture.

"Don't be afraid, Belle. I'm going to track this infantile scum down. I won't let him get to you."

He meant physically, but she took it to mean mentally. "He's already gotten to me, but I'm not afraid," she fired back. "I'm angry. This jerk has no right to try to say what he's saying, to try to poison people's minds against us." Her eyes flashed as she turned toward Zane. "What the hell is his game?"

Her normally porcelain cheeks were flushed with suppressed fury. He'd never seen her look so angry—nor so desirable. Instead of becoming incensed, which he knew was what this anonymous vermin was after, Zane felt himself becoming aroused. By Mirabella.

Now wasn't the time, he upbraided himself.

It was *never* going to be the time, he reminded himself in the next moment. He'd married her to save her reputation, to squelch the hurtful, damaging rumors. Stringing up the person saying all those caustic things about them, about *her*, did not lead to the "and they all lived happily ever after" ending he was after—even if it might prove to be immensely satisfying on a very primal level.

Nothing wrong with a little primal once in a while, Zane caught himself thinking as his thoughts returned to last night.

Don't miss
THE PREGNANT COLTON BRIDE
by USA TODAY *bestselling author Marie Ferrarella,*
available August 2016 wherever
Harlequin® Romantic Suspense
books and ebooks are sold.

www.Harlequin.com

Turn your love of reading into rewards you'll love with
Harlequin My Rewards

Love the Harlequin book you just read?

Your opinion matters.

Review this book on your favorite book site, review site, blog or your own social media properties and share your opinion with other readers!

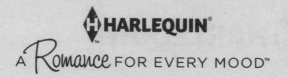

JUST CAN'T GET ENOUGH?

Join our social communities
and talk to us online.

You will have access to the latest
news on upcoming titles and special
promotions, but most importantly,
you can talk to other fans about your
favorite Harlequin reads.

Harlequin.com/Community

Facebook.com/HarlequinBooks

Twitter.com/HarlequinBooks

Pinterest.com/HarlequinBooks